CAPTIVE

OF THE SHADOWS

a novel
by Kaitlyn Weiss

The Fairy Code
Book One

MAGIC DOME BOOKS

Captive of the Shadows
The Fairy Code, Book 1
Copyright © Kaitlyn Weiss 2019
Cover Art © Ivan Khivrenko 2019
Designer: Vladimir Manyukhin
Editor: Meredith Rodriguez
Published by Magic Dome Books, 2019
All Rights Reserved
ISBN: 978-80-7619-064-1

TABLE OF CONTENTS:

CHAPTER ONE

THE DAY STARTED out like any other weekday. Who knew it would be my last day of freedom?

It was a Monday, right after a great weekend camping with my friends. I love the outdoors, and I especially love Golden Lake. The oaks and birches there are huge, maybe even centuries old, and yesterday the air had been clear and especially fresh, with a misty fog emanating from the lake. Lit by the morning sun, it had glowed a luminous golden pink, as if alive...

"He was staring at you."

I yawned into my receiver. Liza always thought that guys were checking me out. "He was looking at anyone who had breasts and long hair."

"But he was especially interested in you!" She insisted. Her tone held a note of accusation. "I notice stuff like that, you know."

"Whatever, Liza. So he took a look, got a thrill, and moved on."

We were talking about some guy who had joined us at the lake. Nothing special about him. For example, when they missed me in the evening, he hadn't tried to find me. Instead, he just hung around camp.

"Okay, Aurora, but I thought he was kind of cute."

"Maybe, but I want more than 'cute.' But hey, I've got to go before the traffic gets bad. See you tonight. And thanks again—you're my guardian angel."

That last bit, by the way, was the truth. Whilst in the woods yesterday, I'd actually lost my way. I was on a little hike and came across a really unusual clearing: it was perfectly round, with lush green grass and strange shadows cast by the trees. I'd sat down and unexpectedly dozed off. When I awoke, I jumped up and headed back to the campsite, and ... that's when I realized I was lost. I found myself wandering around in a circle, always ending up at the clearing. It was as if every path I chose took me right back there. It was only the sound of Liza's terrified screams that broke this strange spell.

And then she burst into the clearing, wrapped her arms around me, and crushed me to her chest like a python crushing its prey.

Ding! Ding! There went the coffee maker and the microwave, meaning coffee was ready, and so was my breakfast burrito. My workday morning was settling into its usual routine, which was breakfast on the run, then a splash of makeup on my pale face - even paler than usual from lack of sleep - dark pants and a fresh, light blouse. For whatever reason, this was the dress code for senior researchers. It didn't matter that 90% of the time I was in a white lab coat. And in the lab. And that the genes we were experimenting on didn't care what I was wearing - I really didn't need clothes at all as far as they were concerned.

Ah, the great outdoors.... As I sat in my car, my eyes strayed out the window. To be sure, we lived in a beautiful town, green, pretty. I can't complain. But the images from my weekend at the lake made me feel like something was missing from my life.

Like usual, the institute was buzzing with activity. As I rode the elevator upwards, I heard all the latest gossip and news. It came mostly from the men, who, contrary to the old stereotype, actually liked to gossip more than the women.

"Did you hear that Lab 5 is in hot water again?"

"Did you hear that Rostova had an abortion — a fling with her junior technician."

"... and they told him to just hand over his cash like a good boy. Yet another scammer!"

"Oh, Aurora, you're so pale! Didn't you sleep well?"

The last question came from Zina, our lead researcher. Around 60 years old, Zina puckered her lips, like usual, making them look like a withered prune below her thin eyebrows.

"I guess not, Zina," I flashed a mischievous smile. "I didn't sleep much, what with the orgy I hosted last night."

Yes, it was a typical day.

My lab was on the tenth floor. Five years ago, the Institute of Molecular and Applied Genetics had moved from an old, pre-war building to modern facilities. Now we were surrounded by light and glass. Our labs new were state of the art in terms of our equipment. Pretty fancy stuff.

I don't know what was behind such dramatic changes. Rumor had it that our institute had been given a lot of money for research and development. But from whom, and why...?

I wondered, but didn't really care. What mattered to me was that we no longer had to worry about securing new equipment and such.

In fact, we had just about everything we needed. And this morning, like usual, instruments quietly hummed, including the genetic analyzer, which was shiny and new, and people were bustling around the microscopes and test tubes. It was just another workday. Ivory-colored blinds shuttered the windows, preventing the sun from blinding us and interfering with our work.

The fateful intercom call came after lunch. I had just returned to the lab and donned my lab coat when the senior technician shouted that Osipov wanted to see me.

My hands grew instantly cold. What did the director of the Institute want from me? I didn't have any transgressions on my record – I'd always carried out the experiments accurately and in a timely fashion, without any incidents.

"Aurora, maybe the old man's lonely," smirked Rostik, the junior laboratory technician.

"Ha ha! That's rich coming from you."

"Don't let the door hit you on the way out," Alice sneered. Unlike Rostik, she sounded downright mean. But that's our Alice for you – kind of like cut glass. She didn't like her position – she'd wanted mine. She didn't like her salary – everyone else earned more.

But it didn't matter. Our lab was the best – young, fun. No one was older than 35. So maybe we were a little irreverent, but we were always conscientious about our work, and really, a little kidding around was okay.

"Don't cry when you think of me," I muttered, taking off my lab coat. I ran my hand over the collar of my blouse, fixed my hair, which was tied back, and for some reason sprayed a little perfume on my wrist. I took a deep breath, and headed for the elevator, still thinking about what could be the matter.

Osipov wouldn't summon me for nothing. In fact, he was a rather rare sight at the Institute. And even when he did show up, all he did was reprimand us, or drone on and on about how grateful we should be for the privilege of working there. I don't know what he expected us to do – maybe fall on our knees and kiss his feet or something.

Our beloved leader was located on the top floor – the twelfth. The reception room was huge, with polished floors, glass walls and a secretary at a long semicircular table. Everything was expensive, stylish, and slightly over the top. Why, for example, did the sofas have to be covered in gold leather embossed with DNA symbols? Or, why the low table made of thick green glass with multicolored splotches suspended within? And these plants in dark, ornate tubs ... It felt cold, more like a cemetery than a reception area.

They were already waiting for me. The secretary glanced up from her computer, waved her hand toward the massive door, and plunged into her work again.

"Hello, Sir," I said, standing at the door. I was doing my best to sound calm and businesslike.

"Come in, Aurora."

Hmm...Was that a quiver in his voice?

I stepped inside, sensed the door close softly and silently behind me, and all of a sudden felt a stab of fear, like I had walked into a trap. I knew that was silly, of course. I was simply standing before the director, who, for whatever reason, was acting like he'd been caught smoking by the teacher.

Honestly, the director really was acting strange. He hemmed and hawed, tapping his fingers on the smooth surface of the table, while something twitched in his neck. Now and then, he reached for a glass filled with a dark gold liquid. I doubt it was apple juice.

"What is it?" I asked, looking from the director to the figure of a man standing next to him.

The latter was the picture of calm. He was tall and too thin. He wore a gray suit, which hung on him as if on a coat hanger. His gray hair and gray face were so impossibly dull that I felt the need to look away. Faded eyes in a forgettable face, and long pale fingers sporting a single, simple ring.

"Aurora, we're sending you somewhere."

I felt my eyebrows shoot upwards. Independently of my will, my hand grasped my own ring and began twisting it. Made of metal fashioned into the shape of a snake devouring its own tail, it never left my index finger.

"Is this a business trip?"

Wait a minute, it's not the director who handles business trips, but the senior researchers. Or maybe the deputy director of research.

"You could say that."

I really don't like ambiguity, especially when it comes to my personal life or my work. "Sir, I have experiments to attend to, so why don't we get to the point. Then I'll be on my way."

"You won't be going anywhere." The gray stranger's voice was soft, yet creaky. It made my skin crawl.

"Excuse me? Who are *you*? And what gives you the right to talk to me like that?"

"I came to fetch you," he said indifferently. "Let's go, I'm out of time. Your master awaits you."

So, who let a psycho into the Institute?

"Sir, I'll come back later." I said resolutely — I had no desire to play these games. What was up with this stuff about a "master?" Had someone been bingeing too much on *Game of Thrones*?

"Aurora, listen to this ... man," the director suddenly said, and I thought I heard fear in his voice. "He is the representative of someone very important to our institute. And so please, just go with him. Moreover, I have already accepted compensation for you."

Compensation?!? What did he mean? Was he crazy? Was I dreaming?

"Compensation, Sir?"

"Yes," he replied, "I sold you."

"You, you... you *sold* me?"

The director pretended to be busy looking at the table. As if he'd suddenly noticed something interesting there.

"Come here, little one." The stranger said. Suddenly, there he was, right next to me, grabbing my hand - the one with the ring. His finger brushed the metal.

And then he sort of...howled... And recoiled, as if in pain. His gray, expressionless face flickered, briefly revealing a completely different visage beneath it. Then I too screamed and pulled away, rushing toward the door.

Apparently, it was I who was losing my mind. *I really need a vacation,* I thought as I swept past the gaping secretary, past the elevator, and raced down the stairs. Away, away from this crazy nonsense.

My work mates opened their mouths in astonishment when I burst into the lab.

"Aurora ..."

"I'm not here!" I snapped, grabbing my bag, "Get back to work! I'm going to the police station."

Everyone's eyes widened. I wondered what they thought. But really, who cares? What mattered much more was getting the hell out of there!

I am a biologist and geneticist who has spent her adult life studying the mysteries of human origin. I know for a fact that no one can change their face, like a mask, in a matter of moments. It's physically impossible!

I dashed outside and ran to the parking lot, to my car, all the while afraid I'd hear the gray man's creaky voice at my back.

My cell phone rang, causing me, already seated at the wheel, to start. It was an unfamiliar number.

"Hello."

"Aurora," I heard Osipov's voice. "Get back here. You ... you, anyway, I can't undo what is done. It is in your interest to go voluntarily. The contract has already been signed, and your stubbornness only worsens the situation and exhausts the patience of ... he who bought you."

"I cannot be bought!" I shouted, starting the car. "Know that I'm going to the police and submitting a statement about your attempted abduction. Selling *people* - what the...! Is it because I'm an orphan? You think no one cares about me?"

I tossed the phone into the backseat, and clutched the wheel with trembling hands. With a shriek of tires, I pulled out of the parking lot and drove toward the nearest police station. I had to find how what was going on here.

No one tried to call me again. But I felt like I could feel the gray man's eyes boring into my back. Now and then I peered anxiously into the rear view mirror, halfway expecting to see him sitting behind me, like in a horror movie. My hands grew cold at the mere thought of it.

Fortunately, I was alone. And, miraculously, I didn't get into an accident. In fact, I drove safely to the police station and almost ran toward the entrance. I didn't feel safe out on the street. I mean, sometimes on the news they show how in the middle of the day people are kidnapped and dragged into cars. Even big men, so what hope would there be for someone as small as me?

It was quiet and sleepy at the station - that post-lunch silence - and the room was rather dark. The officer behind the glass looked at me a little lazily and raised his eyebrows in a question. Next to him stood a white sign: "Senior Lieutenant A.V. Krymov"

"Good afternoon!" I said, somewhat nervously.

"Hello, I'm listening."

"Someone's trying to *abduct* me."

One of Lieutenant Krymov's eyebrows fell into place, while the second remained suspended.

"Who?" He asked. From somewhere in the depths of the room a woman in a uniform poked her head out, and then withdrew it. And that was it. It was like everyone else was extinct.

"My boss," I exhaled and tried to explain, "Listen, I work at the Institute of Molecular and Applied Genetics — I'm a senior researcher. This afternoon, the director of the institute summoned me. He had a man in his office who tried to grab me, saying that he had *bought* me. And that they were going to take me to some kind of 'master'."

I shuddered at the last word, but went on:

"So I want to file a complaint about an attempted abduction!"

Krymov stared at me for a few seconds, then sighed and asked:

"Do you have a recording of the conversation? Any way to confirm what you're telling me?"

"No! Of course not! How was I to know my boss would try to *sell* me? It's *crazy*."

"Right. That does sound, er, crazy. Are you sure he wasn't pulling your leg?"

"No!" I said indignantly. "No! You have to believe me! He was serious!"

"Okay, calm down. Let's get to the bottom of this. What kind relationship do you have with your boss?"

"This isn't like that!" I hissed. "You should see the freak he was with! He wasn't normal, I mean it!"

"Not normal. Right. Got it. Sounds to me like maybe you need a vacation."

"Listen, I'm in danger! Really in danger! I *feel* it, like something bad is headed my way. And those eyes at my back..."

I looked around, but there was no one there. Just a dark room with benches, and posters about battling crime. For a second, it seemed that the shadows in the corner flickered strangely, but after what I'd been through, I realized I could be seeing things.

Meanwhile, Senior Lieutenant Krymov was regarding me rather dubiously. "Ma'am, what's your name?"

"Aurora Black, and I'm 27 years old."

"You're already a senior researcher?"

"That's right. I'm a genius. Don't let my looks fool you..."

"Calm down, Miss Black. You're clearly upset. In fact, maybe I should call a doctor?"

"But they're trying to *kidnap* me!"

"I really do think you need help. Of a medical nature. Maybe after that we can, er, file a report," said Lieutenant Krymov, and I finally got it. I was wasting my time here. Wow. "Thanks, but I don't think so," I said, backing away from the window.

"Wait, miss! Don't go!" said Lieutenant Krymov, and I suddenly got the creeps. *This isn't normal*, I thought. And again, I turned around and fled.

Once on the street I got back into my car, and sat there, thinking. I was seriously starting to feel paranoid. Should I call Liza? I considered the idea for a few seconds, fighting to stay calm and think clearly.

Finally, I shook my head. Involving Liza might mean putting her in danger. I could not do that to my best friend. Gritting my teeth, I grabbed my phone from the back seat, ejected the sim card and tossed it out the window, and then sped off.

What I needed was a hotel. Hotels have security. *Rent a room, lock the door, get to bed,* I told myself. And in the morning, I'd simply call in and ask for some time off since I didn't have any urgent projects going on at the moment. I'd submit my request by email with an electronic signature.

I chose a good hotel, closer to the city center, next to a brightly lit avenue. I opted for a simple single room and dined in the hotel restaurant, treating myself to a couple of glasses of Chardonnay. And yet, all the time I was on edge. I couldn't shake this uneasy feeling. Was it residual jitters? Could just be the Chardonnay, which tonight made my head race with crazy thoughts. When I drink, I almost never get drunk. Generally speaking, wine usually relaxes me, and that's it, but still...

In my room I carefully locked the door, and then, after thinking about it, I dragged a small bedside stand in front of it. There now. Should someone try to break in, the barricade would slow him down.

The room itself was ordinary. A bed with a nice comforter, blackout curtains, a beige carpet and a chair in the corner. A bottle of water and two glasses were perched on a round table. Oh, and there was a menu, in case someone suddenly felt like ordering room service.

Time to go to bed, so that, hopefully, in the morning, everything would seem like a crazy dream. I stripped down to my underwear, flipped the light switch off, and hurriedly climbed under the blankets. The moon glanced through the window, and pale streaks of light stretched across the floor and the blanket.

I was already dropping into sleep, when suddenly something made me start. It's not like I heard a cough, or someone creeping around. It was just this strange feeling that lifted all the hairs on my body on end. I realized ... I was afraid. A wave of fear slowly rose from somewhere in the depths of my being, enveloping me more and more. It was like when kids get scared at night – they hear something strange, or see the play of light and shadows cast by an unseen monster. It's the kind of fear that makes you turn to stone and shrink inside yourself at the same time.

I sat up and looked around at the gray gloom of the room. Everything was quiet, calm, except the thick shadows in the corner ...

There, they moved!

I blinked, deciding that wine and fatigue were playing a cruel joke. And then the shadows seemed to sigh and grow in size a little more.

This wasn't happening!

I caught myself slowly crawling toward the headboard and whimpering in horror. But *it* swept over my head, turning my hands and feet to ice.

"My god..."

But no, I don't know any prayers, not a one.

"This is a dream," I whispered to calm myself down. But instead, the sound of my own voice scared me even more.

The shadows seemed to laugh, as if they were alive. They gradually grew, cascading across the walls and ceiling. They moved closer to the bed, which remained the last island in the looming inky darkness.

I was already crying softly, thinking about how to get to the door, yet deathly afraid to step out of bed. Then I couldn't stand it anymore and snapped into action, crawling across the mattress, slipping onto the floor ... The shadows swung in my direction and quietly, but clearly, hissed.

And I screamed. Because this just couldn't be, it shouldn't be. The laws of logic and physics were collapsing before my eyes.

Let them collapse. I was getting out of there. I rushed toward the door, though it took all I had— I was stumbling in fear.

And then a male figure emerged from the yawning darkness, and moved toward me.

CHAPTER TWO

THE WHINE of car tires, a thump and a jerk. Screaming... lots of screaming.. And the crackling of flames. Pain all over my body, and the feeling that I was hanging upside down. Another jerk... yet one more, the screaming around me was interlaced with moans and the smell of blood and iron.

I jumped up clawing at .... at the air. The last thing I remembered was a man who seemed to materialize from the night, and those strange, pulsating shadows clinging to him. My brain, already exhausted, hadn't been able to process the sight, and so it did what it had to: it dispatched me into a deep unconsciousness.

Or had it been something else that made me faint?

I looked around, at the same time patting myself. Then I looked downward, remembering that I'd tried to flee wearing only my underwear.

Which was gone. But now I was wearing a long white dress made of a very thin fabric. It was so thin that I could see my nipples through the fine material. And my bosom was barely covered by two flimsy panels and a prayer. Meanwhile, the sleeves of the dress were wide, but fit closely around my wrists.

Sexual slavery! The thought flashed through my mind. It would explain everything: my being sold and that stuff about a master. The practice happened more than it should, in my corner of the world. But what brazen audacity! Selling women in broad daylight, at work!

I flitted around the room, trying to figure out where I was. Alas, a smooth, opaque cloth shuttered the window, and try as I might, I could not open the heavy door. The rest of the room was pretty ordinary, although there were some oddities, such as a bed of frosted lilac glass and strange vine-like plants that almost totally covered the walls. Rarely, I could glimpse golden walls beneath the vines.

I really wanted to scream and shout, call for help, vent and rage. But I didn't, because I knew that this would probably make things worse. My best bet was to wait for someone to walk in and then make a run for it. My eyes fell on a black and lilac statuette depicting a woman holding a child. I picked it up and nodded to myself. It was nice, heavy, probably carved from stone.

And before long, someone did show up. I'd been sitting on the bed, silently freaking out, so by the time the door swung open, I was ready to spring. The thought that I might be forced into slavery made me break out in a cold sweat, but it also made me mad as hell.

You know, I probably should have tried diplomacy first. Instead, I rushed at the door brandishing the statuette.

Which wasn't smart at all. I fully understood how stupid it was when I was thrown back against the wall. The impact drove the breath from my lungs, even though the vines covering the wall softened the blow, if only a little. The next thing I knew, my hands were forced against the wall, palms out, and the statuette fell to the floor and rolled away. And I screamed, realizing that I was about to go stark raving mad.

Because staring intently at me in a fury was a pair of eyes, inside of which a kind of darkness swirled.

Then I felt a sharp pain in my right wrist, as if it had been burned to the bone. I screamed again and collapsed, having committed to memory the face of my tormentor. It was as if carved out of granite, the features were so sharp.

Fainting twice in such a short time is a dubious pleasure. Especially since the first time I had nothing to compare it to.

The second time I fainted, I wasn't out for long. The pain is what woke me up. My right wrist was burning with fire, as if melted polyethylene was dripping onto it. It was like when I was a girl and my friends and I foolishly decided to make a fire in the backyard of the orphanage and melt cartons. At least I hadn't ended up with any scars, back then.

I was incapable of jumping to my feet, and so I slowly sat up. Someone had transferred me to the bed. Probably the same someone who sat opposite me now, in a dark armchair of a strange shape. He sat with folded arms, gazing into space. I remembered his dark, swirling eyes, and lowered my gaze.

"What on earth..." I said involuntarily. Around my aching wrist burned a bracelet. Thin, ornate and bright red.

"That bracelet branded into your flesh indicates that you belong to me." The voice of the speaker was deep, and penetrated the very depths of my soul. It suited him, in terms of his appearance. Pale skin, short dark hair, a straight nose and thin, well-defined lips. He sat wearing only black pants tucked into high boots, as if he wanted me to see that every inch of his body was chiseled as if by Michelangelo: Wide shoulders and narrow hips, a six-pack abdomen and armor-plated chest. My heart was pounding, but certainly not in admiration.

The stranger filled me with an instinctive horror.

"I'm no one's property."

"In this world you are. I bought you from your master."

Ah, it seems the chatter about a sale and a master had ceased being fun and had morphed into a real problem.

I took a deep breath and, as calmly as I could, said, "Until right now, I always thought of myself as a contemporary kind of person, you know, *free.*"

As I spoke, I felt the fine hairs rising on my arms. I mean, how to act around someone who thinks he bought me? What I wanted most of all was to get as far away as possible. But, remembering the force that threw me against the wall, I did not dare risk flight.

The man finally deigned to look at his 'property.' And I blinked, trying not to gasp. The darkness no longer filled his eyes. Instead, I saw a dark golden iris with a narrow cat-like pupil. The man grinned, and the pupil became ordinary.

What was going on? Was it some kind of trick?

"You signed a contract at work. According to our laws, your employer is your master. I bought you from him."

"They will be looking for me."

It was good we were talking. The longer we talked, the longer I put off the possibility of being raped.

The man's narrow lips twitched slightly, as if my response amused him. "But of course, they look for everybody. Especially people who were brought up in an orphanage and favored books over friends. Aurora Black, I spent days learning all about you."

His nostrils flared, as if he had caught a scent. "I'll call you Rory."

"And I'm supposed to call you what, 'master'?" I asked sarcastically. "What the hell am I here for?"

"Good, you're not hysterical. You have a strong psyche ... almost like ours. Let's talk, you must have a lot of questions, right Rory?"

"Aurora," I said through clenched teeth, "I'm not a dog whose name you can change on a whim."

"No, you're not. You are my property."

I made a mental note to myself to stay calm — anger is not the way to respond to someone who was clearly insane. And it's obvious that this was the case. Although his tones were measured, he seemed to be barely contained, like a dam about to burst.

"My name is Doran. I am the Leader of the Wild Hunt, the Judge of the Three Courts and the Lord of Shadows."

Alright then, at least he's not Napoleon. I silently hid my face in my hands and laughed. I laughed about the situation I found myself in, about my own foolishness, about everything. Where had I gone so wrong as to end up who-knows-where in the company of crazies?

Strong fingers grabbed me above the elbow. Doran managed to do this without making a sound. "Come here."

"No!"

I didn't want to go anywhere with him, I didn't want to be touched. But Doran easily dragged me to the window, although I struggled and kicked at him.

"Stop that!" he said, intercepting my hand, ready to hit him. My efforts were futile, but I still tried to break free.

"Look, Rory, just look."

Doran easily held my hands behind my back and pulled me against him. I squirmed, but he forced me to stand in front of the window. My bare back was pressed against his bare chest, which was so hot I recoiled. Was he sick? Was he raving because he was feverish?

The dark surface of the window dimmed

and disappeared, giving way to limpid transparency.

And I caught my breath. This was impossible!

Doran's residence towered over the surrounding edifices, and so the city was spread out in a panorama. Strange, freakish. My head began to pound, and my stomach churned. The more I gazed at the lilac and white buildings, the more my head whirled. The city breathed with a kind of insanity, there was no other way of putting it. There wasn't a single straight line, rather, it was a tangle of buildings and streets that seemed to breathe. I didn't see a single tree, nor any kind of green spaces. But there were numerous large statues, and when I looked at them, the nausea was unbearable, although at first glance I couldn't see why. They were abstract carvings from dazzling white stones with dark veins.

"Let go of me...," I gasped —I couldn't take it anymore. Doran silently released me, and even took a step back. And I fell to my knees, shaking and heaving, although my stomach was empty and I could only vomit bile.

Strange, but after that I felt a lot better, and the throbbing in my temples even subsided. Now my head felt more like a bubbling cauldron, which was, somehow, an improvement.

But why had I reacted so physically at the mere sight of a city?

"Don't tell me that you have heightened radiation in the atmosphere," I moaned, trying to catch my breath. "It's..."

"I know what radiation is," Doran interrupted. I literally creaked as I turned my head, and saw that he was standing two steps away. He was looking at me with interest and approval. "Do you feel better now?"

I listened to my body and nodded uncertainly. Better – at least the nausea had passed. My head was still pounding, plus waves of weakness rolled over me, but that could be because of the stress I was under.

"I think you'll be fine in a week," Doran 'comforted' me and added: "Or sooner, if I deem it so."

Deem? *Deem*?!

"Where am I?"

"Ruadh — the city of the Sluagh, Shadows and Chaos. One of the three Faerie Courts."

I couldn't hold it back – I giggled hysterically. Maybe I'd been drugged with some kind of stuff — what was it that caused hallucinations like this? Or, was I actually in a coma after an accident? This just couldn't be real!

"You are not asleep, nor are you mad," Doran seemed to have guessed my thoughts. "In the latter case, I would have to kill you, since you would be useless to me."

"Is that so?"

"It is." He approached again, and I did not have time to recoil before I was jerked to my feet, turned back toward the window, and forced to look at the lilac-white breathing city. For a moment, the nausea rolled over me again, and then it immediately disappeared.

"Ruadh is partially subordinated to Chaos," Doran's voice above my ear vibrated deep into me. "Not every human mind can handle the sight of the city. If you don't claw at your eyes and don't beat your head against the floor, then your prognosis is good."

"So you weren't sure that I could handle it?"

"No, I wasn't sure."

My hands twitched from the desire to slap him. Alas, I lacked the strength and realized that, anyway, he definitely had the upper hand. He was in his element, while I could barely stand, I was so weak.

"When you accept a job, Rory, you should take the time to read the terms of the contract."

"I don't recall anything about selling employees," I managed to snap. I couldn't resist looking at the city, even though I had no desire to. It was like being drawn to something that both repelled and fascinated at the same time.

Get away from me already! I thought. I wanted to be sitting on the floor instead of standing as I was, literally in an embrace with a stranger, a rogue. Whose fingers burned through the thin fabric of my dress, and whose visage frightened me. Not to mention his conduct.

"Sometimes you have to read the fine print. In your case, it was written that the employer has the right to send the employee to higher organizations at his discretion and for an indefinite period."

I involuntarily swore. I *had* read that clause in my contract, and I could never have imagined such a twisted interpretation.. "So now what? Why am I here? Is this a harem? Am I your sex slave?"

Then I exhaled and shouted, releasing all of my accumulated tension:

"What the hell am I doing here?"

"For work," Doran replied calmly. Apparently, he thought he had something resembling a sense of humor.

"What kind of work? Enough puzzles, I hate them unless they fall under my specialty! If my professional skills are what is needed, why not just ask me for help?"

"The Sluagh have never asked for help!" growled Doran.

He turned me towards him again. His iron fingers clasped my chin, forcing me to look into his eyes, which again were clouded in darkness. "If I buy someone, no one will suspect anything. If someone comes to me voluntarily, it means that we are in an alliance. Or that he, or she, is valuable to me. And then that person's days are numbered. Do you know why? Because attachment — is weakness. And we are always on the lookout for any signs of weakness in each other."

I breathed quickly and raggedly, afraid even to lift an eyebrow. I just looked into the completely opaque eyes and listened to the hoarse, growling voice.

"I bought you, Rory, to ensure that you stay alive. Therefore, it is in your interest to submit to me. In Ruadh, without me, you would not last a day. Now, here is my first order: Go to bed and lie there until you stop puking and come to your senses. You will be looked after. I will try to see to it that you adapt quickly. And then we'll sit down and talk. And, by the way, you humans, you know nothing about me and those I rule."

He pushed me to the side, causing me to land rather clumsily on the stone floor. And, wide-eyed, I watched what ensued.

"I am the King of the Wild Hunt and the Court of Shadows."

Doran's voice growled and lowered to a hiss. Strange shadows swirled around him. Absolutely black and terrifying.

"I am he who lives on the edge of Chaos, and in alliance with him."

The shadows slid along his long legs, wrapping around his waist.

"And therefore I can preside in all of the

Courts. For only Chaos is neutral and indifferent to everything. It alone confers the right to render a verdict."

The shadows thickened into flickering shaggy manes with glowing red eyes. The grotesquely twisted muzzles of horses lengthened, replaced by no less grotesque dogs. And all this was delivered in a quiet sort of howling voice that pierced my soul. I didn't realize it at first, but I was sort of howling, too, as I scooted away from him as fast as I could. I felt the leaves of the vines on the wall against my bare back, closed my eyes, and put my hands over my ears. I wanted to block out this nightmare.

I was in serious trouble.

CHAPTER THREE

HAVING SCARED me silly, Doran simply strode out of the room, leaving me sitting on the floor. I sat there another five minutes or so, and then crawled into the bed. I mean I really did crawl, because after Doran's big scene, my legs weren't up to supporting me. I couldn't handle scary stories when I was a kid, and now here I was, thrust into one.

Bed seemed like a fine idea, actually. I still felt weak and wobbly and kind of muddled. It was kind of like having a slight case of the stomach flu, which a friend of mind caught once. I wondered why I felt this way, though.

Despite my unfortunate circumstances (to put it mildly), I was already processing everything I'd gone through. Perhaps this was my body's way of dealing with it all. I was acclimating to my situation. I mean, it's one thing to fly south and take a week to get over jet lag, but I'd been thrown into an entirely different world.

A different world ... it sounded stark raving mad.

My white dress was crumpled. I pulled it off with relish, and crawled under an unusually light, warm blanket. On top of everything else, I seemed to be chilled. I suddenly realized that my teeth were chattering from the cold issuing from deep within me. I quietly sobbed and bit my lip. Then the door opened, and someone new slipped in.

"I brought you food at the order of Doran."

She was clearly a woman. And young. She wore a long dark-purple dress with a deep neckline and long flowing sleeves. Her hair was swept upward, and was an unusual gray color that almost blended in with the color of her face. And her eyes were enormous and black, rather like a bird's. In contrast, the rest of her features were small and sedate.

With difficulty, I looked from the strange being to the tray that she put on the bed. My eyes immediately turned to her long fingers ending in sharp claws.

"Um....wha..what..."

"You can eat this," she explained, and

added, "My name is Aderyn."

"Aurora," I mumbled, trying not to stare too openly at the girl. The food itself didn't appeal to me much. My stomach was empty, but the nausea put me off of eating.

Meanwhile, Aderyn openly gawked at me. She didn't seem hostile, but she also didn't display the slightest sign of friendliness. It was like I was some exotic animal at the zoo. So, I stared right back at her, and asked, "Is there something wrong?"

"Doran told me to make sure you ate."

"I don't feel good."

"That doesn't matter. You should do what he says."

"Or else what?" I asked acidly.

"Otherwise, he will punish me for not fulfilling his orders. You'll catch hell, too. And so if I have to, I'll force feed you."

I could barely stop myself from diving for the plate laden with meat and vegetables and the glass with a strange bluish liquid. The last thing I wanted was to be force-fed by this creature.

"Drink the juice for starters," advised Aderyn. "It will stop the nausea and help you get the food down."

She kept her strange, unblinking eyes trained on me as I struggled to take two sips of the liquid. Then she smiled. Which was unfortunate. Aderyn's teeth were small and pointed, like that of a fish. "I've never seen a human before."

"Back at you," I mumbled, taking another sip. Yes, the bitter juice really did alleviate the nausea.

Aderyn sniffed and said, "You don't stink."

"Is that a problem?"

"Humans stink. Some reek of wickedness, some of lies, and some smell like sex. That's what I was told. But you don't stink at all."

"So what does that mean?" I said, intrigued. What should I smell like, then? A thirst for knowledge?

"Well, either you'll die or you'll adapt to Ruadh. Doran will find out."

What a thing to say. I mean, how very encouraging.

I totally lost my appetite, but Aderyn was hovering over me. For some reason, I believed what she'd said: she could absolutely force feed me. And if I were to spit the food out, she'd bring me something else and make me eat it. Doran's orders were clearly not open to debate here.

"And you're so frail," said Aderyn. I pretended to occupy myself with the meat, which tasted like quail and melted in my mouth. It was good, but I ate just to get it over with.

Maybe I looked frail, but I really wasn't. Most important, I was smart.

"I don't know how long before he'll use you up," Aderyn went on. "Doran is a tireless lover, and humans, they say, are weak."

I almost spat out the food: what's up with this stuff about a lover?! Hello, who said anything about sex? Or was this a unilateral decision on his part?

Needless to say, after Aderyn left, I was beside myself. Despite my weakness and the headache, which had returned, I jumped up and, wrapped in a blanket, paced around the room. Damn, damn, damn! Fortunately, the window was again closed off, otherwise I would have lost the meal that I'd miraculously managed to keep down.

The light in the room was muted, golden. Pacing back and forth, I suddenly noticed how shadows were gathering in one corner. And I immediately guessed that I'd been ratted on.

When Doran, still clad only in his pants, materialized out of the thick darkness, I told him:

"If you touch me, I'll hold my breath, got it? Or I'll beat my head against the wall. Or I'll come up with something else."

And then I froze, waiting for a show of strength or something worse. But there was something strange about Doran, insofar as anything could be strange at this point. He shrugged his shoulders and ... began to peel off his trousers, under which there was nothing but his naked body. I stared wide-eyed, realizing that now, apparently, it didn't matter what I wanted – sex was on the agenda. This was eloquently communicated by the erect shaft straining upwards. It was interesting how devoid of hair Doran's body was. It was like he was carved out of hard wood. Every muscle was clearly etched and spoke of the incredible strength wielded by the King of Ruadh.

"The choice is yours," he said, meanwhile casually dropping his pants on the floor, where they melted into a dark cloud, "You can lay here for a week, puking and passing out from pain all over your body, or you can get into bed and tomorrow you will feel a lot better. My energy will help you adapt faster. How do you call it ..." — a smile slid across his lips.

"Lust," I said.

"Symbiosis," Doran corrected me.

With obvious pleasure he settled into the bed, which suddenly seemed to shrink in size. It was quite small.

The nausea intensified, and for some reason I ached around my kidneys. Well, at least the wrist with my bracelet "brand" didn't hurt anymore, but it itched.

"Hey, you said that since I didn't die right away, that means I'm adapting!"

"Yes, that's right. Only you can adapt the slow, painful way, or you can do it the easy, fast way."

"I don't want to have sex with you!"

"Don't worry, I'm not interested in sex

tonight," Doran yawned. "I'm already sated, so I'm just going to sleep. But remember, Rory, I am asking you for the first and last time. After this, I will not put up with any protestations on your part."

Alright, I wasn't going to be raped after all. Just the same, I stood there, unsure of what to do. I really, really didn't want to jump in bed with a naked man I didn't know. And something I'd read in some trashy book about hooking up suddenly popped into my head. Essentially, it was that you shouldn't sleep in the same bed with a guy unless you wanted to have sex with him. .

At the same time, I had no desire to experience an entire week of "adapting." In all of my 27 years, I'd been laid up exactly twice: Once I broke my leg, and another time I suffered a concussion when I flew off my bike. But I'd miraculously avoided colds and such. Well, a couple of times I'd managed to get heat stroke. But that was it.

I took an indecisive step towards the bed, then another. After all, there was nowhere else to sleep, except on the floor. On the hard, bare floor. I wasn't likely to be given a blanket or pillow.

Doran lay with his hands behind his head and his eyes closed, as if he didn't care: I could lie down or not. His broad chest heaved, as if this ... this beast had fallen asleep.

One more step ... another ...

My nails dug into the palm of my hand; I wasn't at all sure that I was doing the right thing. But I needed strength to get out of here. And there was something else: I'd best be strong in this place, not helpless. Maybe it was Aderyn's gaze swimming in my memory: too predatory and sinister. That's the look one gives to future prey, a victim, not to an equal.

It was scary...

I knelt on the edge of the bed. It beckoned, so soft and warm, and I was still shivering. Not even the memories of Doran's hot touch scared me much. The light suddenly began to fade, as if by order. And in no time the room was plunged into darkness.

Absolutely. Startled, I flew onto the bed and covered myself with a blanket. For a moment, I almost experienced an attack of claustrophobia, so thick was the surrounding darkness. Inky black.

Then, a tiny lamp, invisible among the foliage on the wall, emitted a light, that slowly increased in brightness. It was weak, just slightly breaking up the darkness, but just the same, I breathed easier. And I laid my head on the pillow.

And found myself pressed against a solid, very warm male body. I couldn't stop myself from crying out, startled.

"Symbiosis," Doran said calmly. But his

whisper raised the hairs on the back of my head. I froze, afraid to move, took a deep breath, and blinked. At the same time, I couldn't ignore his still excited male organ pressed against my tailbone.

"Sleep, Rory," he whispered above my ear again, making me shrink. "Tomorrow you'll feel better, and I'll tell you everything. I will teach you how to survive. Do not display fear or weakness to us. The stronger your fear, the more we're attracted to the source. If you show you are afraid, they will devour you. Or, first they'll rape you and then devour you. There are many options."

"Why am I here?" I also whispered, staring into the darkness. Doran wrapped his arm around my waist and held me very tightly.

"You'll find out."

"Are you — faeries?" I asked him point blank.

I didn't know much about mythology, but I did recall a thing or two. I had this Scottish lover once who adored the legends of his people. And often told them. I did not really listen, but somehow, I'd retained something from his stories.

"That's what humans call us. Sleep, Rory, I order you," his was a little louder now, and sounded commanding.

Was he for real? How to fall asleep with some inhuman man breathing in my ear, excited and scary as hell? My fingers were numb and my throat was dry. Plus, our naked bodies were touching. More closely than some lovers embrace.

But all of a sudden, I fell asleep, as if a switch had been flicked off in my head in response to Doran's command.

I woke up to strange whispers and giggles. For a few seconds I struggled to cast off the last vestiges of sleep, and then I jumped up and began to look around.

The laughter quieted down. Near my bed three girls abruptly froze. They looked so exotic, that my eyes popped out of my head.

"Who are you?"

"Oh!" exclaimed one girl, whose hair sparkled in every shade of gold, "She speaks! We understand her! Her! A human!"

She had enormous blue eyes and perfect features, along with an ideal figure, which was barely covered with an airy, bright garment.

"Most likely Doran did what he could," said another, with black hair and opal eyes. Slightly curved horns peeked out from under a canopy of hair, and a tail, much like that of a donkey, poked out from under a black dress that looked like swirling smoke.

"What do they call you, Human?" asked the third, whose appearance was the most startling of all. This was the first time I'd ever seen a creature with membranes between its fingers, long feathers instead of hair, and fangs instead of teeth. Despite this, she wasn't at all ugly. Rather, she was exotic.

"Aurora."

"Aurora, Aurora!" The golden-haired girl clapped her hands "That means 'dawn.' What a beautiful name"

"Shut up, Briallyn," the dark-haired girl said, and then turned to me: "How do you feel?"

Strange. I feel strange. Kind of like a patient in a mental hospital.

"Okay," I said.

And in fact, I did feel okay: The nausea had passed, as had the chills, and if not for feeling weak, I was perfectly fine. Had sleeping with Doran really helped, then? So, had he really spent the entire night there? Where had he gone? Although his whereabouts didn't really concern me. What mattered was that he wasn't here.

"My name is Meldyt," the brunette continued, "and this is Derryt. We belong to the Court of the Shadows now. Derryt was born here, and we were gifted as tributes from our Courts."

"Nice to meet you," I mumbled, wondering

what they wanted from me.

"Before now, we've only seen a human once," Briallyn piped up, "And that was just a glimpse. The poor thing went crazy almost immediately."

I swallowed and asked in a hoarse voice:

"So then what happened to her?"

"They gave her away to the bestiary," Derryt quickly squawked— her voice reminded me of a petulant bird. "Had to find something to do with her."

"You, though, are strong," Meldyt spoke again, her eyes fixed on me, "But you're sad."

"I was sad, too," broke in Briallyn, "when I first got here. Now I'm used to it. When eternity lies before you there's no point in being depressed. You're better off looking on the bright side."

"She won't succeed," Derryt objected. "She'll perish as soon as she steps out the door of this room."

"Hello, I'm right here," I said, trying to get their attention. "What are you doing here?"

"We wanted to look at you. You're pretty for a human. Have you already been with Doran? He's an insane lover, always summoning all three of us at once. Can you walk?"

I felt my cheeks and ears burning.

"I'd rather not talk about it."

"Why not?" asked Briallyn, surprised. All three girls knelt on the floor by the bed, eagerly looking at me. Here they were at the zoo again. And I was the latest attraction.

"Let's move on," I said glumly. "What goes on between two people is private."

I could see total incomprehension emanating from the eyes of my visitors. Then Meldyt blinked and said, "Ahhhh, I heard that humans had hang-ups about sex."

"Hang-ups?" Briallyn gasped. "Whatever for? How do they generate offspring?"

"The same way we do," Derryt said. "Except they do it in the dark and just in twos."

Their chatter was getting to me. Meldyt kept casting covert looks at me with her large, dark eyes, and then she asked, "Are you unhappy? Do you want to escape from here?"

At which a hush fell over the room. The girls leaned forward, waiting for my response. But I silently shook my head and said quietly, "I don't know how to escape. Of course I'd like to."

"I know how," said Meldyt. "There are ways."

I felt a nag of suspicion. Totally justifiable, of course.

"Um, why should I believe you? I've just met you."

"Faeries don't lie," offered Briallyn. "You didn't know that?"

I recalled then that yes, I'd heard something like that before. "And what's in it for you?"

And again they exchanged glances. Then came the somewhat hushed voice of Briallyn.

"Well, what does Doran want with a mistress — a human?"

"I'm not his mistress!"

"Not yet, anyway. Did he promise to never try to take you?"

"Well, no."

I was dying to go home, but something continued to bother me. For example, the fact that these girls I barely knew were so ready to help me. I asked, "Are you jealous, is that it?"

"What?" Meldyt asked.

Derryt explained, "That's when a woman wants to keep other women away from a man and is furious if he sleeps with anyone else, or pays attention to them."

"Ah, well, that's so silly!" Briallyn chuckled. "Doran is the King of Shadows and we are all at his service. Until he finds a Queen for himself. Then, under the laws of our world, they will forever be together. Well, until one of them is bored with living. In the meantime, he can summon any of his subjects. And you are no exception."

Briallyn nodded toward my wrist, encircled by the intricate bracelet-brand. "You belong to him, Aurora. So either make peace with it, or run away."

Make peace with it? With the fact that I, a living person, belong, like property, to some creature? Okay, I had to get used to the reality of having been transported to another world, as crazy as that was. But I wasn't about to become someone's plaything. Should I trust these wenches? I looked over the trio once more.

One kept her eyes glued on me. Derryt shook her head, making her hair-feathers softly rustle, and rasped, "Time's up, Aurora, you don't have any to spare."

"Won't you get in trouble for helping me?"

"Do you worry about us?" asked Meldyt, surprised. "In your place, we'd run away, no matter what the consequences."

"Well, I'm not like that."

"Doran will be angry," Briallyn interjected, "He might even punish us, but he won't kill us. He's used to us. And to kill over a human? Pfff. Besides, he might be able to impregnate one of us, and he knows that. So fear not."

It all seemed to make sense. Too much sense, actually. But I really wanted to go home. What if this was my only chance? What if, right now, Doran was on his way to come screw me silly? The very thought of it drove me crazy. True, I slept fine last night, and at some point, the man's embrace had stopped seeming so very bad. In fact, he spooned me in such a way that our two bodies fit perfectly. But it was one thing to sleep together. When it came to sex, I preferred to be ruled by love rather than by a master.

"What do I have to do?" I still had lingering doubts, but I decided to believe the three wenches. All the more so because they were looking at me so avidly. And they sounded so very sincere.

Faeries don't lie...

"I have no clothes," I said. Apparently, this signaled to the trio to start moving, and they practically jumped around me.

In fact, they'd brought clothes, which all this time had been quietly lying on the floor alongside the bed. Were they so sure I'd agree? Suspicion nagged at me again, but then Briallyn touched my hand, looked gently at me, and the doubts disappeared. Yes, they'll return me to my home! Realizing this, I was elated with happiness, like a balloon. Just a little more, and I would float up, up, and away from Doran and this crazy city.

Fortunately, they gave me a dress that wasn't too long. But once again the cut was rather daring, featuring thin strips crossed over my chest, with a hem made of ribbons, and the fabric was also thin. The color was scarlet and could be seen from afar. I hurriedly pulled it on, deciding not to worry about incidentals like underwear. The main thing at this point was to get back home.

"Ready?" Briallyn took my hand, and a new wave of euphoria surged over me, washing away all my fears. Soon ... I'll be home soon!

But just the same, I hesitated when I saw a thick cloth bandage in Derryt's hand. "What's that for?"

"You are a human being," the bird-woman explained patiently. "Your eyes cannot stand the sight of the palace. Our city is partly in Chaos, and humans are weak creatures. You'd return home stark raving mad."

I didn't want to go crazy, but I also didn't want to wear the blindfold.

"Decide," Derryt said, seeing that I was hesitating. "Doran left the palace for a while, but soon he'll be back."

"Aurora, hurry up!" Briallyn's pleading voice seemed to foster something inside of me that I didn't understand. I felt a warmth toward her, a kind of confidence that just didn't make sense. And yet, I went with it. After all, there I was and maybe this was my only chance to escape. *Let's do this thing*, I thought.

The blindfold covered my eyes, tightly and gently. I immediately felt uncomfortable — I really don't function well in the dark. I grabbed hold of the golden-haired girl's hand. Fortunately, she wasn't about to let me go.

We walked quickly, but carefully, apparently along some kind of secret passages, since I did not hear voices around me. The smooth floor chilled my bare feet, the air grew cooler, and then it started warming up so that my back started sweating. I smelled something sharp and spicy, as if some spices were, in fact, spilling out somewhere nearby. And I couldn't escape the feeling of something huge and alive around me. This living thing was neither evil nor good, rather, it was indifferent. It was taking measure. Of me.

A turn...Briallyn whispered, telling me to step up, so a threshold was in front of me. Another turn, an easy gradient. The tiles under our feet became a little warmer and began to spring a little. How fun.

"Aurora, now is the most crucial moment."

I nodded, communicating to her that I was ready. Only Briallyn spoke. The other two were silent. But I heard their breathing nearby. The feeling of something huge and alive increased from time to time.

"Aurora, you have to crawl up to a boundary. I'll tell you when to stop. The most important thing is to keep on crawling. And utter this phrase.

Briallyn said something in an unfamiliar language. She had to repeat it several times before I could reproduce the words correctly.

"Crawl! When I whistle, take off the blindfold."

Well, okay then. I took a deep breath, and crept forward, repeating the phrase I was told in a trembling voice. The floor really was warmer than in other places. It was even rather pleasant to be crawling, although I wished I knew where I was...

Suddenly the euphoria began to subside, like water swirling down the drain. Then the certainty washed over me that this was a trap. Plus, the feeling grew that I wasn't at all alone here.

And then I heard... A barely perceptible laugh. I could barely hear it, but there it was.

I'd had it!

I pulled off the bandage and jumped to my feet. And then I closed my eyes — from the light and the shock. It was a lot. It filled the huge hall where they sat....no, not people. Creatures, the sight of which really could make you lose your mind.

And they laughed out loud.

The first impulse: plug my ears and run, run, run. The assembly reminded me of facing down the gangs of "troubled kids" at the orphanage. They also laughed at anyone who was weaker than them. I got it before I consciously understood it: the greater your weakness, the more joyously they tore into you. It was probably just like that here.

Slowly and carefully, I brushed off my dress, although there was not a speck of dust on it. Good for them, what a clean palace. Then I looked around.

The space must have been something like a dining hall. Gleaming stone tables were scattered about, on the right was a dais, and strange, as if melting, furniture stood under a huge transparent dome that spanned the ceiling, under which an almost palpable gloom prevailed, making my head spin a bit. Again lilac colors mixed with black and light gray.

The noise of voices, strange creatures, the sight of which made my blood run cold What to say? It's not like they were really scary. No, a lot of them looked a lot like people. But each of them had something off about them—a too-long nose that reached the chin, or eyes all over the face, or four hands rather than two.

I slowly turned to the trio —the girls were clearly enjoying themselves. I asked as coolly as I could, "So what does the phrase I was repeating mean?"

"I'm a dirty slut who wants to suck you off," Meldyt said.

And again the spectators broke out in laughter. Amidst the laughter, I distinctly made out phrases about how I could satisfy my wish. With whomever.

"Ugh!" said Briallyn in response to this. "Do the subjects of the Court of Shadows want to debase themselves with a human?"

"So you're saying I debased myself with her." The voice came out of nowhere. And made quite the impression: the entire room fell silent.

The faces of the trio took on a greenish tint. Although, Briallyn tried to look chipper and even jutted her trembling chin out a little. "My

King, we were just having fun!"

I couldn't tell where Doran was. His voice echoed through the hall, but the Lord of the Shadows himself was not visible.

"Fun?" Doran asked, his voice deceptively soft.

Briallyn nodded hastily and repeated: "I remember, my King, you said — do not harm your new toy. And nothing befell her. We just wanted to get to know her. It is amusing, isn't it?"

Yes, how very fun. I gritted my teeth, doing my best to look calm. Even though inside I was overwhelmed with humiliation as I imagined what all these creatures had seen. Me, crawling on my hands and knees and asking to ...give them blow jobs. Oh, how funny, really really funny.

Suddenly Doran appeared on the dais. There was a ball of darkness, and the King stepped out of it, dressed in black pants and a black shirt of a silky-looking material. A large bright lilac pendant shimmered on his chest, and darkness swirled in his eyes. Was I right in assuming this was a sign that he was furious?

"Rory, how did they get you to leave the room? What did they promise?"

The gazes of hundreds of creatures closed on me, as if piercing me with the finest needles. My skin actually began to burn. Well, don't lie. Something inside was resisting...

"I ..." – I had to cough. "They offered to help me escape."

"And she believed us," Meldyt suddenly laughed. "My King, we only offered to help her leave, but to where and from where we did not specify."

Fool, my inner voice told me, *I didn't ask the right questions.*

"So, you were ready to escape, Rory?"

He turned right toward me. And I involuntarily backed away from the dark, wide-shouldered figure. Because I understood: Doran, to put it mildly, was furious about my escape attempt.

My tactical retreat ended quickly. The faery quickly crossed the hall and grabbed my throat. I could still breathe, but just the same, it was highly uncomfortable. I helplessly clawed at his fingers around my neck.

"You wanted to flee?" The black eyes bored into me. I felt sick at heart and ready to die.

"Yes, I wanted to flee, and I still want to."
He'll kill me.

Doran's eyes spoke volumes. On the one hand, I never promised him I wouldn't run away. And so...

A sharp pain burned my wrist with the bracelet so sharply that I flailed my arms, trying to scream. Doran graciously gave me the opportunity to do so, letting go and letting me fall onto my knees. It was like my wrist had been sawed through: slowly and sadistically. I couldn't even scream — my breath caught in my throat. All I could do was moan. At some point I fell on my side and through the din in my ears I heard the voice of the faery:

"The punishment for attempting to flee, Rory, is extremely serious. Think about that, human."

Through the red veil of pain, I saw the black figure turn towards the trio.

"Did I give you permission to enter the room and approach my human?"

"No, King," the friendly one sang. All of the others were silent and eagerly listened to the conversation.

"And did I really allow you to let her out of the room?"

"But, my King," Meldyt said, "you did not forbid it. You just said not to harm her."

"You're a clever one, Meldyt. It's not for nothing that you were at one time an advisor to the Unseelie Court. How could you be so very stupid?"

I swallowed and tried to breathe evenly. Yes, the pain had definitely waned, although I could not move my hand.

"What do you mean, my King?" Meldyt's voice acquired a tremulous tone.

"Humans are naturally very fragile. She could have been emotionally damaged by this. What would I want with a broken plaything?

Worse still, you turned the magic of the Seelie Court on her. Briallyn, is this your doing?"

"I have done nothing wrong, my King. My magic cannot be used to harm anyone. I just caused her to relax."

"How sweet of you, Briallyn. So very caring of you."

I managed to somehow rise to my knees so that I wasn't lying at Doran's feet. But for the time being, there was no way I could stand on my feet. I was trembling from what I'd gone through.

"Henceforth, I advise you not to feign good intentions. Meldyt, what did you have Rory say? *'I am a dirty slut who wants to suck you off?'* An excellent idea. Today, you three will serve my Hunt."

"No!"

"My King, have mercy!"

"We won't survive!"

"You'll recover," Doran snapped. Ignoring their screams, he threw me over his shoulder and carried me out of the hall. I managed to glimpse a few dozen of the creatures rushing towards the sobbing girls. And then the doors closed, and at once the screams fell silent. Now I could hear only Doran's measured steps, and his breathing. Well, along with my quiet sobs from the mental overload from everything that had transpired.

"You had to be punished in front of

everybody, Rory, so that no one thinks twice about any favoritism."

I was silent, staring blankly at the dark shiny tiles beneath me. What did it matter what anyone said or thought about me? I wanted to go home. Away from this surreal nightmare.

"We're going to sit down and talk with you, Rory," Doran continued calmly, "You have already collected yourself; your adaptation is going well. You're capable of hearing me out."

I'm not going to hear you out. You'd be better off going to hell and back. That's where people like you feel right at home.

"I think you'll be interested in hearing that I need your brains."

So he's a zombie, then? Awesome! How perfectly awful!

"The fact is that we are dying out, Rory. It's been going on for some time now."

For real?!

I wasn't about to tell him about the dinosaurs – not to mention the mammoths. *Sorry, dude, extinction happens.* And yet something in Doran's voice made me bite my tongue, both literally and figuratively, and humbly ride on his shoulder and wait. At the same time, I stole a look around me.

We proceed along wide corridors that were as if carved into the rock. Everything around us was massive and evidently heavy. The creatures whose path we crossed either bowed low or knelt before us. This seemed to depend on their status. And no one was surprised that their King was walking around with a woman over his shoulder.

I didn't see many doors — instead there were high arches, through some of which a pearly fog hung in the air. What was it? Through one arch, I thought I saw something move in the hazy depths.

A strange place, unpleasant. But at least it was no longer trying to deprive me of my sanity. And I was starting to kick my legs when Doran strode toward a foggy opening. Of course, my feeble squirming was totally ignored.

For a few seconds the fog totally shrouded me. It was warm and dry, not at all watery. I tried not to think about what it was composed of. All the more so because we passed through it, and ended up in a spacious room that was very bright with no windows. I could not discern the source of the light.

"This is how we transport ourselves through Chaos," Doran broke the silence. Just when I was starting to feel good about his deciding to give me the silent treatment.

"Teleportation?"

"That is a human word, and you have yet to master this concept you came up with."

I shuddered, because I did not expect that we'd be alone. But from behind tall stone cabinets emerged a man...or, yes, it was another faerie. He could have passed for an ordinary, although extremely good-looking man of around 40. He had a chiseled profile, with a lean face and bright blue eyes, a mane of ashy hair held back with a thin dark band, and a lean body encased in something long and shapeless. Only one thing spoiled the impression: his goat hooves. Well, nobody's perfect, right?

"You seem to be well versed in our terminology," I said, trying to work out a kink in my neck and properly check out the new guy.

Greenish brown furniture cluttered up the room, which reeked of herbs and something else which made my throat start to feel sore.

"I am one of the Hunt," said the ash-haired faerie and smiled broadly, which made my own smile quickly fade as his teeth were triangular and sharp.

"More precisely," Doran corrected, "you are my adviser and doctor, and at the same time a Hunter. This is Rory."

"Oh, she survived the night. This is good. I am Haedyn. I know a little bit more about your kind than the others do."

"I'm a little intimidated by how popular I am," I said.

Doran responded by throwing me off of his shoulder and plopping me into one of the chairs. It looked like it was stone, but in fact it was quite soft and comfortable. I didn't really like having the men towering over me while I sat here, though. Just the same, I threw up my head, meeting Doran's usual gaze, and informed him:

"I hate you."

"Nothing strange about that," Haedyn said, soothingly. "He's hated by a large portion of the Courts. Want to know what they call him? The Dog of Chaos."

"Haedyn, examine her, and then we'll talk."

"What do you mean by 'examine?'" I asked cautiously. "And why now instead of yesterday when I was throwing up my guts?"

Doran shrugged, as if I had asked the dumbest thing in the world.

"I myself can alleviate the period of acute adaptation, but had you perished during the night, then an examination by the doctor would have been in vain. And his energy — wasted."

"I see," I nodded. "Why squander the national wealth on a future corpse."

"She's afraid, but hides her fear," Haedyn commented, turning to Doran.

Doran nodded, continuing to look at me. Then he spoke, slowly and clearly, trying to drive every word into my head. "The gift of a doctor, the gift of a healer is very much appreciated here, as it is extremely precious. Therefore, we surround them with honor and attention. You've demonstrated that you can survive in my Palace. Now, Haedyn will use his gift on you to ensure that you've adapted and are in complete health. If he discerns any problems, he'll neutralize them. You humans are good at ailing, and love it, too.

I flashed Doran a look that communicated what I thought about his understanding of humanity. But that was all. I mean, I really had no desire to experience pain from the 'bracelet' again.

"Okay, stand up," Haedyn said. "This won't hurt at all."

They could pull my teeth out then and there, but I wasn't going to let out a squeak. I had no intention of seeing the satisfaction in the eyes of the King of Shadows, who was, it seems, a covert sadist.

To onlookers, it probably looked like a performance in a two-bit magic show. Haedyn and I stood face to face while he placed his hands along both sides of my head, all but touching my skin. Then, he slowly moved them downwards, along the sides of my body.

In fact, I didn't feel anything at all. Haedyn's face, however, displayed ever-increasing pressure. I saw the hair on his temples darken with sweat, and his pupils dilated so much that they eclipsed his irises.

Doran was silent, but I could not look at him. I was not allowed to turn around. So I stared at Haedyn, whose hands were now hovering near my stomach. Suddenly, our eyes locked, and I saw such pain in his that for a moment I felt uneasy.

"You are ovulating now," he said softly. "You can be impregnated now."

Was I imagining things, or did Doran softly sigh? So...

"It's normal for women to ovulate," I said, trying to stay calm. "So I don't see what the big deal is."

"People have always multiplied randomly without ever thinking about how valuable it is," Haedyn sighed.

"Not true. Right now humanity is crazy about babies and children."

The healer just shook his head, still very sad. And also tense. After completing the examination, he shook his head and made a strange clicking sound.

"How is she, then?" Doran asked rather harshly. By now, of course, I was used to being referred to in the third person. Whatever. So be it.

"That's the first human I've ever examined," Haedyn said obliquely, stepping away from me, "I can assure you that she's healthy. The picture of health."

"So what is it?"

I looked at each man in turn. What was *what*? As regards my health, I was happy to hear I was fine, but it's not like I didn't know that was the case. I mean, I seemed to have good genes.

"Well..." Haedyn was obviously feeling unsure about what he was about to say. "Doran, perfectly healthy just doesn't happen."

"That's what we say, as well," I cut in. "That being said, there are things we know little about."

"I gave you a very thorough examination," the doctor said.

"Quiet now," Doran said. "Haedyn, besides her remarkable health, what is it that gives you pause?"

I bit my tongue, lest I let loose a snarky response. I had the feeling that any outbursts from me wouldn't help. In fact, they might worsen my situation.

"I'm at a loss," the doctor said, "Perhaps it's the result of her exposure to Chaos. I don't know, Doran, she seems to be fine. And yet something isn't quite right. But I'm repeating myself: neither she, nor her life, are endangered now. So you can make full use of her."

I couldn't take it anymore and coughed. My mind suddenly supplied me with images of how the three wenches were being "entertained" right now. And Doran was looking at me so thoughtfully, as if pondering whether to eat me right then and there, or have some fun tormenting me.

I gulped and asked, "Well, now that we know there's nothing wrong with me, then maybe you can finally tell me what I'm doing here? I mean, it clearly doesn't have anything to do with the fact that I'm ovulating?"

Haedyn chuckled and muttered something in an incomprehensible language. And suddenly it dawned on me.

"Why is it I understand you?"

"Because I gave you the ability," Doran said. "Have a seat, Rory. Let's talk."

He extended his hand to me, but I looked at it with righteous suspicion. Although at first glance, I had no reason to fear it. It's just a hand, extended by a strong man, with a strong wrist, and long, sinewy fingers, one of which sported a gleaming silver ring. But I remembered how they'd grasped my throat.

I hesitated, and then extended my hand. And very softly exhaled when our fingers touched. Why was Doran so hot? He was like a stove. His heat penetrated under my skin and froze there.

It was a strange sensation.

He led me to a wide table carved from a greenish stone, which was silky and warm to the touch. It was only now that I noticed plates covered with silver lids on the surface of the table. And I realized that I was ravenous and even had cramps in my stomach.

"Let's eat, Rory." It was like he was ordering me.

Silently, I took the lid off of the nearest

dish. Some kind of meat under a strange golden sauce, and some kind of vegetables.

"You can eat everything," Haedyn said, as if hearing my thoughts. "Your kind can eat our food. So feel free to eat whatever you want."

The meat turned out to be juicy, succulent, and the sauce imparted a delightful piquancy to the dish. I couldn't begin to say what it was, though. The vegetables were like a combination of potatoes and eggplant, with a consistency that was 'al dente' on the outside, and tender on the inside.

Doran himself poured me a glass of the bluish beverage, and said, "Drink, it's good for you."

What would be good for me would be to get back home, but that's a luxury no one could provide me here.

I drank the drink, all the while imagining tossing it into Doran's stone face. And as soon as I put the glass down and took up the fork and knife, he began speaking. Haedyn silently chewed and listened closely.

"Rory, our people can live forever. We are not affected by illness, and it's quite difficult to kill us. We can choose to die if we lose our appetite for living and slip over the border into Chaos. Several hundred years ago, we lived side by side with humans. Our chronicles depict the legends of these days of yore."

I silently nodded, and began cutting the

meat into neat little cubes.

"Our worlds split apart when humanity began to develop too rapidly. Perhaps the technological leap somehow impacted the structure of the world. And we left, came here to Alfheim. In the legends, it is called Avalon, Alfheim, and there are other names, as well."

"Are you afraid of iron?" I asked, remembering how Gray had screamed in the Director's office.

"Some of the lesser nations are quite allergic to it," nodded Haedyn.

"So you have quite a few, umm...um..." I snapped my fingers, trying to find the right word. "Races?"

"Yes, many races," nodded Doran, "and we all ended up here." He drank a silvery beverage from his glass and continued, "In your world and ours, time is not the same. I can't be sure about when we first started noticing that something was wrong. Even before the schism between our worlds, we rarely had children, and after we all ended up here, we stopped altogether."

Whoa, that made me uneasy. I mean, what with Haedyn going on about ovulating, fertility, how very healthy I am.

"Are you planning on making a breeder out of me?"

The doctor was about to take a sip, but then he stopped, his eyes bulging. He looked bemused, to say the least.

As for Doran, his impenetrable composure was no doubt the stuff of legends. He looked at me closely and said calmly. "No, our need for you is of a professional nature."

Whew. What a relief. Kids are great, don't get me wrong, but no way did I want to be anyone's incubator. "Can you give me more details?"

"I can," said Doran politely, "I want you to study our genetic makeup and restore our ability to bear offspring."

"Ah, I see," I thought about it, and said again, "Ah."

Then I burst into somewhat hysterical laughter. And I laughed for several minutes, releasing all of the tension I'd accumulated. With effort, I managed to get myself to stop before my ragged laugher turned into sobs. No way did I want to cry in front of these two. A voice within me told me that crying was not respected here.

Doran and Haedyn patiently waited for my bout of levity to pass. But it did seem that the King's sinewy hand gripped the handle of his knife rather hard. The table knife was beautiful, gilded, with small diamonds set into the handle. There were a lot of valuable gems here. I even saw entire panels displaying them on the walls.

"Gentlemen Faeries, are you serious?"

"Do I look like I'm joking?" asked Doran,

very softly. Under his gaze, my laughter was instantly quenched and banished. Again, his pupils became like slits.

"You appear to be an intelligent faery," I responded diplomatically, trying to choose the right words. "But I can't do what you ask all by myself, understand? It ... it sounds simple enough, but in fact, it would require the whole institution to carry out. Okay, maybe a state-of-the-art lab with solid professionals, the best equipment, reagents. Can you provide me with all that?"

"Give me a list, and we'll find what we need."

"My god!" I exclaimed, putting my head in my hands. "No, no, you just don't get it. I can't pull this off on my own. All the more so because you aren't even humans, and I don't know your DNA, your physiology, and so on. Why did you think you needed *me* for this? Look at all of your abilities!"

"Our abilities can't help us," Doran snapped, rising from his seat slightly. "And your institute is a sad joke that's only good for hemorrhaging money. Who do you think invested in its development? Your former boss is up to his ears in debt to me, and for what? It's all smoke and mirrors, what he does. Yes, it's true that I understood this before I provided him with some of our genetic material. But you are the one to do this. And do you want to know why? It's because you alone managed to put together a strong team and produce some solid results."

"He showed me your work," Haedyn said. "You did not even have magic, and yet you applied science to the task and made great progress. I lack such knowledge, I am not able to change how each cell in the body functions, plus delve into anomalies, hunt them out. We do things a little differently here. I see what's what and I heal. If I don't see it, I cannot heal it."

"You know what, this is crazy! It's stark raving mad! I really feel for you, I do. But what you want — it's impossible."

I suddenly stopped, overwhelmed by my thoughts. And then I cautiously suggested, "Although, if you let me go home, then I could go back to my lab and..."

"No," Doran roared so loudly my hair stood on end. "You will stay and do what you can right here."

"What do you think is going to happen? Do you think I'll wink and nod and say "Oh, I see, you're lacking this and that in your DNA, so just take this magic pill and you'll all be fine?"

"If you succeed, I'll let you go," the King softly said.

I froze and right then realized that we both were standing, palms on the table, staring intently at each other. And we were practically yelling.

But yes, he was dangling quite a nice carrot in front of me.

"But what if I can't do it?" I asked, almost involuntarily whispering. And even though it was hard, I resisted the urge to avert my gaze. Doran's eyes almost burned a hole in me.

"I'll give you to my Hunt. First you will be devoured, then your remains will be thrown into Chaos, and you will return as a red-eyed skank."

I swallowed and suddenly said, my voice hoarse, "Well, your offer is just so-so."

"Rory, I will help you get everything you need to carry out your research," said Haedyn, whose presence I'd almost forgotten about. "In general, I'm here for all your questions."

I almost collapsed back into the chair and covered my face with my hands. My head was spinning with thoughts, but I couldn't seem to focus on any of them. It was as if Chaos had invaded my head space. Right now, Doran's order seemed like the ravings of a madman. I'd been almost sure that the King, despite his obvious brutality, was still a smart man. But then to be given such an order. And he was clearly confident that I could do it.

Of course it's nice when others think more of you than you do yourself. At the same time, it can lead to certain pitfalls.

I was absolutely sure I did not want to be thrown to the Hunt. But I didn't know how I was going to carry out Doran's order.

I slowly lifted my head from my hands and sighed. Whatever, it's not like I had a choice. So I had to move forward one step at a time. "I'll start tomorrow. And the first thing I need is to learn your entire history, all about your species, your races, and your abilities. This is just the start."

I felt like a tightrope walker on a thin wire with no net underneath. One step in either direction and I'd fall into the abyss. It's not like if I failed, Doran would issue me a fine and shake his finger at me.

So I had to do my best.

I suddenly felt incredibly tired, no doubt from the information overload I'd been swamped with — it was like I was seeing double, even.

Doran noticed how pale I was and said, "You need to get some sleep. You haven't adapted to our cycle of life here. Let's go.

Right. Cycle. There was something I wanted to ask, but I couldn't remember what it was. The thoughts that had been racing through my mind seemed to slow down. I felt lethargic, and I couldn't keep my eyes open. It was easier to think of this as simply a matter of acclimating to this place.

I was glad that, rather than carrying me, Doran simply walked beside me. True, I had to keep up with his long stride. This wasn't easy given how sleepy and shell-shocked I was. Again the fog-enshrouded Archway, a barely noticeable resistance field, light warmth, and we found ourselves in a wide corridor with a dark, flickering ceiling, empty and echoing. The light had an unpleasant, reddish cast, which looked like spatters of blood here and there. We were alone.

"Why is this place so empty?"

"There are lots of people here," said Doran, not breaking stride. "You simply can't see them yet. Here we are."

I recognized the door to my room: tall and dark gold with obscure symbols. And, reluctantly, I stepped inside.

"Is something wrong, Rory? What is it?"

"It's nothing. It's just that I have some bad memories associated with this room."

Doran's eyes swept round the room as if he was seeing it for the first time. Then he looked at me and said, turning back to the door. "Follow me."

I definitely preferred the new room. The furniture was dark, but I felt especially comfortable here. Maybe this was because of the many strange golden lights stationed around the room, or maybe it was because the room wasn't as spacious as my last chamber. And I didn't feel like a rabbit on the high plains.

"Does this room suit you?"

I looked around again and nodded. "Yes, it's perfect. And I don't have to worry about any unexpected visitors, right?"

Doran grinned. "Don't worry, Rory. I don't share my toys."

"Especially when it's an educational toy, right? You're not afraid you'll break it?"

"Are you referring to how I had to punish you?" Doran's eyes narrowed, and he stepped closer to me. I felt my insides tighten up, but I stood my ground, hoping that my chin wasn't quivering with fear. It wasn't the King's height that was so intimidating, although he was a full head taller than me. Rather, it was his aura. I don't know how I managed to not fall to my knees. I could clearly see why he was the King. He didn't have to even try, he simply exuded power and might.

"Rory, you tried to run away. You never promised not to try this, but I had to punish you in public to demonstrate to everybody that you were no exception. To me and Haedyn you're a scientist on whom the survival of the species depends. To everyone else, you are my property, and as such, totally off limits. That's for your own safety. And so behave yourself, so that we do not have to again mete out punishment."

"Why this secrecy?" I had to ask. "You're all facing extinction, yet you alone are worried about it."

For some reason my breathing was impeded by our close proximity. It was like the air itself was infused with his aura. And his fingers suddenly brushed my cheek, as if scorching them. I couldn't stand it, and shied away from his touch.

"Because I alone am able to swallow my pride and clearly see what's happening here. Get some rest."

He walked out the door, leaving me pensively looking after him as I bit my lips. *What's happening here...*

I was full of questions. But I did the only thing that, in my opinion, mattered. I set off for the bathroom. It was situated in the same place as in the lavender room, behind a door in the far corner. It was spacious, with mirrors everywhere, and a glossy stone floor and shower that cascaded down like a waterfall from an artificial cliff. The toiletries were arrayed on flat stones, in silver jars. Shampoo, soaps...they all looked like a rainbow of multi-colored gels.

Afterwards, I barely made it to the bed, casting off my dress en route, and then climbing under the covers and passing out. I wasn't tormented by thoughts because my brain had simply decided I needed to rest up for the labors that awaited me.

I don't know how long I slept. I know only that I was awakened by what I'd expected, but didn't want to be right about.

Actually, what first awakened me was an exquisitely delightful sensation. The sensations started down *there* and filled my core. *Oh, yeah.*

Someone's fingers were tantalizing me, and I was already hot and wet. The fingers expertly fondled me, sending sharp stabs of pleasure throughout my body. My breath caught, I was so aroused.

This went on until I finally shook off the deep slumber. Then, the delicious pleasure was abruptly replaced by a tremor of fear. Here I was, naively hoping for the best, but here we go again!

I silently started to fight back, realizing now whose hot form was pressed against me from behind —so tightly that I could feel his throbbing member against my back.

Strangely, as soon as I started kicking at him, he let me go. I rolled off the bed, my knees hitting the stone floor, and turned around, shielding my chest with my hands. Yes, it was futile, but I still had my pride.

Of course, it was Doran. He sprawled across the bed, resting on his elbow. Naked and aroused. In the semi-darkness, I could barely see the green glow of his eyes.

"What the devil!?" I cried out, although in my head I was thinking "What the faery!?"

"I think I should sleep here with you to ensure your safety."

Maybe I was imagining things, but his voice seemed deeper than usual, and sort of purring or something. Like a huge beast ready to mate.

"And touching me is also part of your security measures?"

"You were aroused," he said. "I was just helping."

I stared at him, waiting for an explanation. And, sighing, Doran deigned to provide one. "We attract people to us. Perhaps you have yet to realize this, but your subconscious is already in the know. When I arrived, you were evidently dreaming of something that caused you to moan and stroke yourself. This state could hinder you from thinking clearly."

"So for you it's just fine to climb right into bed and start... joining in?"

"Sex is simply pleasure. Well, or torture, depending on the situation. You humans ascribe too much to it."

"While you simplify it too much," I retorted, continuing to cover myself while hiding behind the bed. I had this totally awful feeling of complete helplessness. Because if he wanted to carry on, there was nothing I could do about it.

Meanwhile, Doran contemplated me thoughtfully until I began to freeze, kneeling on the bare floor. Although it was certainly warm enough in the room itself.

"Your condition may interfere with work."

"It's not like I'm at work right now. And yes, I appreciate your concern, but it's not warranted."

"Okay, but bear in mind that you'll get no

leniency from me." With these words, he simply stood up and left, while I stared after him, dumbfounded. So that's the way it was going to be, then?

Another five minutes passed before I felt that I could trust what was happening and go back to bed. Where I sat and thought. A thoroughly aroused man had just left who had not really insisted on finishing the job, so to speak. It was kind of...well, strange, maybe.

Although, it just hit me, he is the King, after all. Why should he struggle or force anyone when all of the women at the Court were at his service? How many did he have at once? Two, three? Who cares? What mattered, really, is that now I could sleep.

Which is easy to say. All I had to do was close my eyes to see the image of Doran in all of his naked glory. His slightly narrowed eyes, perfectly chiseled muscles, narrow hips and throbbing cock, so very big and kind of scary.

Damn! Again I was overwhelmed by lust. No, it wasn't all about Doran. I was just really horny.

I tried counting sheep, but they melted into vibrators jumping over a fence. Then I tried meditative breathing, but this just excited me all the more. What was going on? I hoped that this was a passing phase, because I had no desire to turn into a raging nymphomaniac.

My fingers slid under the blanket to the

sweet spot that Doran had so recently caressed. In no time, I came. I gritted my teeth, arching in a flash of pleasure and relief. And then, almost immediately, I was overwhelmed by a drowsy fatigue. *Alright then. Let's get some sleep.*

CHAPTER FOUR

IT WAS A WEEK before I really got the difference in times between the worlds. No, not because I'm slow, but because so much had transpired in such a short period of time, starting with my being transported to Ruadh!

By the way, Doran turned out to be right: After just a night and a half in bed with him, I felt almost right as rain. Almost — every now and then I would feel this heat enveloping me inside, which would always evolve into chills. But Haedyn assured me that I was fine, and that this was most likely the residual effect of habituating to Ruadh. He told me that, generally, mortals didn't fare well in close proximity to Chaos, and then expounded on energy flows and so on.

As for Doran ... it's complicated. After his attempt to seduce me, he seemed to either give up or lose interest. But, over the course of the week, I would catch him looking at me. Like today, for example. I was sitting in Haedyn's laboratory compiling a list of supplies. I worked on this kind of thing in the evening, after spending the morning learning all about faeries. My sources were primarily the books written by healers.

Doran had been a rare presence in the laboratory of late. I primarily talked with Haedyn, who thus far struck me as the most level-headed of all of the faeries in Ruadh. Then again, I was strictly prohibited from going anywhere alone, so there was virtually no one else for me to compare him with. And I knew that if I dared disobey, I would again face punishment.

"What?" I asked, lifting my eyes from the list I was compiling to the figure of Doran.

He'd appeared in the laboratory, again dressed in black with silver accents, and now was looking me over. His expression was enigmatic. "Are you doing okay?"

I listened to my body, and answered him candidly, "I'm thirsty and want to go out, but generally speaking, I'm fine. Why do you ask?"

"Don't you feel drawn toward me?" Doran came right out and asked. "Or toward Haedyn?"

I narrowed my eyes and looked at the doctor, who winked and then got back to work on his patient. I knew her. It was Meldyt. She lay on a long, low table, sunk in a deep sleep. Haedyn was leaning over her, scanning her condition. The Hunt had fun with the three wenches for four full days, after which two healers had patched them up and left them to heal.

"Should I?"

"Humans respond very strongly to us," Doran explained, sitting opposite me on the edge of the wide table at which I was working. "It is thought that after a night with a faery, humans — male or female — will never be able to forget their lover. Especially if their faeries are Gankoners."

"Well, sorry if you're disappointed. But what is that?"

"Gankoner? That's a flute-playing faery who seduces the girls by playing his instrument. In the past, mortals would call him their 'sweetheart.' Once a girl met a Gankoner, she was fated to love him until the day she died. And it wouldn't be long before the unfortunate lady would wither away, refusing to eat."

"There you have it," I said, "instantly addictive and a harsh comedown. Sounds like a bad drug habit. Perhaps his flute playing was hypnotic, or had another narcotic effect."

"Rory, the laws of science do not explain

everything."

"Oh, well. I can only try."

Doran sighed deeply, but didn't argue with me. Instead, he asked, "Have you finished the list?"

"Well, I guess so, more or less. I wrote down everything that I could think of."

Doran extended his hand, obviously expecting me to trot up to him and hand it over. I'd used my ballpoint pen, which had been returned to me. Along with my purse and all the contents, including my laptop. I had high hopes for the laptop, despite the fact that it didn't work at all. I couldn't power it on. Likewise with my cell phone.

I looked at his hand, and simply pushed the list in his general direction. It wouldn't kill him to reach for it. "It's possible that you have a special pheromone that attracts people, and possibly causes an addiction. Like, for example, ants and the *lomechusa pubicolli*, which secretes a special substance."

"Nice," I heard Haedyn say as he stood up, having finished the scan. "You're equating humans with ants, then?"

"You're the one comparing us with them," I retorted. "How is she?"

I tried not to look at Doran. Every time I did, I ended up feeling everything inside me start to grow hot. It was a combination of anger, desire for revenge, and a sexual charge. The fact is, I'm not made of stone! Even though the King was on my list of enemies, I couldn't deny his ability to arouse me. I've always been drawn to strong, powerful men. And he was all of that and more. There were those pheromones, as well. I was sure that the pheromones were causing me problems.

"She's okay," Haedyn responded. "A few days of sex never hurt anybody, but now they've learned a lesson. Hey, come in and get her out of here!"

In response to his summons three pint-sized faeries entered the lab. I already knew that these were of the Dobi clan. Dumb as a brick and useful, plus, they stayed silent even under the most brutal torture. They looked kind of creepy: pale, withered faces with big red eyes. The Dobi picked Meldyt up and silently took her from the laboratory.

I began to breathe easier. Yes, what the trio had done was revolting, but still, the punishment was harsh.

"A genetic analyzer," Doran read out loud, a strange expression on his face. "What do you think, will the Hogmani understand what I mean when I tell them to make one of those?"

The Hogmani are small, extremely vicious faeries who lived somewhere in the hinterlands of Ruadh. The King valued them for their ability to craft almost anything. They were blacksmiths, artisans, and so on. No, they aren't up to making a genetic analyzer, but they could come up with something of the sort. It stands to reason it would be powered by magic. Electricity was unknown around here.

"What do you suggest? Drawings of some sort?"

"No," Doran said, and my heart sank. That was the same smile he'd had when he'd dispatched the trio who'd pulled a joke on me on a violent three-day orgy. "No, Rory, sit down and describe each item in detail. What it's for, what it looks like, and what its function is." Provide plenty of detail. Time isn't the issue, don't worry."

And then I remembered. "Doran!"

He raised an eyebrow just a little, indicating that he was listening.

"How different is time here compared to on earth?"

"You're not aging, if that's what's worrying you. The mortals who find themselves here stay young."

"But once they go back home, they immediately acquire all of the lost years and grow old?"

"Clever girl," nodded Doran. "Yes, there is a legend. But it's not true. In fact, years may pass here, but only a few days there. So have a seat, Rory, get to work."

All I could do was grit my teeth and get back to the cursed list of supplies. I grabbed more sheets of paper, because I had a lot more writing to do. In a way, though, this delay was a good thing, actually, since I'd been afraid to return to my room for the past two days.

I had just cause for my fear. You see, for the past two nights I'd tossed and turned. I only managed to get to sleep with the overhead light on full blast. But if I left just a single floor lamp on, then it got really creepy in that room. In the corners, shapeless shadows would form and slide across the floor, a soft whisper would sound, which chilled me to the bone. And a real horror would take over me. It was so bad that I wanted to hide under the mattress and whimper.

So I would end up not getting enough sleep and rising in a foul mood. I was suspicious that this was Doran's doing. Like, "that's what you get, wench — if you don't want me, have fun with the Shadows."

On top of this, I couldn't shake this feeling that I was being watched. By an invisible presence. Not an angry being, not a curious one, rather it was something totally indifferent.

I rubbed my temples and almost angrily turned my attention to the list. Doran left, and Haedyn didn't come back. A silence settled on the laboratory, which smelled of chemicals and spices. And flitting through my head were numbers, documentation, and matters related to the equipment that I needed. Why, though, wasn't there any electricity here? It would really make things easier! I almost spat and ground my teeth as I angrily scribbled down notes. Sheesh! It's been a century or so since I've had to write so much by hand!

On page 10 of my description of the ABI Prism 3130 genetic analyzer, I couldn't take it anymore. It was so quiet and cozy in the lab, and the overhead light was muted. There were no Shadows lurking about. I yawned, and then yawned again...

"Just five minutes," I muttered to myself before dropping my head onto my hands. I hadn't fallen asleep like that since back in college.

The squeal of brakes ....a thud......bam! Everything spun before my eyes — screams, groans, and the feeling of an unutterable loss. As if inside some invisible threads had snapped...

I lifted my head, staring dumbfounded at who it was who'd walked into the laboratory.

"Rory?"

Ah, I'd managed to surprise Doran. A faint gleam of satisfaction flashed through my sleepy mind.

"What time is it?"

"It's late morning. Have you been here all

this time?"

"Someone told me to stay here and write," I snapped back. "Damn, I'm still not done! Well, at least I got some shuteye."

I yawned, covering my mouth with my hand, and asked, "Is Haedyn back yet?"

"No, he's still sleeping," Doran said. He was already right at my side, looming over me, reading my notes. To my surprise he grinned and nodded, "Not bad — we've got something that the Hogmani can use."

And he suddenly clapped his hands. In a flash, a few dozen Dobi literally crawled into the laboratory, dragging boxes. Ordinary boxes from my home world. Thick, cardboard boxes.

I silently watched what was happening. Maybe I was still sort of dreaming? Because before my eyes the little faeries opened the boxes and unpacked... laboratory equipment. Including a genetic analyzer, which weighed around one hundred thirty kilograms, and an automated DNA extraction system, and much more. But if the microscope and reagents weren't much to wonder at here, as they could function just fine in this world, I was mystified by the equipment that required electricity. For a moment or two, anyway.

"What's the use of all this?" I asked after the Dobi had everything unpacked and had left.

"The Hogmani can study this device so that they understand what we want from them."

"But how..."

"I read the list, Rory. That's all I needed to do. And your former boss can't refuse me."

"So why did you insist I write all this down?"

"It's good for your brain cells," Doran grinned. "And it kept you busy. I'll have to explain to you what I want."

At that point, I really, really wished I was the Incredible Hulk and could go berserk. I'd smash everything to pieces and throw it around.

Doran was evidently waiting for me to go ballistic. And to be sure, he was practically bursting. I had to swallow hard to hold myself back. But I felt like smoke was streaming out of my ears.

Suddenly, an idea came to me. I mean, I am a genius, am I not? "You jumped the gun. I have a proposal for you."

"What, Rory?"

"Maybe you don't need to put all this on your Hogmani. You can use a diesel generator to power the equipment."

A vertical crease appeared on Doran's forehead. "I don't recall what that is."

"It's a great thing to have, trust me. If it works, then we'll make swift progress."

The way the King looked at me, I almost started trembling. But I restrained myself and even smiled, hoping that my smile didn't look like a smirk.

"A diesel generator," Doran drawled. "All right, Rory, my subjects will secure one for you. But you're going to have to wait. It's not so easy entering your world."

"Can anybody enter it?"

"Only the Wild Hunt. And this adds to the resentment of the other Courts."

"Is there anybody at all who actually loves you?"

"Love is a sign of weakness. When you love someone, you are vulnerable, and everybody knows who it is that wields influence over you."

I nodded my head. Okay, yes, for sure, I'd had to listen to stuff like this on Earth, too. Mainly from macho types who needed to explain why they played around. Why they felt they had to tell me about it is still beyond me. Apparently, they thought that I was too clever to be just a fling.

"Rory?"

I started and realized that for a few seconds I'd been lost in thought. And Doran noticed. Now he was standing close by, touching my shoulders. Again I felt the heat from his fingers penetrating me deep inside. And something inside me made me raise my head up.

It was a very strange, scary feeling.

"Rory, aren't you sleeping well? You're sluggish, and you look tired."

Seriously?

"Doran, you kidnapped me and transported me here, I lay in bed for days, was humiliated by your subjects, and on top of all that, for two nights now your envoys have been torturing me. It's a great creep show, though. I'd wet the bed if I were a kid. But what's the point? You're the one who told me you needed my brains."

"What are you talking about?"

I sighed and shrugged off his hands. I leaned on the table, aware suddenly that I probably didn't look like much. My back was slumped over, I had shadows under my eyes, and my hair was a mess. "For two nights now, when I turn off the light, they infiltrate the room."

"That's impossible," the faery snapped. "You have guards."

"Really? Then what is that shadowy shit that crawls out of all of the cracks?"

Wow. Again I've surprised him. At least, Doran's pupils narrowed into slits. "You can't see them!"

"Is that so? Then why do I, in fact, see them?"

The King of Shadows ran his hand over his slightly thrust out chin and shook his head. "I don't know, Rory. That's your guard, my Shadows. But humans can only see them when I want them to. These ones were supposed to remain invisible and provide security."

We stared at each other. My heart was skipping beats. I wasn't sure, but it seemed like Doran wasn't happy about my wide-eyed astonishment. So displeased was he that his aura began to almost physically apply pressure on me. As did his dark aspect. Had I done something wrong?

The beating of my heart was thundering in my ears, and the fingers of my clasped hands were white when Doran said: "Right. I had no idea things were so bad."

"What are you talking about?" I was afraid that, right now, he'd decide it was better to just kill me rather than dealing with all this nonsense.

"You saw something that you weren't supposed to be able to see. This can only mean one thing." He sighed again, and I was all ears. "Our strength is waning. And I don't know why."

Well, I guess today's not my day to die. My heartbeat gradually slowed down, and I started breathing easier.

"Could it be that the Shadows simply disobeyed you?"

"That can't be," Doran snapped. "The Shadows are part of my essence, and are connected to Chaos. It would be as if I was disobeying myself. Strange...."

Well, lots of work for me here — where should I start? I wanted to see his....genes. "Are there any other explanations for why I can see them? Or could your waning strength be linked with your infertility?"

"Well, if you were a faery you could see the Shadows, but Haedyn already checked you. Have something to eat, Rory, and then get to work."

Quite the sudden change of subject... But yeah, I was hungry. "Will they bring me something to eat here? I like it here, and wouldn't be opposed to sleeping here if they'd bring me my bed. That would facilitate the workflow."

"Haedyn's got dibs on this space," Doran laughed. It dawned on me then how almost-human Doran looked when he smiled. At least, his mask of absolute authority would slip off then.

But yeah, he's a despot, no doubt about it.

Though, to be honest, we'd definitely exchanged glances today. But I had a good excuse: I'd never seen such eyes before. Such strange, mercurial eyes...

The doors in this place opened without a sound as soon as anyone approached them. I would have thought photocells were behind this, but it seemed that magic was what ran everything. Which was something I could not yet comprehend.

"Brother, I'm waiting for you, but there you are with your new toy." The beautiful contralto belonged to a no less beautiful woman.

A faery, of course. She was tall and surprisingly limber, with an elegant, chiseled figure clad only in a patchwork of black fabric held in place by chain-linked belts. They made a slight tingling sound as the woman sidled up to Doran, who was frowning slightly. The resemblance was striking. Except that the lady's blue-black hair fell in thick tresses to her waist, and her features were much more delicate.

"I didn't get to see her last time," the woman cooed, lightly touching Doran's chest. Clearly, this was fine with him.

"Really? I thought you all looked her over, Aerona."

"It was fun. But it was over too quickly." Aerona turned to me, her hand still on her brother's chest. It's too bad I was standing so closely by him, but my pride kept me there. Aerona deftly grasped my chin with her second hand, forcing me to lift my head. At the same time she casually turned it this way and that, as if inspecting a prize horse. At least she didn't ask me to show my teeth.

Her eyes were dark, but lighter than Doran's. And flickering in her eyes was haughtiness, rather than the serenity that comes from power.

"Pretty," Aerona concluded, her eyes gliding over my face. I looked at something above her head and thought about my last academic project. That's how I kept a grip on myself.

"Doran, be a dear and let me have her for awhile? If only for a couple of hours. I promise to return her safe and sound."

I couldn't stand it and threw a quick glance at the King, which caused Aerona to laugh, "She's scared, Doran. How very exciting!"

Wow. Clearly this place was all about sex, what with the brother crawling into bed to "assist" me, and now this one clamoring to get in on the action. Or was I simply a spoil-sport?

"Leave now, Sister," Doran said quietly, "Rory will come, but with me. You know I don't like to share. You're surrounded by multiple options when it comes to sexual fantasies."

The faery made a moue with her lips, but released my chin. And she also stopped caressing Doran. Instead, she crossed her arms and stretched, looking slightly peevish.

"Greedy. I'll wait until you're tired of her." She winked at me and slid out the door as silently and gracefully as she'd sidled in. And I realized that I was trembling: quivering with disgust.

"What was that all about?" I said, involuntarily.

"Don't mind Aerona. It's not....easy for her."

"Are you for real? That's how she releases stress?"

"You might say so." Doran stepped

forward. I didn't have time to step back, and felt his hands on my shoulders. He bent over me a little so that his face was so close to mine that I felt his breath on my lips. And I smelled an unfamiliar spicy scent that made my head spin a little.

"Aerona really wanted to have children with her husband. They were joined by the Tree even before we all left for Alfheim, as were all of our couples. This meant that they could bear a child. But hundreds of years have since passed, and they have yet to conceive. My sister is slightly off-balance, mentally."

"Have you tried to heal her?"

"That's why I've brought you in. You see how much we need your help."

"And that's why you've set me up here like I'm your…. sex kitten." We were almost whispering now, our foreheads all but touching. The laboratory itself seemed to be holding its breath, as was I. Behind Doran, a huge Shadow briefly loomed, like huge wings. I blinked, and then it all disappeared.

"No one would mistake you for a sex kitten. You do not know the other Courts, Rory. Ours is the most, how to say, democratic. The Court of Shadows grew out of outcast fairies, those who were too dark for the Seelie Court and too bright for the Unseelie. We are not loved because we did not perish. Rather we succeeded in coming to an agreement with Chaos. Which is why we are now the Wild Hunt, endowed with the right to judge all of the Courts. Imagine the indignation of the elite Seelies, forced to submit to my judgment? There are forces that are higher than us. It is thanks to this that we live. And this infuriates them. If it becomes known that I have entrusted a human with the secret knowledge that we are dying out, they will kill you."

"You mean their impending doom doesn't bother them?"

"The snobbery of the Seelie Court boggles the mind. And the Unseelies are too proud and egotistical to accept help from a human. They'd rather pretend that everything is fine."

"That's crazy. Alright then. For all intents and purposes, I'll be a sex toy. But why couldn't you be candid with me when you approached me? I could put on a good act, and so on."

"Faeries can easily see through any falsehoods, so it had to be authentic. So don't try to lie. You're better off just telling the truth."

"Uh-huh," I nodded. "Like you do. Okay, I got it. I'm safe as long as everyone thinks I'm your sex toy. But this totally justifies my hatred for you."

"As well as the lust."

I gasped, and took a step back. Doran let me go, but followed me with an inscrutable expression on his face.

"Excuse me?"

"I feel your desire," the King said casually, as if we were talking about the weather. Well, good for him, but I felt my face flush from embarrassment and anger. Lately, anger was always at the edge of my consciousness, occasionally indicating its presence by a tingling at the back of my head and in my fingertips. I was sorry I had to keep it in check.

"I'll take care of my lust on my own."

"I'm sure you will. Just don't let it interfere with your work. Come on now - our plans have changed."

"What now?"

"You will be present at dinner. It doesn't look right for me to keep you stashed away. Aerona's incursion just now revealed this to me. Come on. Let's go."

I extended my hand to him and quietly spoke in a tone of finality:

"Just remember, King, our collaboration is a matter of necessity. I'm not your ally."

"I know," he nodded, pulling me toward the door. "What do I care, Rory? You'll still do as I say. You have a lot at stake."

I kept judiciously silent. I was silent as we passed through the Foggy Arch into an unfamiliar corridor with low ceilings and bright lights. I was silent as we entered a spacious room, where, in a whirlwind of Shadows, stood a white-haired, lean faerie who created a dress literally out of thin air. I was silent while they got busy fiddling around with me from all sides and ululated in "birdspeak". But I couldn't stop myself when they dressed me in a gown. At least, this was what the white-haired one called a gown.

"What is this?" The lament welled up from deep inside the depths of my tormented heart. What a shame that it made no impression whatsoever on Doran.

"What's wrong, Rory? You look magnificent."

I looked around in agony. The room had mirrored walls, and my reflection was multiplied in all of them. I blinked and tried to at least adjust the so-called gown. Well, at least the hem was long and at first glance a good length. At first.

I was frozen to the spot and didn't feel any air on my bare legs. The fabric was a solid pale blue, and the skirt was comprised of multiple strips extending from the waist right to the hem. But with ever move I made, my legs and hips were exposed to all. To add insult to injury, an artful cutout revealed my bosom such that I felt completely naked. Even my hair was pulled back in some kind of complex braid intertwined with blue and silver ribbons. I wasn't permitted to wear shoes. I guess human slaves were supposed to walk around barefoot. At least in public.

I had to literally bite my tongue until I felt

pain. But better this then announcing to the world that I'm not a slave, and so on. Doran's look was enough to make me keep a hold of myself.

"So what about underwear?" I asked evenly. The dressmaker, a faery Doran introduced as Emlyn, look me over somewhat haughtily and said that she had nothing to do with such human items. They were not worn around here.

"I'm supposed to just wear this at the dinner?"

I turned toward Doran, secretly hoping he'd side with me. But he only shrugged and said,

"Rory, just try to look at it from our point of view. And relax."

"But I am not one of you."

"You belong to one of us. This means that you should behave as our society dictates, not as in human society. And from our point of view, you look fabulous."

Doran nodded slightly, obviously thanking Emlyn for her work.

She bowed and said, "Come by with your human female, my King. I will personally create outfits for her which will send you over the three moons with desire."

"I think Rory will appreciate the honor shown to her, Emlyn."

I asked a question only when we were back

in the corridor, where the Shadows had been frolicking, as if they were playing tag. When Doran appeared, it was like they dissolved in the corners. "Why is a dress from Emlyn an honor for me? Do people walk around in rags around here?"

"No, humans need to be well taken care of, as you are so fragile and perish so easily."

"Why didn't you enslave us all, given your views of us?"

We walked along the corridor, which had opened up and become more spacious. Not that I'd noticed when. It was like we'd just passed by gray stone walls, but now they were black with golden sparks. The ceiled soared high above us while the floor was like a mirror. I looked at it, saw myself and blushed. God, how could I get some underwear for myself?

"You cannot be enslaved," Doran said seriously, "you multiply and grow too quickly. You make up for your mortality and fragility with the fast tempo of your civilization — which out-paces ours."

Maybe that's why we had to leave this world. Nature is wise in all its decisions.

"And so that's why you simply snatch us one by one?"

"Only the best of the lot."

Doran smiled thinly and suddenly stopped. I took another two steps before I realized that I he was behind me. I swung around and saw something thin and shiny in his hands. It only took me a second to realize what it was. It was a collar. It was darling, elegant and yes, utterly revolting.

"Rory, don't look like that. You've got to look the part. At gatherings such as this, sex toys usually wear collars. Everyone has to see what your status is. If not, the rules can fall by the wayside. As the King, I must set an example."

"The more I know of you, the less I want to help."

"You have no choice," Doran said. And he fastened the collar on me.

It felt nauseating. As if the subtle clicking sound was saying to me: *You're property. You're nobody.* And, perhaps this is what breaks many people - the touch of metal around the neck.

I couldn't stand it, and grabbed the collar with my fingers, pulled and angrily muttered some foul language. At least to myself, under my breath.

"Rory, all this would go a lot easier if you'd simply accept your situation."

In the distance, a group of fairies appeared, and I stopped tugging at the "necklace." It looked pathetic, stupid. I proudly raised my head: let them see a human being. I had their fate in my hands. If I repeated this enough, I'd be able to endure a lot.

True, I didn't expect the chain attached to

the collar. Doran, his face stoic, folded it in his fist and gently tugged at it, saying in a low voice, "Keep a step behind me."

I hate you, hate, hate, hate you...

Fortunately, the faeries paid little attention to me. Well, after bowing to the King, they flicked a glance at me and moved on. Apparently, they didn't impinge on other people's property. Especially when it belonged to royalty.

I was like a prized pooch. I should demand better chow and a silk-lined doggy bed.

We met more and more faeries. They were in the corridors, streaming out of foggy niches, and materializing as if out of thin air. Doran proceeded right by some of them, looked at others, and graced still others with a little nod. Apparently, that signified that the recipient enjoyed a special status.

I kept my mouth shut, not knowing if I should talk to the King in front of anyone else. But there was plenty for me to see.

"Wowza!" I whispered involuntarily.

We walked into an unbelievably cavernous hall with a deep blue ceiling. I absolutely caught my breath. Without thinking, I strode in front of Doran, and didn't realize at first my *faux pas*. He growled rather menacingly, and tugged on the leash. I had to check my stride, and seethed with indignation. Really, I had to do something, or else I'd simply burst with anger.

There were no solemn speeches, no trumpets to herald Doran's arrival, nor a loud recitation of Doran's titles. But for whatever reason, everyone in the hall immediately noticed him, and opened a wide passage to the throne as the King approached.

"Rory, don't violate our rules," I heard his barely perceptible whisper as a soft paw touched me. I flinched a little.

I wouldn't violate them, but only because I truly care about my own well-being.

For some reason I believed what the King said to me. About my behavior and keeping me alive. Although, I was in a red-hot rage over having to play the role of a pet poodle on a leash. Unfortunately, I had to somehow stomach this for now.

For now....

I had to find out how to remove the bracelet-brand. And get out of here. I had to escape.

But right now I trailed after Doran, feeling the warmth of stone slabs under my feet, as if they were heated. All around us were faeries of all shapes and sizes. I had to steal looks at them, my head held high. I saw some other humans in the throng, also wearing collars. And I bit my lip. Why not put some collars and leashes on a faery or two?

Doran strode a little ahead of me. Broad-shouldered, in black and silver, impassive as a stone. He glided along, smooth and silent.

Ahead of us was a stone dais on which stood the throne. One look at it, and I forgot all about everything else around me. At first, it looked like a bunch of Shadows. Then, I could see that the throne was solid, material, but that the Shadows were swirling around it, like bees around their native hive. Looking like sculptures, there were guards along both sides of it. Huge, absolutely bald faeries with greenish-gray skin. Except for their faces, they were covered in thin, opaque outfits, like jumpsuits.

Three more steps and we were in front of the throne. And then I stumbled, having seen where Doran was going to station me.

A blue pillow near the throne, god help me. Silk, large enough to sit atop. At the feet of the King.

No, it was too much. Too much!

My feet were rooted to the floor. I couldn't move, even when Doran pulled the chain so that it was taut and the collar dug into my throat. I was quivering inside from the urge to scream *"Hell no!"* and slap Doran's face, and then...then...well, end up as the next hound for the Wild Hunt.

All this flashed through my head in about three seconds. Then I grit my teeth so hard that they hurt, and took a step, then another.

Screw this pillow. I'll use it to smother the

King.

I had a heck of a time figuring out how to sit on it. Especially considering my attire. Especially with everyone looking at me. But I did it and briefly closed my eyes, repeating like a mantra: "It's all a game, it's all a game."

Everyone around me merged into one big colorful blur. It took me a moment to realize this was because my eyes had teared up a little. I blinked once, blinked again, and then decided to act as if I was a statue, mute. Yes, I looked murderously at Doran's foot, clad in a high black boot. I imagined the look on the faces of his courtiers if I suddenly bit it. I reveled in the thought for a second, and then I realized that this made everything easier to bear. Right, I just needed to breath in and out and try to apply irony to my situation. Then I just might be able to hang onto my sanity.

I sat, tucking my legs beneath me, and almost pressed my back against the throne. It was...well, alive. True, the Shadows were still swirling around it. I saw one of them up close. It looked like an ink blot, kind of like a dog with pointy ears. And then I felt Doran's heavy hand on my head.

He was petting me as if I was a dog!

And then it struck me: I had to live through this, if only to avenge myself.

Do you really think women like to be broken? Not me, no way! God no! I was going to come up with the most sophisticated, elegant revenge.

My breathing became easier. And I managed to straighten my shoulders, look around, listen to what was going on around me.

Something interesting was happening. Apparently, dinner was when the latest news from other Courts was passed around, and faeries from elsewhere visited.

Doran's people sat at semicircular tables; the closer to the throne, the more distinguished the occupants. Among those seated at the nearest table, less than two meters away, I spied Aerona next to a tall, thin, black-haired faery, with bright green eyes glowing from a narrow, arrogantly handsome face.

Doran's sister was literally dazzling: She wore a long, transparent, dress embroidered with countless tiny gems. They glittered under the bright lights of the hall. The green-eyed one at her side seemed morose in his shapeless dark attire with shoots of lilac threads.

They set a square table of translucent, dark purple stone in front of Doran. I couldn't stop myself from touching the massive legs of the table, and was surprised: the stone was warm, silky, not at all cold. And the smells from the dishes! My stomach rumbled, reminding me that I'd been too busy to eat. I wondered if Doran would know that it's time to feed me. Although...probably I'd be better off if he didn't figure it out. I didn't want to have a plate set down in front of me on the floor.

I looked around: The human slaves sat at the feet of their masters. One of them — a pretty blonde girl, laid her head on the knees of a broad-shouldered faery, whose chestnut hair fell to his waist and was held up by a purple band. He lazily tickled her chin like she was a cat. Ugh!

Other fairies chatted with each other, laughed, some kissed. Just like people. Almost. Just the same, they were different. Their morals, laws, these were alien. I sensed the alien ambience in my bones.

And the Shadows. They danced all over the hall, snaked along the dark walls gleaming with golden specks, glided among the tables. Sometimes one, then another Shadow would suddenly wrap around this or that faery. But it was as if they didn't notice. Interesting, was there a symbiosis between them? I'd have to find out more about them from Doran.

I looked down and almost screamed: A small, slender Shadow was wrapped around my wrist. Like a little snake. Its touch was warm, and barely perceptible.

I swallowed and looked cautiously at Doran. Did he notice? He did. And he raised his eyebrows, clearly, he was surprised. "Rory, is everything all right?"

"I'm not used to being in this position."

I had to speak quietly so that no one else could hear. I made a point of not looking at my hand. As I understood it, as a human I wasn't supposed to be seeing this. So we'll just pretend everything is fine.

The shadow encircled my wrist for a bit, then flew off elsewhere. And I could finally exhale. True, my respite was brief.

"Rory, you need to eat."

Well, at least a bowl of something. I could bang it on the floor so that all of the food splattered on the King and his entourage. But, as luck would have it, Doran had something better in mind than a bowl. He had it in mind to feed me by hand. "Eat, Rory, soon you'll see something interesting."

Near my mouth appeared a piece of meat that smelled absolutely tantalizing. I swallowed my saliva and hesitated. This was so humiliating. But what choice did I have? If I were to refuse, I'd still be hungry and for how long was anybody's guess. And it's not like I could refuse the King.

"I'll deal with you later, you bastard," I thought, and carefully grasped the meat with my teeth. I took pains not to touch Doran's fingers, but did not fully succeed. Looking into my eyes, the King of Shadows put his fingers to his mouth and licked the meat juice. Then he reached for a small silver glass, into which he poured a dark rosy beverage.

"Drink, and have some more to eat."

My heart was pounding as I drank something that was tangy, yet also sweet. It wasn't wine, but I felt a warmth within me, and also a little calmer.

Right up until Doran's strong, calm voice filled the hall. It wasn't as if the King was straining his voice, rather, it seemed to echo off the walls. "The Court of Shadows is renowned for providing shelter to any faery, regardless of their origin. We will receive those who request entry into the Court. We will decide their fate. And then we will greet our new brethren in befitting manner."

The shouts and whistles of approval led me to expect an orgy, or more. I hoped that I wouldn't end up having nightmares.

Doran handed me a piece of pastry. At the same time, three figures entered the hall through the huge doors, now open. Suddenly, I could no longer think of the food. A faery strode in, the sight of whom made everything around brighter. It could be due to his dazzling red hair, which fell to his shoulders. Or his translucent, pearly skin. Or his bright green, slightly slanted eyes. The image was completed by his green and gold attire.

I didn't pay much attention to the others. I mean, there are faeries, and then there are *other* fairies. But this one, well, you could admire him for time immemorial. You could peer into the shining depths of his eyes, caress his radiant, blazing hair, feeling how soft it was, smelling a scent that made the heart flutter.

I shuddered and realized that for a second I'd been carried away. I again looked at the handsome redhead, but now more soberly. It was like something clicked into place within me. Sure, he was striking, but around here who wasn't? True, many of them had flaws, and he, well, he was perfect...

"Jioladh," Doran said, "as always first in line. I heard, that you, the beloved of the Queen of the Seelies, fled from your patroness. Did you come seeking peace among us?"

"Doran, King of the Court of Shadows, as always in the know about everything," said the redhead. His voice was beautiful. I mean, it was *beautiful.* That's how a man should sound - so that your head spins, and unspeakable lust wells up from deep inside.

And again, inside, something silently clicked, putting my thoughts in order.

"Yes," Doran confirmed calmly. "I know that you fucked all of the fair Queen's entourage, along with her lady-in-waiting. It seems that Ornia alone wasn't enough for you. So were you able to save your manhood from her vengeance?"

"In fact, I would like to start anew, free of the cloying ambiance."

"In you, the Unseelie part passed down

from your father is stronger than that of your Seelie mother. It's a pity that Ornia did not notice this, enchanted as she was by your physiognomy.

"My physiognomy isn't half-bad at that."

I didn't look at Doran, but I could tell that he was smiling a little. "Don't try to play the jester, Jioladh. I'm no friend of Ornia's, but I won't stand between her and her enemies. You're not an enemy - just a faery that is rather inclined toward a wayward life, rather than a life of domesticity. Nevertheless, I grant you the right to live at the Court of Shadows. And abide by our laws."

"I respect you, King of Shadows. And I do not want to become the prey of the Wild Hunt."

"Excellent, then."

I made a note to myself to find out what the faeries did with themselves in their day-to-day lives. It's not likely that they sat around twiddling their thumbs.

The redhead, whose name was hard to pronounce, bowed and stepped aside. Doran spoke to the other two fairies, while I sneaked a glance around the hall, now and then returning to this Ji ... Jioladh. He stood out even in such a vibrant, remarkable crowd.

I felt Doran's fingers in my hair. And I realized that he had already stopped talking to the faeries being welcomed by the subjects of the Court of Shadows. I lifted my head and met the gaze of the King.

"You were looking at Jioladh?"

I didn't see any reason to pretend otherwise. "Yes, I was looking at him. What of it? I love artistic representations."

"Explain what you mean."

"Don't you look at paintings? And sculptures? Why not look at the faeries?"

Apparently, only Doran heard me speak. Everyone else was talking and waiting for Doran to finish with me. "But you don't feel insanely lustful when you look at pictures."

"Ummmm, well, I guess not."

"But when you look at Jioladh, you should."

"Sorry to disappoint you," I shrugged. "So far no."

Doran let go of my hair and thoughtfully stroked his chin.

"Strange," he finally said and momentarily lost interest in me. Which made me happy. By now I got it: the less attention I attracted, the better.

Evidently, it was pretty easy to make it into the House of Shadows: All you had to do was to walk in and swear fealty to the King. True, Doran would then warn you that his word was the law. And if he could look the other way when it came to small infractions, he would personally mete out punishment for serious ones. I looked at the Shadows flickering around and thought: *Is it they who report everything to the King?And can all faeries see them?* All sorts of mysteries here. Candidly, it was all starting to drive me bonkers. Right now, I didn't even know where to start in terms of work. And here I was, stuck at this feast instead of at the laboratory or getting some rest.

I looked at the faeries more closely and realized that many of them had deformities. It was jarring: a gorgeous exterior, but then a serious disfigurement. For example, that tall graceful beauty with a thick mane of black hair, in a dark emerald dress bedecked with jewels. She had a sexy figure and … no neck. I could tell when, as she sat with her profile to me, she tossed her hair from one side to the other. So no neck, but hey, great hair! I was glad I didn't easily get sick.

Three eyes, a long thin tail, a huge nose, membraned fingers — I saw all sorts of things before Doran again took the floor. And again, the hall fell silent. The Shadows, alone, kept on gliding along the dark, shining walls.

"There is a time for love, a time for celebrations, and a time for punishment. The laws of the Court of Shadows are harsh, but fair. We do not deny refuge, but cruelly punish those who transgress our laws. I love my people. But there are times when I must render judgment, though it be a difficult matter.

A hush fell over the room and I felt myself

clench up inside. Something bad was about to happen.

"Of course," Doran continued in a voice that made me, at least, squirm from a feeling of impending horror, "I see all — nothing is hidden. He who thinks otherwise is, indeed, a fool."

Even the Shadows froze, looking now like black, smokeless flames.

"For the first time in centuries, one of our women found herself with child - pregnant. Yes, from a human, but so it was. A half-breed, yes, but even this is, for us, a rare event."

"Who is she?" I heard someone ask.

"King, even a half-breed is a great joy!"

"Who is it that was so graced by fortune?"

Doran made a strange sound, kind of like a muffled growl. And the queries abruptly stopped.

"Devin, from the family Ellroynov — you are guilty of beating your wife Dyran upon learning of her pregnancy, and of inflicting multiple stab wounds on her, causing her to miscarry. She was unable to bear the loss, and threw herself into Chaos. I hand you over to the judgment of the Shadows."

The hall was filled with the sudden clamor of angry shouts and exclamations. There was movement at one of the tables: a faery with short brown hair in a dark brown garment shot with gold thread tried to rush out of the hall.

I couldn't stand it, and quickly crawled to

the side, which I could do as Doran had dropped my leash as he slowly rose from the throne. At his back, the Shadows rose like gigantic wings filled with concentrated horror. My chest grew cold, but my eyes remained glued on the King. At his feet, where I had just been sitting, the thickened darkness acquired the form of giant creatures. They were like dogs, hyenas with red eyes and sharp ears.

They silently overcame Devin, bounding toward him and surrounding him. They didn't growl, they just stood and watched.

"I didn't want it!" shouted the accused.

The dogs remained silent, their eyes glowing like burning embers. Throughout the hall, the spectators intensely watched the proceedings. I noticed that Aerona gripped the table so hard that her knuckles were white. She bit her lip until she drew blood.

And now, as if on cue, the dogs looked at Doran. And he uttered, as if exhaling it, a single word. "Guilty."

And the hall erupted: Shouts of *"Kill him!"* *"Punish him!"* were heard, and worse still, from all sides. Meanwhile, Doran simply raised his hands, from which ribbons of Shadows streamed.

Devin screamed. He was lifted above the floor and turned face up. I watched, aghast, as the faerie's body twitched, contorted, as the Shadows wrapped themselves around him, crushing him. Devin screamed at first, but then gasped harshly as he was spun around in the air. He no longer looked like a living person, rather he resembled a broken doll.

But he was still alive. And this is what scared me most of all. At some point, I had to close my eyes and cover my ears to block out the hoarse, rasping sound that cut through all of the clamor from the onlookers. As if from far away, I heard Doran speak.

"Put him in the iron cage until he dies."

Almost by force, somebody pulled me to my feet and hustled me out of there. I opened my eyes and found myself looking at Haedyn.

"This way, Rory. Doran told me to take you to your room. You've seen enough for one day."

I felt at one and the same time something burning inside me, and a sort of stoicism, as if all of my feelings were hidden behind a thick transparent wall. I simply followed Haedyn, like an automaton. I stared down at the gleaming floor below me, numbly wondering what had happened to my collar.

The bedroom was lit by three floor lamps which cast golden reflections on the walls covered with a leafy carpet. Haedyn led me to the bed and asked, "How are you holding up?"

I sat down, silent, and looked at the doctor in such a way that he frowned, and carefully took my head in his hands. He squinted slightly, and then exhaled with relief.

"You have a very strong psyche, Rory, very. Get some sleep, and in the morning, we'll get to work."

"These Shadows," I said, still feeling like a robot, "only Doran can control them?"

"No, all of us can. But only the King can control all of the Shadows of the Court. The rest of us can only control the ones that respond to our summons. They're rather like domesticated animals. But it's more accurate to think of it as symbiosis. They give us strength, and we give them the ability to revel in emotions."

"Can people control them?"

"No. They usually drive people insane. That's why Doran ordered them to not reveal themselves to you. But during punishments, they always become visible. Was it so bad...?"

Yes, but for a different reason. As I listened to Haedyn, I realized that I wasn't supposed to see the Shadows in the hall until the punishment.

Except that I *did* see them. I guess it was a special human gift of some kind or the other.

The wall of ice inside me slowly began to fracture. I was glad. I'd been thinking that I'd lost the ability to feel for good.

Haedyn sat with me a little longer, and then left, saying finally that he'd see about having a passage made directly from my bedroom to the lab.

I stayed as I was for awhile longer. Then I

got up, and stripped off my dress. It fell to the floor with a whisper, now an airy little pile of blue. And then I suddenly felt so chilled that my teeth began to chatter. I jumped into bed and wrapped myself in a blanket. But I was still shaking, and could not escape the image of that mutilated body. And a hot lump welled up inside me. It became unbearable, and suddenly burst through the frozen dam inside me.

My tears gushed out in a salty stream, soundlessly, but heartrending. I smothered my face in the pillow, sobbing and shaking. I was overwhelmed by it all. I'm not made of stone. I have no desire to be a hero. All I wanted was to get back to my regular, everyday life. A life without Shadows that could mutilate you just like that. A life without strange beings whose customs and ways of thinking were so alien. Where no one would force me to eat from their hands.

That last bit was especially offensive.

I don't know how long I cried. No doubt it was awhile, as my nose was swollen and the pillow was soaked. I had already begun to hiccup from tears, when the mattress bent a little under the weight of someone who'd just sat down next to me. I didn't even have to look — I knew who it was. In a flash, every cell of my body was on alert and tingling.

For a while longer silence reigned, save for my intermittent hiccups. But I was through with crying.

"Did someone complain?" I asked, a bit nasally. I heard him sigh behind me, as if he'd made peace with my mood now.

"Rory, I told you that there's nothing that can escape the all-seeing gaze of the King. The Shadows are an extension of me. And ...faeries don't cry unless it's really bad. That's why they immediately reported to me. You should have told Haedyn how upset you were. He could have induced a healing dream."

I abruptly sat up, not caring that I was naked, and the blanket slipped off of me. Doran sat on the edge of the bed, dressed only in shreds of darkness, and stared at me. Yes indeed, the big bad King had to come by to find out why his pet human was so upset. There are all kinds of stupid out there.

"I should have told him? Is that right!?! Put yourself in my place!" I wasn't shouting. I was hissing. "You bought me! *Bought* me! Do you have any idea what that feels like?! And you gave me outrageous conditions. And I'll do my best to meet them, because I don't want to be some kind of bitch for your Hunt. I'll do my best, even if it's all in vain. And you know what? I'm sick of you and everyone else. Honest, upstanding faeries, who are actually just elegantly lying to themselves, hiding from the truth. So you can't produce offspring? Maybe that's just nature's way of disposing with you, like dead wood!"

Again I felt tears rise in my throat, but this time not of despair, rather of anger and frustration.

"What did I do to be the chosen one, huh? Why do I have to put up with your barbaric customs? 'Don't go there, play along with it, eat from my hands, or else!' And threats, threats, and pressure. What a great environment to get work done. Fantastic!"

I almost shouted that last word right into Doran's impassive face, realizing as I did so that I was making a big mistake. But I couldn't stop myself. I'd been keeping it all bottled up inside for too long, and trying so hard to quash the fear and panic deep inside. Now it all burst out, unabated. Damn the consequences!

Yeah, and what about a good slap to the face? But this was just a fleeting thought. I didn't want to get into fisticuffs. Words can inflict a lot more damage.

Something flashed across Doran's face, and I realized I was in for it. I scrambled to the side, but the King was stronger. In one swift move he pinned me to the bed. He loomed over me, clamping my arms above my head. Behind him, the Shadows were as if enraged.

"You've had it with us?" a low rumble echoed against my breast. "So I bought you, and it's too bad? You don't have any say in anything? So deal with it, Rory. Don't rant and rave. That's what weaklings do. You are strong. Humans don't live in Ruadh, but here you are."

What about those other people wearing leashes? I thought. But right now, that thought was neither here nor there. Right now, I was more concerned with my current situation — Doran was pressing against me so hard that I could hardly breathe.

"You're facing a challenge," the King growled, his breath searing my cheek. "So you want to go home? You hate us? Great! I gave you my word that I'd be happy to send you home again after you've found a solution. So maybe you should stop feeling sorry for yourself and start working at attaining the goal."

He pupils again turned into slits. I swallowed, but wasn't about to give ground.

"How am I supposed to attain anything with you dragging me around on a leash and displaying me to everybody?"

"I told you," Doran thundered, "if I stash you away, they will start to wonder about things. If the King singles someone out , then this could be his weakness."

He gave me a strange look and spat out, "And you'll be no weakness of mine."

We glared at each other. I felt in my skin how the surrounding atmosphere was heating up from the tension. What an idiot I am! I insulted him. Brilliant! I sucked in air, and whispered through gritted teeth,

"Let me go, Doran..."

Alright, I was about to whisper. But just then something happened, rather like a small earthquake. Evidently still enraged, Doran leaned over and simply covered my lips with his own. No hint of tenderness, simply rage. And this feeling hit me, my blood started boiling and I couldn't help it. I bit the King's lip - hard.

He recoiled, but did not stop. In the golden light, I could see the blood on his lower lip. And now, scarlet drops seeped onto his chin.

Doran thoughtfully licked his lips and suddenly threw me a very ambiguous smirk:

"Our kind often mixes blood with sex."

"Let me go!" I demanded, starting to kick at him.

"I will not," said the King without missing a beat. "Do you know why?"

Even before he slipped his hand down low between our bodies, I already knew the answer. Waves of lustful desire were roiling through me from deep down, damn them! They were fueled by anger and demanded release.

I shuddered when Doran's finger slid between my legs, touched my clitoris, and briefly teased it. Making everything in me coil up like a spring.

"You're dripping wet, Rory," the King smirked, raising his finger up. "And I'm the reason why."

"Ha!"

To hell with it all! I raised my head and now it was I who demanded a kiss. And he gave it to me. Tough, merciless and completely maddening. I bit the King's lips again, he answered me with the same, now and then licking the bites with the tip of his tongue. Meanwhile, his hands slid along my body, cupping my buttocks and pulling me tight against him so that I felt how hard he was. No romance or tenderness, just raw, naked passion.

My head was emptied of thought, like a slate wiped clean. And the feeling expanding within me filled me to the brim, totally and completely. And just when I thought I couldn't stand it anymore, Doran thrust himself inside me. He grabbed my hips and entered me with a single, hard thrust.

I screamed from the stab of overwhelming pleasure intertwined with a twinge of pain. He was huge. I moaned, trying to shrink back from it, or at least somehow accommodate his gigantic cock. Doran silenced me with a kiss and started moving inside me. Faster and faster, each time thrusting deeper and deeper. And he continued kissing me — long, bruising kisses.

But I wasn't passive in this "skirmish". I gave as good as I got, scratching him and responding to his rhythmic thrusts.

"Scream, Rory," Doran said hoarsely, looking at me. "Scream, let it all out, let go! Do it!"

And he was grinding so hard that lightning shot through my entire body. I sucked in air and again screamed. Louder and louder, feeling like everything was building up to a crescendo. Doran loomed over me, covering the entire world. His eyes glowed, and their fire poured like lava into my blood, my shoulder muscles tensed up with each push. Which increased in tempo, harder, faster. I arched and clenched the sheet in my hands. I couldn't endure much more. And the waves of pleasure began to roll over me one after another, taking my breath away. Through the sheer ecstasy, I felt Doran bite me on the shoulder, shudder, and groan. And this forced me to curl up in one more explosion of pleasure.

I was hysterical and then — silent. I was stretched across the bed, realizing that I couldn't even lift a finger. It was like all of my emotions had been drained from me, leaving only fatigue and wild relief. I felt Doran lying next to me, and was silent. I didn't want to speak, didn't want questions, didn't want to think. I just wanted to sleep. The Shadows had disappeared somewhere. Were they satiated with all of the emotions we'd expended, or stunned by what had transpired here? Although, what was I saying?

"This is what life-giving sex is about," I thought sleepily, before falling into a deep, dreamless sleep.

CHAPTER FIVE

I AWOKE to a wonderful feeling deep inside me. A soft flame was burning down low within. I ached all over, as if I'd been working out. I wanted to arch my back and stretch like a big cat. This probably had a lot to do with the hot male body pressed against me from behind. Doran....He had one arm wrapped around my waist with his hand cupping my breast, which tingled with excitement.

What was I in for, now? The role of a brood mare in heat? I tuned into what I was feeling and decided that, yes, I was really hot for this guy, but it was manageable. What a relief! A clear head was integral to my work.

I squirmed and started when Doran

playfully pinched my nipple - it sent shoots of lightning through me. I was already kicking at him, trying to free myself in earnest when he reluctantly let me go. I turned over and found myself face to face with him — the source of my unabashed ecstatic screaming and the ensuing release.

Fortunately, my head wasn't spinning from a sudden rush of love and tenderness. The sex was amazing, no doubt about it, but my heart was still my own.

Silently, I looked at Doran in all his naked glory: the massive shoulders which I'd clutched in the throes of passion fueled by anger and pleasure, at his muscular arms, at the face with its edged features, too severe to be strictly handsome, but just the same remarkably compelling. What a faery. His dark eyes, nothing out of the ordinary now, were scrutinizing me, as always calmly and even a little lazily. And there wasn't a trace of the bite I'd given him on his lips. And I'd also scratched him rather seriously.

The silence dragged on, but I had an urgent need to "attend to business," so to speak. "Doran, I want to get to work sooner rather than later."

Yes, I know, quite the romantic opening after such a passionate night. In response, the King produced a wide smile. "Sounds good, Rory. So you're no longer in the mood to throw yourself at me?"

"I'm not saying that, but I can contain myself. And, of course, I'm taking heed of your counsel: I'll get to work, fulfill my mission here, and then be gone."

"How do you feel right now?"

I tuned into my body: I discerned a slight rumbling in my stomach and the need to get to the toilet right away. "I need to eat and also visit the bathroom."

Doran silently got up and left, not bothering to get dressed. I suspected, though, that this kind of thing was the norm around here. And I, too, slipped out of bed, and then gasped: It may be the norm, but I wasn't going to do likewise just yet. Quietly exclaiming, I bent over the dress which I somewhat gingerly picked up and held out in front of me. It wasn't exactly what I wanted to wear as I conducted experiments. Although, yes, it'd be perfect if I was a porno star playing the role of an alien scientist. I had to ask the King for something normal to wear, this was the first thing. Next, I had to talk about my working hours. The third item was to talk about how I could go about working with specimens. Yes, that's right, I'd already started referring to the faeries as 'specimens' and 'test subjects'. And by the way, there was, indeed, a place for thoughts about natural extinction. With qualifications, however. Why is it the process had begun in this world?

I dropped the dress back onto the floor, and, still naked, marched into the bathroom. I was beckoned by the rushing sound of the warm shower fashioned after a waterfall spilling down a cliff. I had to ask about the source of the water here. I felt strongly like I was really out in the wild here. And the dark stones of the 'cliff' were warm and covered in greenery. I could sit right on them and relax a bit.

I closed my eyes and thrust my face right into the warm water cascading down. My mood was almost serene after the sex. As for Doran, I'll exact my revenge, and then I'll forget about him. And my vengeance will be sharp and ever so exquisite. Because I don't care if it's for my own good, no one, but no one gets to treat me like a prized poodle.

As for the sex …. okay, why not? I felt that given my situation in Ruadh, I really had to release tension on a regular basis. I just had to see about obtaining contraception. I wasn't likely to get pregnant, but better safe than sorry. Pills, condoms, either would do. After all, what did he need a pregnant scientist for when his entire species was facing extinction?

I moved away a bit from the waterfall and immediately bumped into someone behind me. In a flash, masculine hands slid around me from behind and cupped my breasts.

"Gotcha," a voice murmured in my ear, making everything inside me vibrate.

"King," my voice went up an octave, "what are you doing? What is it?"

What "it" was doing was insistently poking me in the ass and lightly throbbing. I blinked and realized that I had no choice. Now was the time to broach the subject. "Doran, do you want me to work on your problem, or are you trying to impregnate me?"

His arms immediately released me. "You're not likely to get pregnant."

"I agree," I said, turning to face him, "But why take risks? I used to take the pill."

Doran's pupils again extended into slits. Leaning against the stones, the faery literally glared at me. It was a little intimidating. "What are you saying to me?" the King asked in a too-quiet voice.

"Doran, I know that to you, pregnancy is just great. We also regard it as a blessing. But it's got to be right..."

"Rory, these pills of yours, they'll stop you from getting pregnant?" interrupted the King. Obviously, he was still horny, but I could tell that he was also thinking twice about acting on it.

For whatever reason, I gulped and said, cautiously, "Well, yes."

Doran sighed so deeply that it was as if he really did need some air. His cheekbones became sharper, and there was a deep crease between his eyebrows. He was clearly trying to get a grip on himself, but his eyes clouded with darkness. I swallowed again: was he really so bothered by my simple request for protection? I mean, I fully understood their problem, but given my situation, it would really be inconvenient if I got pregnant.

"Lucky for you that I can keep my cool." Doran's growl chilled me to the bone. And he quickly strode out of the bathroom, leaving me caressing the warm stones and blinking in surprise. So I guess he was all for getting me the pill? Darn it, I'd forgotten to ask for something to wear.

I hurriedly finished up in the bathroom and stepped into the bedroom and screamed: there stood Haedyn. His hair was combed back and he was attired in dark gray waistcoat and trousers. His goat hooves were shining, as if he had buffed them with something.

"Oh, Chaos!" he rolled his eyes. "Calm down, now. Do you really think I've never seen breasts before? My betrothed has four of them, in fact. Get dressed, shrinking Violet."

Covering myself as much as I could with my hands, I saw some clothes on the bed. It was an outfit that was almost like Haedyn's, except it was a bright azure. No underwear, of course, which was fine. I hurriedly began pulling everything on, at the same time asking,

"You're engaged?"

"Yes," Haedyn nodded. "Why is that so

strange? The Tree blessed us back when we moved to Ruadh.

"Actually, I've read about that," I nodded, tightening the belt of the waistcoat. "Each of the three Courts has its own Tree, which unites each couple. So is that like getting married? Doran told me that you don't feel love"

"The blessing of the Tree signifies that a couple can produce offspring."

"Is it a genetic analysis?"

"It's just magic, Rory," Haedyn sighed. "If you're ready, let's go. We'll have breakfast in the laboratory and try to get the diesel generator going."

"You mean they've brought one in already?"

"Doran said to bring everything that you required posthaste."

"Oh..."I froze halfway to the exit. "Haedyn, there's..."

Well, who else could I talk to about this? This guy was a healer and a scientist. So I told him about my recent conversation with Doran and his reaction to my request for contraception. Haedyn listened, lightly tapping his hoof on the floor. "Rory, you are most fortunate."

"Meaning?"

"Our kind see children as a blessing," Haedyn said abruptly. "All is well when children are about. To interfere with a child or his or her mother is a major crime. Do you understand?

And you tell Doran to his face that you don't want to get pregnant, and that you insist on pills so that he can't knock you up. Do you know why he didn't strike you down then and there? Do you know why he will bring you these cursed pills?"

Silently, I waited for him to continue. I was afraid to speak. Haedyn was bent out of shape, but held himself in check.

"Because he understands: If you get pregnant, then our work will be suspended for some time. And so his own viewpoint is at variance with reality right now. And for the sake of his people, he must accede to your wishes here. Imagine what he's feeling right now, Rory. And, moreover, he knows that you would give birth to a half-breed. And you would not be able to deal with such a child. If Doran wasn't the King, then you don't want to know what would come next. "What's wrong with half-breeds?" Doran is, after all, smart, you can't argue with that. I felt a brief pang of pity for the King of Shadows. He was, indeed, facing a tough choice. It wasn't easy going against your very way of being.

"Half-breeds are rare. There are less of them born than faeries, even. They have a human appearance, they are mortal, but they possess our endurance. There is only one destiny for them in our world: they become someone's toy. They cannot survive in the human world. They would perish from a longing for our people."

They were toys? I shuddered. Barely containing myself, I said through clenched teeth, "And the parents, then, are okay with their children being someone's plaything?"

"Well, in fact, not so much," responded Haedyn glumly. We stood in the middle of the room, arms folded, looking at each other.

"Rory, what kind of parent is okay with giving up their child? But they are stolen, sold, lured. A half-breed is more susceptible to the influence of faeries. So you see..."

"Wait a minute," I interrupted him, "So in the hall yesterday..."

"Yes, they were all half-breeds, born fifty years ago. In the land of faeries, they live twice as long and don't grow old until the very end. They were all stolen from the Court of the Seelies."

"Why didn't Doran intervene?"

"In what? Such matters are best handled between families. And perhaps I was exaggerating when I said they were 'stolen.' All of them voluntarily elected to be with their chosen ones. Rory, not everyone wants to spend their lives in the bosom of their family."

"So you're able to give birth to half-breeds."

"Nowadays, this is a rare event. You saw Doran's judgment. That was the first faery to get pregnant in half a century. You can imagine how angry he was. No, they're not faeries and, in fact, half-breeds don't belong to any Court. Their lot is to live off of their families. But! Any birth, any child, would be a harbinger of hope."

"Wow," I said. "Well ... Okay, let's go work." But I was stunned. Really. So it really was possible for Doran to impregnate me, and I had every reason to believe he wouldn't be opposed. Too bad for him that wasn't going to happen. And good thing he really needed me. More precisely, my know-how, my intellect.

Actually, he could avoid giving me pills or condoms by simply opting not to sleep with me. Which wouldn't offend me, actually.

I trailed after Haedyn, simultaneously exploring my own feelings. First, according to Doran, faeries don't feel love. So don't go getting any ideas. Second, to them, engaging in sex is akin to drinking a glass of water. So I guess I'll look at the sex as a nice bonus. I need sex. I love sex. Doran was spot on about that.

And it will have no impact on my revenge.

To my surprise, I found that I could work out this stuff while on the job: discreetly and a little detached. As if it was another person shouting the King's name at night and clawing at his back with her nails.

"Doran will have a passage made between the bedroom and the laboratory in a few days," Haedyn said, opening the door to the corridor.

"In the meantime, I'll show you the way. Do not leave your chambers on your own. In Ruadh, especially in the palace, humans are always in danger."

"And collecting ma....," I began, and almost ran into Haedyn, who'd abruptly stopped. I stood on my tiptoes to carefully look over Haedyn's shoulder. There you go! Directly in front of us stood the handsome redhead. One glance at him made me again catch my breath. For a second. Because it is impossible to remain indifferent to a man with such a gorgeous body, barely covered by what looked like a short dark purple toga.

"So it's true," Jioladh's voice oozed out like thick, somewhat bitter honey, "Haedyn, the King has a full-blooded human who has managed to adapt to Ruadh! I'll be damned!"

His beautiful green eyes, too gorgeous to belong to a man, were trained on me. And I just froze, trying not to pant. The main thing was to stay put behind Haedyn. For some reason, this seemed to be really important. I must not approach this redheaded creature, because even from this distance my head was spinning slightly.

"She is not the first," there was a barely perceptible warning in Haedyn's voice. Who was it intended for?

"But I've never seen a human. I need to tune into her. Haedyn, may I?"

The healer hesitated, and I asked: "What does that mean, 'tune into me'?"

"He's a healer, Rory, like me. Doran did not prohibit your being examined. And I don't see anything wrong with it."

I almost held on to Haedyn as he stepped aside. But I held myself back. So what was it Doran had said about this redheaded devil with that difficult name? He is a Gankoner. The guy who seduces girls with one look, who then wither away, right? So we're definitely not going to fall for that trick. As for the instant seduction thing, yes, well, Jioladh definitely was compelling, and I certainly felt like touching him, but then, isn't that a perfectly normal reaction to a handsome man?

I remembered Haedyn's examination. He hadn't touched me at all. All he'd done was move his hands down along my sides, as if scanning me with them. And Jioladh did the same. But his presence ...

He smelled of honey and freshly cut grass. This smell enveloped me in a warm, thick cloud. His eyes were like an endless summer, and his blazing hair was like molten gold. They sparkled so, his eyes, compelling one to look at him, and then look again.

I hastily stepped aside and almost immediately ended up in Haedyn's arms.

"No Enchantments allowed!" he barked, holding me. I continued to see the blazing hair and glittering green eyes before me. I shook my head and asked,

"What *was* that?"

"Sorry," Jioladh said, "It's a habit. And yes, what a fun girl." He winked at me and dropping his voice a little he added more intimately, "Full of surprises, I would say."

"You must dispose of your Seelie habits," Haedyn said. "We don't have a place for Enchantments here. The Shadows dislike them."

"I'll quit using them, then. And I'll drop by your laboratory, Haedyn."

"You'd best not."

"Why?" Jioladh asked, surprised. "Or are you engaged in something illicit there?"

"The lab is my home. I do not like uninvited guests. Moreover, I doubt Doran will keep you here at the palace."

"He wants me in the Dungeon of Darkness. He said that that's just the place for me to rid myself of my Seelie nonsense. Post-torture healing."

"The King has a sense of humor," Haedyn responded without a hint of a smile. "Welcome to Ruadh."

And he led me along the corridor, where the light was barely noticeably pulsing in time with my breathing. The mirror-black floor reflected our two forms and also those of whoever approached us. Today, almost nobody paid me any attention.

"What are Enchantments?"

"Illusions," Haedyn said, nodding to a passing fairy with stiff white hair. "We all possess them, but the Seelies have raised Enchantments to the level of a cult. Enchantments don't work well on us, but humans take the illusions at face value. By the way, the Enchantments are why many legends have it that we faeries possess an unearthly beauty. The Seelies use Enchantments to hide their deformities."

"Why don't you do that? And why don't the Unseelies?"

"The Unseelies think that it is a weakness to hide disfigurements with Enchantments. They don't care about them. Moreover, the Shadows are nervous when it comes to Enchantments."

"Why?"

"I don't know, Rory. Probably no one knows. Shadows are the direct creation of Chaos, and their motives are unknown to us. We only know that Doran managed to somehow form an alliance with them. And while he is our King, Ruadh is under the protection of the Shadows, and the Wild Hunt can hold court. And he is the Chief Justice."

Again I was floored once I stepped into the lab. Doran had kept his word: a diesel generator stood on the floor. And next to it was fuel and oil canisters.

And then the fun began. First, Haedyn

called the Hogmani, at the sight of whom I almost dropped to the floor, as they resembled dwarves right out of, well, a fairytale.

True, they were very angry dwarves. They were about 4 feet tall, with huge fangs protruding from under their lower lip, and small rat-like eyes. The Hogmani didn't speak much, and when they did, it was in low voices and all about work.

And, they emitted a horrible stench of something rotten. Later on, Haedyn told me that they favored a diet of raw meat. This was because it supposedly increased both their stamina, and their magical powers. Fortunately, they did not like human flesh; rather, they feasted on some local creatures that lived near Ruadh. I didn't even want to think about what could survive so close to Chaos. But I was certain of one thing, and that was that the Hogmani were real bad-asses. And that is was best to get right to the point when talking with them.

Since Haedyn had no idea what a diesel generator was, it was on me to do the talking. Somehow, I managed to explain how the generator functioned. The Hogmani listened attentively, without interrupting. After I finished my explanation, they asked a couple of questions and got down to business.

But it was a no-go - the generator. There was no spark. It simply wouldn't start up.

I watched in silence as the Hogmani tried to start it over and over again. It was as if they'd been thrown a challenge and refused to give up.

"What's going on?" Haedyn asked me.

"It's not starting. I have no idea why not. It might have something to do with the battery."

One of the Hogmani silently walked up and fixed his gaze on me.

"I don't know what to say," I mumbled. "Listen, do you have amulets that can accumulate and store magical energy?"

The Hogman nodded.

"Great, well, a battery stores electrical energy. This is my world's energy, which runs our devices."

"We've heard of electricity," said the Hogman. "I understand."

The next three days melded into one continuous nightmare. Doran wasn't around, but I knew that my requests were reaching him. And yes, I was provided with the pill. And the way this was done spooked the hell out of me. In the evening, a Shadow in the form of a two-headed dog slipped into the bedroom, threw the package onto my lap and disappeared, leaving behind him the faint aroma of rain. After a 'visitor' like that, I felt rather shaken.

But the diesel engine was a bust. What a waste. The Hogmani thought about it and decided that the battery was drained as it was transported here. It needed a charge. But how to get one? Then I suggested we try a gasoline generator. It could be activated using a hand crank.

They dragged in the generator, but it, too, wouldn't start. At least the Hogmani appreciated the aroma of the gasoline. It was a lot like the urine produced by some of the Bokks.

Then they brought in a bicycle-powered dynamo. The Hogmani perked up at the sight of it, while Haedyn asked how it worked. I somehow described how it functioned, and they seemed to understand.

Doran was a no-show for three days. I was ever more sure that the King wasn't interested in anyone who opted to take contraceptives. But, anyway, I had no time for him. I slept no more than three hours, and spent the rest of the time on the quest for electricity.

A senior Hogman volunteered to have a go at the dynamo. He was a rather block-shaped dwarf, with a chipped canine attired only in a fairly greasy apron with a lot of pockets. For their own safety the Hogmani would shave all of their hair off. Apparently, their work was very dangerous, and so they were better off without any hair to get in the way. That being said, many of them had serious scars on their pates. I didn't even want to consider what that was about.

Kalvag, the elder of the Hogmani, straddled the dynamo. And he began to pedal. I and Haedyn, along with the other Hogmani, watched from the side.

Nope. No electricity. Zilch. The damn electricity refused to comply with all our efforts.

"Try pedaling harder," I suggested, biting my lip in vexation. I mean, what a hassle! I needed my stuff! Without my equipment, I could not see how I could carry out any experiments.

Kalvag threw himself into pedaling. Right then, I glimpsed some movement at the door. Turning, my eyes locked with Doran's. I swallowed a lump that had materialized out of nowhere in my throat, and tried to turn away. But it was as if the King's look forbade me to do so.

Doran was in black pants and a black shirt, unbuttoned, thereby exposing his chest. As always, he looked like a walking remnant of the night. The only contrast to the black was the silver amulet on a thin chain. And also the alabaster skin on the exposed portions of his frame. The shadows encircled his ankles like a barely noticeable mist.

It was like we could generate electricity with our protracted exchange of glances. I, at least, felt sparks fly. I was, in fact, sizzling with anger. I was also relieved. I still was well aware that my safety was in Doran's hands.

On the other hand, if not for Doran, I'd be living my life in peace right now rather than doing my damnest to generate electricity in faery-land.

I communicated all this to Doran silently, with a look. Yes, he was holding me captive, forcing me to work for his benefit. But he'd better not think that I was okay with that fact.

I could temporarily roll with the situation whilst waiting for the right time to act.

Doran seemed to answer me that it was all the same to him. I had to do what he told me to do. And then I could vamoose out of there. Me and my pills.

Our silent conversation was interrupted by a loud clang and crash. I spun around and saw that Kalvag had gone too far. The dynamo was now a pile of rubbish. And the Hogman was just now picking himself up from the floor, a bit worse for wear.

"Oops," I said. "Maybe we should try solar panels?"

"We have no sun," Doran announced, stepping out into the middle of the lab and pushing the pedal from the dynamo aside.

"Kalvag," he said to the Hogman, "just take all this human stuff and make something analogous to it, but which operates under the laws of our world. Haedyn, has she been sleeping these past few days?"

"She's here," I said grimly, "and she's been sleeping."

Meanwhile, swift and silent, the Hogmani picked up all of the equipment, including the genetic analyzer, and slipped out with it. And they didn't leave through the door. Rather they exited their way, through a portal behind a huge stone shelf lined with thick books.

"Haedyn, leave us."

"I'll go find Kiara. It's been three days since I've seen her," the healer quickly got his things together and disappeared through the door. Traitor!

CHAPTER SIX

WE WERE LIKE two duelists facing off. No kidding, I half-expected to see a sword in Doran's hand. A gun just didn't fit the scenario here, so yeah, a sword.

He seemed to be *sans* his Shadows. Everything in the lab came to a halt, and the air crackled with tension. I noticed that I stood as if ready to bolt.

"You knew, didn't you, that it was futile to try to generate electricity here," Doran stated quietly. The way he was looking at me was sort of bemused, almost, like I was a house pet that had snarled at him for the first time ever.

"I suspected it would be futile."

"And yet you forced my subjects to cart all

this.... machinery here."

"Suspecting is not the same as knowing. And, by the way, you gave the orders. If you thought it was futile, why did you let me move forward on this?"

"It's like you said: suspecting is not the same as knowing."

And like night and day, Doran smiled, dispelling the tension, if only a little. But I began to breathe easier.

I sank into a chair, exhausted, and automatically reached for a glass of water. I always felt like drinking water here. Haedyn told me it was the dry air. He had suggested I also use a moisturizer on my skin. I had found one on a shelf in my bath chamber. Now I smelled faintly of lavender and grapefruit.

"So, Rory, what's next on the agenda?"

Doran paced around the table in a circle, turning over one of the books I was reading in his hands, and stopped beside me. I again felt it difficult to breathe. Apparently, the King's aura still had a major effect on me.

"My plan is to make a genetic map, select subjects, identify mutations, if any, and what they are, conduct a hormonal analysis and ... Oh, am I making sense to you?"

"Yes, absolutely."

I felt Doran's hands touch my shoulders and shuddered slightly. He signaled that I didn't have to break off, that I should keep talking. So I continued,

"Okay, but I have a question."

"Ask away," Doran said, meanwhile sliding his hands first down my shoulders and then up them again. I carefully swallowed, trying to ignore little things, like how my skin tingled wherever he touched it.

"You mentioned a Tree that united all of your couples. Can I see it?"

"Why?"

"You said that the couples united by the Tree would give birth. Before the exodus to this world."

"Yes, before the exodus. The Tree also appeared in this world, in each of the Courts, in the center of the palace, but it no longer unites couples."

I bit my lip and asked gently, "Could I see it and try to collect a sample for an analysis? To study it? Did it stop pairing faeries as soon as you arrived here?"

"No, this happened over time. At first, there were some births, like I said, but then, more and more pregnancies ended in miscarriages. Then there was nothing at all. The Tree was no longer active. But it is alive."

Doran walked around me and extended his hand. "Let's go," he said. "Take a look, get what you need."

I took his hand. What happened next was strange, indeed. And even a little scary.

Doran pulled me in so close that our lips almost touched, and said in a low, resounding voice that made everything inside me vibrate, "Help my people, Rory, and I'll do anything for you. But if you don't help them...."

Alright, no need to finish the thought. An unspoken threat has more of an impact, right? But why kiss me whilst threatening me – this I didn't understand. But I found myself responding with a surge of anger and passion.

It turns out that it's really sexy kissing someone you secretly hate and yet also have a thing for. This wasn't tenderness. Rather it was something deeper, incendiary. I felt fire coursing through my veins, which alarmed me. What if I were to burst into flames?

Struggling a bit, I broke away from the kiss. My lips were swollen and felt really red.

"Let's go, Rory," Doran said again, this time in a commanding voice, his eyes still glued to my face. My hand still in his, he pulled me out into the corridor. Once there, he let go of me so that I could walk a step behind him.

Right. In Rome gotta do as the Romans do, after all.

I thought that we'd get there by foot. And was anticipating perusing the faeries we passed with the eyes of a scientist. It had occurred to me that I'd need a sample of all of the different types for my analysis. Based on my reading, I figured there were more than ten of them.

But again Doran surprised me, leading me to a misty arch in a deep lilac color. It emerged rather unexpectedly. I'd recently traversed this corridor with Haedyn, and I was certain that I hadn't come across anything like this arch. But here it was, right outside of the lab, with waves of thick lilac fog whirling around it.

I slowed down as we approached it and candidly said, "It looks rather sickly."

"Humans don't really enjoy passing through it," Doran responded. "But this is the fastest way to get to the Tree. Let's go."

"What do you mean they 'don't enjoy' it? Can you elucidate?"

"It induces nausea and dizziness."

Sounded more or less like business as usual here.

I totally expected to be thrust right into the thick of the fog. But in fact, it wasn't so bad. Sure, I felt a little muddled, but not for long, and I wasn't at all dizzy. But just to give Doran a good show, I pretended to stumble and clutched my temples.

"Is that where we're going?" I asked in a weak voice, pointing at a set of huge doors painted an unexpectedly warm green. We were in a huge circular hall with a high ceiling and no windows at all. There was nothing else there. Nothing except the arch at our backs. The pale lilac walls were etched in black hieroglyphs, and muted light poured down from somewhere above. Washed in the light, Doran's face was paler than usual, and his eyes emitted dark flashes.

"Yes, beyond those doors is the Tree of the Court of Shadows. Just walk up to them, and they'll open."

"Pull the rope, and the door will open," I laughed to myself, and took a couple of steps. And then I was hit by the sudden realization that I had to go in there by myself. I had to be alone.

The premonition was so strong that I stopped in my tracks and backed off. I simply knew that I could not go in there with Doran. I mustn't!

"Rory?"

"Can I enter on my own, alone?"

"Why?"

The King wasn't going to make it easy for me. And really, what did I expect? I coughed and tried to explain. "I have a strange foreboding. It's like I need to go in there by myself. Is that forbidden or something? Is it dangerous?"

Doran looked at me like I was an idiot, but he responded, "No, it's neither dangerous, nor forbidden. I just don't understand why you want to go in there by yourself."

If only I knew! But for some reason everything inside screamed with one thought only, and that was not to appear before the Tree with the King at my side. My legs were even trembling, and my teeth were chattering.

"Listen, we can stand here and bicker, or we can just get down to it. All I need is a piece of bark, or a leaf."

"Alright, get to it, then," Doran growled. "I don't understand it, but I see no reason not to allow it."

Good, then, I had the blessing of the King and so I could get on with it. I felt better right away. And my legs were then able to convey me through the sanctimonious doors. I wondered what the Tree looked like. For some reason I expected it would be something epic, massive, like a magical oak in a fairytale.

The doors opened, releasing into the corridor a gentle light and a fragrant aroma. It was so pleasant, that I took a deep breath, and momentarily closed my eyes. A feeling of calm flooded over me. Which was rather strange, considering my situation.

I looked back at Doran and stepped across the threshold of the hall. Where are you, Tree?

I didn't have time to think twice. The doors slammed shut behind me. And then I was literally thrown for a loop. The ceiling and the floor seemed to switch places, and everything around me disappeared in a dark gray cloud.

I felt like I was falling down an elevator shaft, and I couldn't even scream because the speed of the fall took my breath away. It was only at the very end that I slowed down. Even, though, the landing was rather hard, I was okay. I gasped from the blow to my knees and palms, then awkwardly jumped up and looked around. I no longer knew what to expect. I didn't know what was happening.

The Tree didn't smell like one. It smelled like...fear. More precisely, it really stunk. I tasted iron in my mouth, paralyzing my will. Although my first glance down the corridor, or wherever this was, wasn't so bad, really.

I sat in the middle of a huge space, with three wide corridors around me. As usual, the predominant colors were black and lilac, with flashes of silver. But the light was brighter, although I did not see any windows. Nor was there any furniture or plants. Just bare walls. That's it. For some reason, I had the feeling that I was in a basement.

And then, from the gloomy depths of one of the corridors, I heard a swishing sound. The kind of *swish* made by a long, heavy robe. It didn't do anything to improve my mood. Why not? Because in the short time I'd been at the Court of Shadows, I'd learned one thing for sure: I had no friends here. And given what they thought of humans, I wasn't ever likely to have any. Therefore, moving very slowly, on tiptoes, I began to creep backwards into another of the corridors.

But behind me, I heard another rustling sound. And a chilling kind of horror wafted from somewhere down that corridor. I also heard a strange cackling sound.

On top of all this, I could not understand where I was, or how I'd gotten there. So this wasn't where the Tree was. Got it. Well, where, then, was I? And what was I doing here? I hadn't had time to cultivate any enemies. And who would risk going against Doran?

I dared not enter the third corridor. If only because it was the darkest and most forbidding. On the other hand, I had to do something, right? Or maybe I should just stay put?

And right then, two cackling thingies appeared from one of the two corridors. Seeing them, I gasped, and then, because I couldn't help it, I screamed. And I kept on screaming as I backed away.

I twisted my ankle on the slippery floor, fell on my butt and began crawling away. My scream turned into a hoarse rattle. I could not process what I was seeing. They were shapeless creatures in black robes with cowls under which there was nothing. Meaning, there was only darkness under the robe.

They kept on cackling, incessantly, sending waves of horror over me. I wanted to roll into a little ball and become invisible. Instead, I backed away and tried to scream, though my throat was now raw.

I heard steps running up to me from behind, and I spun around, sure that this was yet another creature. Meanwhile the two creepy creatures kept on slowly moving towards me, clearly enjoying my fear. Their cackling increased in tempo, the sounds resounding in my head.

But the other new arrivals weren't creatures at all, although they weren't much better. It was Jioladh and Aerona, barely clothed, staring at me in surprise.

"Did she forget something here?" The first to find the gift of speech was the King's sister.

"Who let the brollachans out?"

"Well, let them have her!" Aerona snapped, annoyed. "That's what she gets wandering around without an escort."

"I wasn't wandering around!"

"Shut up," the "good" faery advised, "Jiol, let's just leave her. Let them share her. The brollachans will get off on it, and crawl away. It's just a human, after all."

"We don't want Doran finding out that we didn't help her. We don't want to get fucked up our asses and everywhere else, do we?"

The redheaded faery stood between me and the brollachans. He didn't seem to fear them. Meanwhile, Aerona was keeping her distance from them. But she gave me a little kick and hissed.

"Crawl away, little girl. You interrupted our coitus."

"Why don't you crawl away?" I snapped.

"Do you think you're special?"

Aerona's pupils widened, and she would have rushed at me, but suddenly there was music. No, not music, rather it was something that was unexplainable. It sounded in the very atmosphere, the air around us.

The sounds issued from a small pipe that had suddenly appeared in Jioladh's hands, and they were so beautiful that tears ran down my cheeks.

I wasn't the only one. Aerona fell silent, and gazed into space, her eyes wide as if she had seen something that she alone understood. I felt infinitely happy and somehow amorphous. I simply sat there with a stupid smile on my face, absorbing the sounds. I heard in them hidden longings, dreams, hopes for the future, peace and harmony. And Jioladh was the source, the most beautiful creature in the world ... oh, to touch him... Just brush him with my fingertips...

The brollachans had stopped approaching and now rocked from side to side, fascinated. They also seemed nice. Not as good-looking as the redheaded faery, but also not bad at all...

Then, a dense bundle of Shadows burst into the intersection of corridors, breaking the melody apart until it stopped. I blinked in confusion, and Aerona, who was behind me, moaned weakly and muttered something in an unfamiliar language.

The illusion flowed away like thick, sugary water. In the meantime, the Shadows, now in the form of armored beasts, kind of panther-like, attacked the brollachans, who grumbled with displeasure and retreated further and further down the corridors.

Doran appeared in a dark whirlwind, sweeping Aerona, me, and Jioladh to the side. The latter somehow managed to stay on his feet, but the sister fell on her knees and stayed there. Apparently, for good reason. I looked at Doran and hastily cast my gaze downward: The King was truly frightening. No, it's not like he suddenly had horns or extra limbs, but that darkness in his eyes, and his aspect itself... How did the redheaded faery stay on his feet? Oh, he, too, had fallen to his knees. He bent over and froze.

"Who?!" Doran roared, making the brollachans cringe and finally fully melt into the depths of the corridors. The Shadows trailed after them.

"My King," Aerona sounded scared, but not hysterical, "We heard shouts and came here. And found your toy ..."

My eyes still glued to the floor, I felt Doran's eyes on me demanding an answer.

"Yes," I said, meekly, "Jioladh came to the rescue with...that music."

I looked at the King. He'd already transferred his gaze to Jioladh, and growled,

"Desist from playing your tunes around my toy, understand? You could damage her mind and break her. This would upset me very much. If anyone's going to break my things, it's me."

"My apologies, King. My strategy was to drive them off, and then clean up the mess."

"Thank you," Doran suddenly changed his tone. "Today you did, in fact, save both the human and my sister. She would not have been able to repulse them."

He arched an eyebrow, clearly assessing the couple's state of undress, and generously added, "Carry on with your fun. Follow me, Rory."

He grabbed me under the arm, forcing me to rise, and pushed me down the corridor from whence Jioladh and Aerona had come. The misty arch was literally thirty meters away.

We exited into the now familiar corridor leading to my room. For some reason, it was usually pretty empty.

"Doran, I don't know how..."

"Of course you don't know," he interrupted me, impatiently. "And I don't know who the foul bastard is who is now so brazen that they put an Unseelie spell on the Tree's chamber. Moreover, you were so affected by it, that you were compelled to see the Tree on your own!"

This really was no joking matter. I flew into the bedroom, which seemed to me like a real sanctuary now, and said hoarsely,

"What kind of spell is this?"

"Calm down."

"Sorry, but I don't feel like calming down! You said that you'd ensure my safety."

Doran strode towards me and I jumped to the side but didn't manage to get very far: The Shadows, which had darted to the side, swarmed around me like a straitjacket and dragged me to the bed.

"What's this now?" I asked, trying to untangle myself from the Shadows, but they encircled my wrists and ankles and pulled me across the bed so that I was spread-eagled. It was humiliating. On top of everything else that had happened, I now felt helpless.

"This is so that I can talk to you instead of chasing after you."

Doran sat down beside me and said thoughtfully, "There's something else: how did anyone else know that you were planning on seeing the Tree? Only I and Haedyn knew about this. And I'm sure it wasn't from either of us."

"Are you?"

"I am," the King nodded. "Haedyn has sworn an Oath of Honor to me. If he breaks it, the Shadows will carry him off to Chaos. Once there, he would undergo as much torture as they wanted to inflict on him."

"Could someone have overheard? With your Shadows all over the place, how could anyone cast a spell?"

As we talked, I noticed that a small Shadow sitting on my chest had turned into a kitten. I didn't let Doran know that I saw it, though. He also glanced at the 'kitten' and then responded, "There are no Shadows around the Tree - not in the Tree's chamber, nor in the corridor near the chamber. They are incompatible - the magic of Chaos and the magic of Life. But what's strange is that you were taken to a place where the Shadows are at liberty to roam. If they wanted to kill you, they would have sent you outside the palace, where you would not be easily found. As it is, it's as if they were just trying to scare you, or issue a warning."

"So someone found out why I'm really here?"

"Well, I wouldn't rule it out. For the time being, no more trips to the Tree for you. You have plenty to do as is."

"What about the series of tests and so on? Damn, I at least need to get to know your kinfolk."

"My what?" Doran asked.

"It's an expression. I meant that I need to get representative samples from the different genera that make up your subjects. By the way, what's the nature of that pipe Jioladh was playing?"

"So you like it?" Doran asked in a strange tone, for some reason moving his gaze over me lying there.

"I wasn't the only one," I grunted, recalling Aerona's rapturous gaze. "Is it a kind of magic?"

Doran gently touched my cheek with his fingertips, then traced a line to my neck and lightly stroked it. A careless little caress. I bit my lip, trying to calm my quickening breathing. What is it that they give you in the army? Bromine? I could use some bromine about now to control my libido, okay?

"It's magic," the King's voice dropped a little. "Even fairies cannot resist the sound of the Gankoner's flute. And human girls are totally entranced by it. That's when the Gankoner has sex with them. And from then on, no one else will do for the girl, who withers away and dies."

"I've heard about all this already."

Meanwhile, his fingers were now encircling my nipple, which was hard and erect and straining to pierce through the fabric of my waistcoat. First the one breast, then the other...

My heart was wildly thumping. I need that bromine, asap!

"It's like a very strong aphrodisiac," Doran went on calmly, continuing to explore my quivering body. "I showed up in time. You could have been seriously enchanted."

"Like Aerona?" I asked in a broken voice. I took a deep breath and tried to count to ten.

"Oh, she's depressed over her inability to conceive."

One ... two ... five ... seven ...

The fingers were now probing under my waistcoat and stroking my stomach, flirting with my waistband. Then they slid inside the waistband, and I caught my breath.

"That's why Aerona is trying to lose herself in sex," Doran's voice was like velvet now, caressing my skin along with his hand. "Furthermore, she's hoping she'll get pregnant from someone or the other. Hence the orgies and the desire to bed any High Fairy she crosses paths with."

"What if..." I swallowed — my throat was dry, I was so aroused, "...I invite her to take part in the experiments? In any case I'll need volunteers, and ..."

I broke off and moaned a little, as just then Doran's hand had slipped into my pants, slid between my thighs and touched me. I was so wet, so ready.

"I'll consider your suggestion."

Apparently at Doran's command, the Shadows released me after briefly wrapping me with a slightly warm mist. Then they disappeared. Along with my clothes. Which were now on the floor.

"Turn over."

His voice was like a velvet paw that set my skin ablaze. He didn't wait for me to do it myself, instead flipping me over and pressing me into the bed with one arm. I heard a slight rustling, then a clink as his belt buckle hit the floor.

"This is ..." I began, but then I felt the King pressing into me from behind. I started as he showered kisses on my shoulders.

"Disobedience turns me on," I heard his muffled voice. "And so does your anger."

He noisily inhaled, his breath hot on my neck, and added,

"And desire turns me on, too. You smell like sex and rage."

"Because I hate you!" I hissed, at the same time feeling his excitement where his hips met mine. I couldn't stop myself from pressing into him as he moved against me.

"Hate and passion are two sides of the same coin. It's indifference that kills lust."

And then Doran wrapped his arms around me and started entering me. Slowly, so that I felt every inch of him as he gradually filled me up inside. It was so tight that there wasn't any room to move at all. I clenched the sheets with my fists and moaned softly from the overwhelming totality of it all. Then he was fully inside me, and he groaned, his head thrown back. "This is unbelievable!"

I felt a rush of sheer pleasure with each thrust he made. I bent my head and moaned, my voice ragged. And I moved my hips in rhythm with him, harder and faster, arching my back.

"Turn over to face me, Rory."

I turned around and Doran immediately kissed me, crushing my lips and demanding a response. He grabbed my hair with one hand, lifting my head up higher. My lips parted as he forced his tongue in. I felt as if an invisible fire was scorching me. I didn't even notice how we were now even more closely entwined and moving with an even greater urgency.

Doran moved ever faster, and his ardent thrusting sent shockwaves through me.

"Faster!"

It was almost painful. It was painfully sexy fucking, really. I clawed the sheets, shredding them.

Could I really keep this up without going crazy? I felt like I was on the edge of absolutely pure ecstasy. And inside I felt an increasing pleasure that was a little frightening.

His probing was ever more insistent, while the sound of our bodies slapping together with each thrust could probably be heard beyond the bedroom walls. I looked around again and locked eyes with Doran. And that's what did it.

"I can't take it anymore!" I said.

"Then come, Rory!" he roared with one last push driving my stomach into the bed and leaning over me from above.

And waves of pleasure swept over me from all over, filling every cell of my body with a delicious sense of ecstasy. It was unbelievably strong. So strong I wanted to scream, but my voice was shot. All I could do was writhe in sweet convulsion.

And I realized that something had been planted inside me, a deep contentment, something that I wanted more of, and then some more.

Doran rolled over on his side, propped himself up on his elbow, and listened. Yes, Rory had fallen asleep almost instantaneously, and now he felt her quiet, sonorous breathing somewhere deep inside him.

How strange...

He couldn't help himself, and leaned toward the girl's neck and inhaled deeply. The smell of her made him again rage with desirer. He managed to get a grip on himself, but only with an effort. Rory was a human, after all, and could not take any more lovemaking tonight. He's already had his way with her for two full hours. No wonder she'd fallen asleep right away.

Still, he ran his finger across her back, feeling the smooth, still moist skin, then touched the softness between her thighs and realized that his breath was already labored. Before he burst, he wanted to straddle Rory, and hear her moaning in ecstasy again. He wanted to know that those moans were his.

Instead, Doran very slowly got out of bed and stood there, waiting until he'd calmed down. But just then Rory stirred, a dark strand of hair slid over her shoulder, and again he was forced to take a deep breath to calm the fire raging inside him. Enough already. No, she definitely wasn't going anywhere. Rory was his. And she needed to rest before starting her big job.

He slipped through the shadow portal he'd created, feeling the instant surge of cold, and immediately exited into the laboratory, startling Haedyn, who put down the thick, ancient Talmud he'd been perusing.

"Were you torturing the poor girl?"

"Was your examination of her thorough?" Doran asked, looking around the room. In his absence, the Hogmani had already produced one of the converted instruments. In the morning, Rory was in for a surprise.

"In the sense of is she okay? Does she have health problems?"

"You said something was wrong with her."

"She's fine," Haedyn sighed. "It's just that it's been quite awhile since I've examined a human. Calm down. She's fine. By the way, what will happen if the girl finds out about your real plans?"

"She won't," Doran answered shortly. "It's for our own good that she doesn't. Haedyn, you'll be participating in the experiments."

"Of course, that's a given, actually. Good,

there's me, then, and who else?"

"I'll be talking to Aerona."

Haedyn sat up, and almost dropped the Talmud, he was so surprised. Speaking carefully, he asked, "Aerona? Your sister?"

"That's right."

"Well ... you are the King," Haedyn said diplomatically, at which Doran only grinned and turned toward the exit, casually saying over his shoulder,

"Get the Hogmani to hurry up.. Rory still has to figure out how to operate the new equipment. By dinner tomorrow, she should be ready to start."

Then Doran proceeded to his sister's chambers. The Shadows let him know that she was there, showing him an image which made Doran shake his head.

The misty arch led to the chambers close to those of the King of Faeries. They were one level below the chambers of the King himself, in one of the most protected areas of the Palace.

But how protected were they, actually? Chaos was full of surprises. And but for his alliance with the Shadows, their Court, most likely, would gradually disappear. For example, only Doran dared descend into the nether regions of the Palace. And he alone knew how to move through the Shadows. The rest only saw them or were able to communicate a little.

He exited onto the level housing the

chambers of his sister and also Haedyn, when he wasn't overnighting in the laboratory. The chief of the Palace Guard also lived here. They, and no one else. Everyone else either lived a couple of levels lower, or had houses in the city of Ruadh itself.

The Shadows opened the doors to his sister's chambers. The King immediately smelled the sweet scent of an incense that stirred the blood, and heard moaning. The large room was semi-dark, lit only by two red lamps levitating in the air. Almost all of the furniture was masked in darkness – only a massive bed with bodies on it was visible.

Aerona, sandwiched between her husband and Jioladh, was moaning deeply, her hands on the chest of the red-haired fairy lying beneath her. The fourth participant, a young, pretty lady's maid, caressed her mistress's breast. As the King entered, she looked a little startled, and then a little longingly at him. Apparently, she wasn't getting enough attention from the two men.

"Aerona!" Doran's voice penetrated all corners of the chambers. The intimate atmosphere was immediately dispelled. At least, his sister's husband, Katel, and Jioladh tensed up, whereas Aerona just looked at her brother and purred, "Do you want to jump in?"

"Everybody leave, except you," Doran responded abruptly. Aerona, obviously displeased, rolled onto the bed, while her paramours, bowing to the King, left the chambers. The sister simply stretched atop the crumpled sheets and asked,

"What's your reason for spoiling my fun and games?"

"What are you willing to do to have a child?"

Doran was calm. It was suddenly so quiet, the Shadows couldn't miss a beat. Aerona's pallor intensified, and she dropped all artifices.

"What are you talking about, my King?"

"I asked you a question: What are you willing to do to conceive, and give birth to a child?"

The sister swallowed and seemed to shrink inside herself. The ardent, passionate lover was now gone. In her place sat a desperate woman exhausted by hope. "Anything."

"I can't hear you."

"I'm willing to do anything," Aerona repeated, louder now. "Anything at all, do you hear! Anything, anything, *anything*!"

Doran stared at his sister for a couple of minutes, watching as she grew even paler. She was telling the truth. She really was willing to do whatever it took.

"Then get on your knees," he ordered her. "Give me the Oath of Silence, and I will tell you everything."

Deep inside, he had to give it to Rory for

her suggestion regarding Aerona. She was truly obsessed with the notion of conceiving a child. That's why she dragged everyone to bed, hoping that someone would give her what she so passionately desired. She was probably a little crazy when it came down to it, but Doran couldn't blame her.

CHAPTER SEVEN

HOW DO YOU go about drawing blood without looking suspicious?

This is what came to mind the next morning, as I stood under the waterfall-shower, trying not to groan due to all the aches and pains throughout my body. Sure, I'd had no deficit of sex in my life before I'd met Doran. But I don't recall ever having to fall out of bed on all fours the day after, practically crawling to the shower.

And yet just the slightest memory of it made my body light up with the desire to have another go at it. That's why I opted to think about drawing blood — I needed to banish thoughts of Doran from my mind. All the more so as that's what really mattered right now —

the blood, I mean.

The problem was that in 'faeryland,' there was no concept of medical examinations and analyses and such. From talking with Haedyn, I understood that faeries would come to see him for issues such as amputations or disembowelments. Faeries were self-healing beings, just like dogs, except for extreme situations.

The hot shower did wonders. I could now breathe a bit easier and move about almost fluidly. I wondered who would be escorting me to the lab today.

I returned to the bedroom and hastily pulled on a vest and pants, braided my hair, and glanced into the mirror embedded in the wall, framed with dark green ivy. Hmmm...What to say? There was no hiding a wild night like I'd had. I cautiously touched my bruised red lips, and even thought it wasn't a bad look for me. Right, the "wanton wench" look.

The door creaked open and I turned around, expecting to see Doran or Haedyn. I certainly wasn't expecting Jioladh. Naturally, I was startled, and I spun around to face him. But the red-haired faery was calm and business-like. He was even dressed; when I'd seen him with Aerona, I could tell that he felt just fine without clothes. Now Jioladh favored the colors of the Court of Shadows: black and lilac with a hint of silver. Form-fitting dark pants, high boots and a vest that highlighted his masculine chest which was totally devoid of hair.

"Hello, Rory."

I was silent, not knowing what to expect. I'd found that with faeries it was best to listen. It didn't matter what Court he or she hailed from.

"I hope you didn't have any nightmares?" he went on, somewhat solicitously. "A mortal facing off with a Brollachan is no laughing matter. The mortal could go crazy from such an encounter."

"I'm fine."

"Can you tell me how you found yourself there?"

"Why don't you go first?" I asked, spontaneously.

"Me and Aerona?" Jioladh smiled, leaning on the door jamb and toying with his hair. "Aerona loves kinky places, you see. And what's kinkier than sex in a dungeon, with all sorts of creatures like the Brollachans wandering about? Doran keeps them around because they're part of the Hunt. And except for that, they live in the darkness, in the nether regions. But it's not advisable to go down there. So you're a lucky girl."

"They could've eaten me?" I asked, my voice faltering a bit. Those had been some foul-looking creatures. They vaguely reminded me of the Dementors in *Harry Potter*.

"That's right. They'd consume you,"

Jioladh nodded. "They eat everything that crosses their path. Including faeries. So you can imagine how I felt when Aerona dragged me down there."

I kept silent, having no desire to meddle in other people's proclivities. And mentally summoning Doran. Behind Jioladh, I suddenly saw the familiar Shadow that looked like a kitten. He slipped between Jioladh's legs and sat between him and me. I made a point of ignoring the shadowy beastie.

"I doubt if Doran would approve of your presence here."

Jioladh grinned wryly and nodded. "So true, mortal one. Do you want some advice?"

"I want you to leave. Otherwise I might well be the one to get it."

"Do you like being a toy?"

Jioladh's red hair again brought to mind molten gold. And yes, he was like a bright ray of sun in the kingdom of darkness and shadows. No wonder I wanted to simply touch him. I dug my nails into my palm so that the pain would help me get a grip on myself.

"Enchantments," I said hoarsely, trying to look away. The shadow kitten walked up to me and rubbed its tail on my ankle. Strangely, I felt a little better.

"In the Seelie Court, they love mortals," continued the faery, now no longer Apollo-like, but still an amazing looking creature, even if no longer radiating sunshine.

"What of it?"

"There is always a choice, Rory."

And with these words Jioladh stepped out the door, after giving me a look as significant as if he'd just proposed to me. Yet I did not feel any lust; rather, it was like a strange kind of admiration.

Against my will, my glance fell on the tattoo that circled my wrist. So I had a choice? Sure, sounds good. But what kept me here was revenge and slavery. It's not likely that this brand-bracelet was a simple matter. More likely than not, it wouldn't let me stray beyond the borders of Ruadh. And neither would the ubiquitous Shadows.

I looked down the corridor and immediately spied Doran headed my way. And he wasn't alone. Aerona was with him. His regal sister looked strange. I couldn't even explain exactly what it was about her. "Follow me, Rory.

So, it seems they'd talked. I obediently followed them. Again I wondered why no other faeries were around. Was this some elite floor? The royal quarters?

The now familiar misty arch conveyed us to the laboratory. And there ... there I stopped and felt my eyes grow wide in amazement. In the center of the laboratory stood Kalvag, his chest swelling with pride, and next to him was a mound of instruments which defied description.

"What is this?"

"Instruments for your research."

I looked at Doran, not sure that I'd heard him right. He was the one so fixated on secrecy. Yet here he was with his sister and...

Then I was in store for another surprise in a morning already full of them. Aerona took a couple of steps so that she was facing me, and then she dropped to her knees. And clearly, she did this of her own volition. When she looked up at me, I almost dropped to the floor myself. The face which so recently was a model of arrogance and malice now reflected the deepest despair.

"Your first test subject," Doran said.

"If you can help me, then I'll do whatever I can for you," Aerona said, haltingly. "Whatever you want, understand? I mean it! Just help me, help!"

It was all so pathetic, really. I leaned over and tried to lift Aerona up. For whatever reason, though, she resisted, and she was much stronger than me.

"Enough of this show," Doran said. "So we have one test subject. How many more do we need?"

That was the King, always the picture of composure. I gave up my efforts with Aerona, and stood up to face him.

"Ideally, we should have dozens of each of your species. Healthy males and females. And preferably, they'd be couples united by the Tree, and also lovers in general. But I have no idea how to make this happen without causing a stir. I'd need more than just a drop of blood."

"I know," Doran replied, and Haedyn sighed and muttered something about having to "work around the clock again."

"We'll announce a games in the name of Chaos. Many will come to participate in them. And Haedyn will collect blood from whoever we need."

Right, what's the problem, really? If we needed blood, let's simply create some carnage.

It must have been obvious from my expression what I thought of this, because Aerona, who was still on her knees, cut in.

"These games take place once a year. It's the only opportunity for faeries to challenge whoever has offended them to a duel. They can cleanse themselves of shame in a bloodbath, or they can avenge themselves in public, for all to see. Sometimes entire families take part in battles."

I gulped, and asked, "So this is the only time anybody gets to fight?"

"No. If someone feels the need, they can request permission from the King or his counsel. In extreme cases, a duel is permitted. But most of the time, any offender is simply incarcerated until it's time for the games."

I transferred my eyes from the still prostrate Aerona to Doran.

"That's one way of keeping the peace."

"It's effective," he responded. "Senseless slaughter isn't to anyone's benefit. And while awaiting the games, there's plenty of time to investigate any offenses. Often, most of those accused of wrongdoings are eventually cleared."

"Does anyone ever attempt to exact revenge on the sly?"

"Never," Doran responded coldly. "Even if one were to succeed in doing something like that, he would immediately be banished from the Court of Shadows. He would then be an outcast, as no other Court would have him."

"And women?" I wasn't content yet. "Do they also take part in these games?"

"Of course," Haedyn responded, "but less often. And they prefer to use magic to fight rather than physical force. You'll see. Doran, when will the games take place?"

"They're slated for a week from now, but I'll move them up to tomorrow evening. I'll say this is to please Chaos. Rory, do you want to look over the new equipment?"

"I do. In a minute." I looked at Aerona, not knowing what to do with her. "You said that should I succeed, you'll do anything for me?"

"Yes!"

"Then listen," I said, trying to keep my voice steady. "Swear that if you become pregnant and your brother nevertheless refuses to free me despite his promise, that you will help me return to Earth."

What I asked of Aerona would not endanger her. If she was pregnant, then no one would dare lay a finger on her.

Doran truly disliked this turn of events, of course. I glanced at the King. Indeed, his already impassive face was even stonier, with his cheekbones clearly etched under his pale skin, and the darkness was flashing in his eyes. At least for a moment.

"I swear!" Aerona's serene voice reached me as if through a haze. I blinked and realized that Doran and I had been standing there with our eyes locked. And the tingling frost along my skin was from his gaze.

I really didn't know what to expect from him. Doran wasn't the hysterical type, but I could feel his displeasure, even when suppressed, in every part of me. He waited for me to break away first, and then said, somewhat mockingly,

"Whenever two women get together, it's always the men they blame for their woes. It doesn't matter what species they are."

There you have it. I guess I didn't know Doran at all.

"And now, Sister of mine," Doran said in a completely different tone, "leave us. And remember your Oath of Silence. You could lose not only your life, but also any hope of bearing a child. Not to mention more than one child."

That's right, King, let's raise the stakes even more. 'Scale of dragon, tooth of wolf,' or whatever.

"I'm leaving, King, and know that you can trust me."

I was astonished when Aerona, after bowing to her brother, then bowed to me. I could only nod briefly, but I certainly appreciated it. I mean, it wasn't so long ago that she'd called me a toy and all but threw me to the dogs, figuratively speaking.

"You don't trust me, Rory," Doran said, as soon as Aerona had left. It wasn't a question. He was stating a fact.

"I don't trust anyone here."

"She's a quick learner," Haedyn added. He was circling around the instruments, and I cast a dubious eye on them. The learned healer looked a little dazzled, but also quite into the challenge. True, he wasn't actually fiddling with anything, but he was studying them with a judicious eye.

"I gave you my word," Doran said.

"King," I said politely, deciding that now was the time to be candid, "you said that you would let me go home. However! With all your abilities to influence the human psyche, you may arrange it so that I start thinking of Ruadh as my home. And so either you promise to convey me back to Earth, safe and sound, to my hometown, without trying to impose your will on me, or I'll turn to Aerona for help."

Silence filled the laboratory, and it was, well... formidable. Even Haedyn stopped pacing around the instruments like a curious tiger, and stared at Doran and me. I dug my nails into my palms and tried not to tremble. Really, every conversation with this fairy was a serious test of nerves.

"You deserve respect," Doran said suddenly, and added after a short pause: "But do not deign to be impertinent, or make plans to escape. Now, would you like to see what the Hogmani have put together here?"

I was taken aback by Doran's ability to so swiftly change tracks.

But sure, the equipment, why not take a look? Otherwise, I could be distracted by matters related to the King and forget about the main thing.

These weren't just instruments, no. These were THE instruments. It was like night and day, the difference between these instruments and their earthly equivalents. I was, after all, in a different world. I found myself looking at something that had been taken right from a mega-blockbuster fantasy computer game. It featured major firepower, test tubes filled with liquid lights, and also Shadows. The Shadows were an integral part of the instruments.

How was I supposed to operate these things?

"Doran, where are the user manuals?"

"I wouldn't mind looking at them, either," Haedyn said. "Kalvag, where are you?"

It turned out that he'd disappeared during the showdown between me and Doran, but as soon as Doran called him, he appeared as if out of nowhere. Wearing only an apron, his eyes burning, he looked at me and said,

"You have only to will it to activate the instruments."

"Great instructions," I nodded in approval, "The main thing is they're easy to follow. "But since I'm a mere mortal, can you expound on them a little? I mean, do I simply fill the tubes up with blood and imagine what I want to happen?"

"You are quite clever for a mortal," Kalvag said diplomatically, "Yes, that's essentially the way it works."

"So it runs solely on magic?"

"No, not just magic. We lack your electricity, and so I replaced it with magical energy, which is generated here," the Hogman indicated some glass spheres in the center of the instruments holding a dark gold liquid of some sort. "That's what activates the instruments."

"And the Shadows?"

"They capture your thoughts, your vision, and track what's happening. You'll catch on to how it all works. Your equipment takes a long time to figure out, but ours requires only that you get a feel for the instruments."

Right, what I felt for them just then was that they were going to give me a few headaches. But what other options did I have?

"Thank you, Kalvag," Doran said. "As always, you're on top of things."

The Hogman bowed to the King and departed without a word. He left as stealthily as he'd appeared. That's why I always had the thought at the back of my mind that all these faeries had some kind of secret tunnels that they used to get around.

"Well, Rory, are you ready to try out the new equipment?"

"I'm ready"

In fact, I was dying with curiosity about how this setup was going to work. I caught myself circling around the instruments just like Haedyn. We exchanged glances, and he winked at me. Really, he was a good sort.

"Give it a go, Rory," Haedyn said, encouragingly. "I think it'll work for us.

Well, why not? We had the entire day before us. I straightened up, feeling sort of high, like I always did when carrying out complicated experiments. It was like a mixture of excitement with the desire to prove I could do it all.

"Give me some blood, gentlemen," I said almost cheerfully. "I need your blood to learn how to run this equipment, because I don't see any other donors around here. Or is the King unwilling?"

"My blood is at your service, Rory," he responded. Yes, someone was clearly in a good mood. What a pity to have to spoil it.

"You know what else? At the same time, let's conduct a semen analysis, since I have reagents and a microscope now."

"What's that?" the King and the scientist asked in unison.

"It's a test to assess your fertility and any potential problems with your reproductive system. In other words, you need to give me sperm so that I can study it. Usually it's provided in a jar."

I'd certainly become good at shocking faeries. Even Doran was a little green now. He looked at me in amazement, as if I was joking. *No, my dear, I'm totally serious.*

But Haedyn was all about business.

"So I should masturbate into a jar, then?"

"Well, yes, that's right. Ideally, of course, you should have abstained from sex for a couple of days. But as I understand it, that's not realistic with you guys, so let's work with what we get, and then see what happens. Maybe it's totally different here."

The men stared at me somewhat reluctantly. Well, what did they expect? Some kind of virtual analysis?

"Listen," I definitely hated their silence, "listen, I know that to you, what I'm asking is outrageous. This is a waste of semen, a precious substance that could impregnate a woman. But you have to realize that I need to analyze it. I need semen, and it has to be from a jar. I can't use semen from intercourse."

I paused, and then added, "If it's taken, well, from sexual activity, the data might be compromised. And the guidelines of the World Health Organization definitely frown upon using semen ejaculated during sex. Seriously, you're both intelligent. You surely understand that there's no other way. So you can either donate some sperm, or, forgive me, all our efforts are an utter waste of time."

Alright, I felt like it was a little easier to breath now. At least they'd stopped staring at me. Well, not Doran, who was still fixated on me. But Haedyn sighed and went over to a distant table.

"Will these do?" he asked, coming back with two jars that looked a little bit like they'd once held baby food. They were a thick, greenish glass with some kind of symbols on the outside...

"Are they sterile?"

"Absolutely."

"Okay. Then they'll do. Go for it."

Haedyn handed one to Doran, turned the other over in his hands, sighed, and muttered something in an unfamiliar language. Then he went into the next room. I'd never been in it, but

I suspected that was Haedyn's ad hoc bedroom here at the lab.

Doran stayed put, his eyes still fixed on me.

"King, do you have a problem? I just want to get everything ready for when Haedyn is done configuring the equipment. I myself lack any magical know-how. And what if it turns out that the problem is —how to say? — in the seed?"

Was I right in thinking the King's eyes darkened for a moment? The urge to kill a certain mortal had no doubt flashed through his head. Suddenly and almost imperceptibly, I felt my scalp tingle. The work of a scientist always comes with a risk — there's no escaping that.

"So what you're saying," Doran said deceptively, gently, "Is that I am to sit down somewhere and jerk off into this bottle? I? The King of the Court of Shadows?"

Well, yes, when you put it that way...

"That's right. Listen, I'm doing my job. The one you brought me here to do. It's you who ordered me to figure out your reproductive problems. So then, any questions?"

The shadows suddenly whirled around the King in a cloud and in a flash, vanished.

"Yes, I do have a question," he nodded, grinning. "Won't you help me?"

At first, I didn't understand. Then I felt my cheeks grow hot. Was he suggesting that I ....that I...do him? Judging by the King's wide smile, he was reveling in my perplexity.

He stood, arms crossed, and then he put the ill-fated jar next to him on a table laden with books. Involuntarily, my eyes dropped down to the region requiring my assistance. The right thing to do would be to adopt a serious look and say that the King should service himself while I got ready to analyze the results.

But I just stood there looking at him, while running my tongue over my now dry lips. Hmmm...I could touch it...he was obviously already aroused. It was like I could feel his warm resilience, and velvet skin...the fire under that skin, ready to burst out. I remembered how it pulsated inside me as I clawed Doran's back crying out in ecstasy, over and over.

It took me an incredible effort to look way. My wanton eyes, though, again strayed to the King's pants. And I had to clench my fingers into fists, as they were itching with the crazy desire to reach over and touch him.

"You can command me to help, of course," I said hoarsely, "but I think it makes more sense for me to get everything ready for testing your, er, output. I also need to draw your blood."

Speaking of, my blood was already pounding like a drum beat in my head.

"So, you're refusing to assist me?"

"You can do just fine without me. And it'd be quicker, too."

Yes, I want to throw myself at you! And

yes, feel you in me again.

I gently exhaled and was rather surprised that I wasn't breathing fire. It felt like my blood was about to boil. And down low I felt a pulsing sensation.

"Alright, if that's the way you want it, Rory." he said, mildly, but I knew. The King was offended. He hadn't expected me to refuse him.

I had to force myself to turn in the direction of the reagents, microscopes and all sorts of laboratory trifles that didn't care what world this was. What do we have here? Yes, a pipette, glasses, indicator paper … ah, yes, a microscope. Moving like an automaton, I pulled everything I needed out, and spread it atop a stone table. I didn't immediately realize that Doran was headed for the exit.

"King, please don't go far. I need fresh sperm for the test."

"I'll be right outside the door and I'll be fast," came the cold reply.

"In terms of?"

"Rory, any woman at the palace is ready to assist me. Especially when the task is so insignificant. And don't worry, she will not ask too many questions, she will be discreet, since the Shadows are omnipresent, and I will immediately know if she talks."

"But...but it's easier if you simply do it on your own."

"I don't want to."

Well, to be sure, he is a king, after all. I turned around, and again set about readying everything for the tests. Right, the disposable pipettes, sealed. The glasses too, but the microscope ... well, it needed adjusting. And the displays...what's this?

Would he choose a beauty? Well, really, weren't they are all beautiful here? Even if they were scary, they were scary-beautiful.

I felt like hundreds of small needles were pricking my face. Like you feel after stepping into a warm room after being out in a frost. For some reason I was moving a glass from one spot to another.

Will they do it right outside the door? Or does Doran keep a room here for convenience's sake?

Let's see, test tubes go here.

Why was it taking Haedyn so long? And Doran, was he going at it with some little faery-whore, or just watching as she did him?

Was I jealous, or what?

I put my hands on the table and shook my head. And as luck would have it, just then Haedyn came out his room triumphantly carrying his flask.

"Rory, how are you going to conduct the tests? What's the matter?"

I straightened up and tried to look busy. But something cold was still prickling me in the face, and also the back of my head.

"It's all pretty simple. Let me show you."

Haedyn was obviously interested, and I was glad I had a distraction. No, I wasn't jealous at all, not about the faery. I was just going about my business, and, yes, letting off steam. Anything to keep it together.

I had just finished showing Haedyn how to use the microscope to count spermatozoa when Doran walked in. He had the jar with him. It was full. Without a word, he set it down next to me and looked at me. I had a hard time not dumping it out onto his head. What stopped me was my cool head and the understanding that this would be a sure-fire way to really mess up my life here.

"Thank you," I said. I stopped myself from adding sarcastically, "You can go now," and instead picked up a pH meter to measure the acidity of the ejaculation.

"What's that you're doing?" Haedyn jumped in. I felt like kissing him. His questions helped me keep on track emotionally with the work.

Doran could just stand there watching me do my thing. That's right. I was working. Wasn't it time for the King to also go about his business?

"I'm measuring the acidity. Humans have a normal pH of about eight. You have ..." I paused, then said, "Your acidity is slightly higher, but not by much. Now I'll take a look at the liquefaction and so on, and then we'll be using the microscope."

How nice that we had five of them. Doran and Haedyn also wanted to take a look and do some counting, while I explained everything in detail. It was something else — two faeries and a mortal, heads bent over microscopes. I had to explain what a sperm counting chamber was, how to perform a sperm count, and why the cover glass had to be a specific size. Of course, there were countless other questions.

And then we were done.

"Well," I said, turning to look at Doran and Haedyn, "You're both just fine. True, your sperm count is a bit lower, and they also move a little slower, but, after all, you are faeries, not humans. That's probably just the norm for you. But I don't see how that could negatively impact your virility. So now let's focus on blood and hormones. King, give me your hand."

You done good, faeries, by arming me with all my 'toys'. I picked up a tourniquet, indicated a chair, and said to Doran,

"Have a seat and make a fist with your hand. Or do you need a sexy little faery to help you?"

Doran gave me a scorching look, and then asked, "Is something bothering you, Rory?"

"Not a thing," I replied, extracting a needle and several collection tubes out of a disposable package. "I'm just glad it worked."

To hell with it all. I drew blood from Doran's vein with a steady hand, removed the tube and said calmly, "Next."

"Haedyn, you're in charge," Doran told the healer, rolling down the sleeve of his shirt. "I'll be gone from the palace until nightfall."

"Yes, my King."

And I noticed how the now familiar tiny Shadow in the form of a kitten slipped into the lab. I noticed, and so I pretended that I was busy with Haedyn, who'd already sat down at Doran's place. Why did I pretend not to see it? Because I saw how the King first froze, and then quickly glanced at me. As if he was checking to see if I saw it or not.

Something inside me told me not to let on that I did, in fact, see it, and to just go about my business. Pretend that the kitten-Shadow wasn't spinning around my ankles, exuding a barely noticeable heat.

Doran stood there, thinking for a for more seconds, and then he left. And the 'kitten' slid after him in a dark, smoky stream. For some reason, this made me feel a little sad, and small. It's funny, of course, that the Shadow seemed to have a thing for me. Or was it simply an energy vampire feeding off of my emotions?

But this wasn't the time for further musings about the little Shadow. We were finally getting down to business. I was about to try working with the new equipment.

CHAPTER EIGHT

GOOD GOD, how am I supposed to operate this stuff? What's up with no instructions? True, the senior Hogman had explained the basics, and at least Haedyn seemed to grasp it all pretty fast. Now, for the third time, he was trying to show me what to do.

Those are the samples, and right there are the Shadows, and over there are Shadows as well, and that's the unfiltered magic and then here go the Shadows again. *Sheesh!* The Hogmani had replaced electricity with magic and Shadows. And so the genetic analyzer was now around four feet across and about as high as my waist.

It was all too much for me to process. My

brain might as well have shrugged and said, "Do whatever you want. In any case, I have to think about it."

"Rory, assemble the tests," Haedyn said. "You don't possess any magic, but here it's what powers everything, like your electricity. So I'll operate this equipment. Meanwhile, you put your hands here."

He indicated a luminous handlebar, inside of which something viscous and dark gurgled.

"All you have to do is grasp it and imagine what should happen. The Shadows will capture your thoughts and let me know when I can start it up."

It wasn't easy to grasp the handlebar. I looked at it and kept my cool. Haedyn didn't rush me. I think he understood my misgivings and was giving me time to adjust.

Just then the kitten showed up. It looked like a wisp of smoke jumping onto the rail, arching its back and flashing bright green eyes. It paced back and forth, and stretched. I glanced at Haedyn, but he didn't seem to see the Shadow.

Meanwhile, the kitten was obviously trying to assure me that I had nothing to fear. He played with an invisible little ball, pounced at it a couple of times, and tried to bite his own misty tail.

So where'd you come from, you smoky little beastie, eh? I'll talk with you later, when we're alone. I threw a look at the kitten to let him know I'd have plenty of questions for him next time,. Then, finally, I laid my hands on the handlebar.

I was neither hit by a blast of magic, nor hurt in any way. In fact, nothing happened. But then I heard the instrument emit a faint buzzing sound, and the specimen dropped down into a network of transparent pipes surrounded by Shadows and containing those clear, liquefied golden flames. From there, it disappeared from view. Meanwhile, Haedyn was clutching a handlebar on the opposite side in which the Shadows were mixed with a golden light. He was frowning as he stared into space. I could see that his eyes were glowing a little with a golden light. Wowza!

This process went on for three minutes at the most. Then the kitten disappeared as suddenly as it had appeared, and Haedyn straightened up and exhaled. "That's it. It worked."

"Now we just have to wait," I muttered, wiping my brow with my hand. I'd broken out in a light sweat. I guess I was nervous.

"Does it usually take awhile?" Haedyn asked.

"I want to start by carrying out an analysis of the DNA structure, and then breaking it down into fragments for further analysis. So it should take around a day. At home, on Earth, I used computers for all the data, so I didn't have to track everything myself. But here..."

"You told the Shadows what you needed them to do," Haedyn cut in. "And I'm acting as the end-of-session signal. In other words, once the Shadows are done, they'll alert me by summoning me. Have something to eat, Rory. You look like you're played out, again."

"Really?" He was spot on. I wiped my hands on my vest and asked,

"Can we eat somewhere else for a change? Do you have a cafeteria or something like that? If I have to stay inside these four walls another minute, I'll go bonkers."

"Yes, there is somewhere else," Haedyn said. "But Rory, remember what happened the last time you ventured out?"

"Are you referring to the Tree? Speaking of, when might I see it? I really do need some samples. They're essential."

"You'll have to wait a few days. A thorough sweep of the place is underway right now. Then you'll have to ask Doran."

Haedyn ruffled a shock of his hair, looked at me and suddenly smiled. "Come on. I think we can find somewhere else to eat. Especially now, because there won't be too many others there. Only, I have a request: don't leave my side. Stay right by me. Got it?"

"Got it!"

I really wanted to see another part of the

palace. Otherwise, it was ridiculous: here I was in a completely different world, but either confined to this lab or my chambers, not allowed to see what's what out there. I'd clearly adapted physically and wasn't sick at all when I passed by windows. In fact, I could even see in Ruadh a rather crazy kind of freaky beauty.

"Haedyn, can you tell Aerona that I'll want to see her in a day and I'll also draw some of her blood then. I've got to analyze her hormones. So for the next 24 hours, she needs to abstain from drinking, sex, and stimulants."

"You gotta be kidding....," the healer muttered. "So what's the nature of this analysis?"

"I want to take a look at her reproductive system and see if you have thyroid hormones. I know for sure you do have a thyroid – I studied one of your books on anatomy. And there are other little things I want to look at. We have to approach this from every angle, Haedyn. To be honest, I'm really intrigued by what's going on with your people. Even if I wasn't my freedom depends on my ability to quickly find and solve your problem.?"

We walked along a wide corridor dominated by dark brown and purple hues. A mirror floor, lamps recessed into the walls, niches with sofas, and statues that gave me goose bumps. And also faeries. A lot of faeries passing by one by one and in small groups. All had very business-like looks. Some were loaded down with books, others carried strange vessels with who knows what inside.

I was curious and so asked Haedyn, "So what do the subjects of the Court of Shadows do with themselves?"

"They live their lives."

"Ha ha, very funny. It's just that I see all these faeries living in the palace. I doubt Doran allows them all to freeload."

"You're right," Haedyn grinned, turning right and starting down some stone stairs. I was right behind him, having noticed that the kitten, in turn, was now following me.

"You know, Rory, that the Shadow Court accepts everyone. There's just one caveat to that. Everybody has to work. Half the inhabitants of Ruadh are scholars of some sort. Doran is cunning. Both the Seelie and the Unseelie Courts are stuck in their ways. They are loathe to accept any changes. So Doran draws the scholars in. Including historians. We are the only ones who judge all three Courts. Doran is constantly looking for precedents to various crimes perpetrated throughout our long, rich history. This makes it easier to work things out. Sure, the magic of the Wild Hunt can always point to the perpetrator, but that's not enough. You also need the tools to analyze the situation."

"Wait a minute! I'm one of a slew of

scientists, then?"

"Yes, you could say so."

"What the hell do you need me for, then? Can't you all get together and figure it out?"

"Rory, we study Chaos and everything about it. But when it comes to reproductive issues... alas ... stereotypes and pride come into the picture. Even we scientists have problems with it, and we're the most reasonable inhabitants of the Three Courts. Doran is probably the only one who can honestly accept that we are dying out. Even I have a hard time with it. I can't help but think we're going to live forever. And the most important thing is that we simply don't possess your knowledge. We're used to solving all our problems with magic. I don't even know how to conduct the simplest of blood tests."

I was in a city of scientists who didn't know the first thing about applied science. It doesn't get better than that!

"I have one more question," I said, glancing at the kitten, who was amusing himself by first disappearing into the wall, then jumping out again. "People never see the Shadows?"

"Not unless Doran lets them. Your vision is different from ours. At most you might catch sight of something foggy at the edge of your vision. But at the request of the King of Shadows, they may manifest to you. We see them, but they can disappear whenever they want. Only the King is in constant contact with them."

So this meant that I definitely shouldn't let on that I could see the kitten. Or was this Doran's doing? Yikes! I sure didn't want to ask him. Who knows what would ensue...

I suddenly realized that, except for work, I myself was like a kitten here, except a blind one – totally helpless. One false step and I was doomed. Most likely I'd be punished for getting it wrong. I automatically rubbed the intricate bracelet-tattoo on my wrist. The pain I'd suffered was burned into my memory – I wouldn't soon forget it. Nope, better to avoid a repeat performance.

But yes, I felt somehow better when I thought about how I'd get my revenge on Doran. Someday, somehow, the great sex we had together notwithstanding. I still wasn't sure how I'd exact my revenge, but I knew one thing for sure, and that is that it would be unforgettable.

Yes, I really did feel better just thinking about it. And "my" kitten puffed up a bit, as if it could tell.

"So what if a mortal is suddenly able to see the Shadows without Doran's help?"

"That means they aren't mortals," Haedyn said, yawning. "But don't worry about it, Rory, you're a human, that's all. If you had the slightest drop of faery blood in you, we'd feel it right away."

Alright then. I literally and figuratively bit my tongue to keep myself from letting on about the kitten. My intuition was simply screaming at me to keep it to myself for the time being.

"Haedyn! Haedyn, wait!" I heard a voice that made me flutter inside and see everything in rosy colors.

Sighing, Haedyn turned around. Just then, Jioladh caught up with us. He was attired only in pants held up by an incredible buckle: it depicted an unfamiliar beast smiling broadly, with flashing purple eyes. The stunningly handsome face framed by the flaming red hair was as hunky as it gets and so very.... *very...* Whereas Doran's aura got me all worked up, Jioladh simply made me want to bask in his presence, as if he was emitting rays of sunshine. It's strange that I'd initially regarded him as dangerous. But perhaps that's because there was something monstrous about all faeries. But unlike monsters, they were possessed of reason, which actually made them even more frightening.

"I can't get into the lab – it's locked," Jioladh said. "And I need to get in there. Oh, hi there, Rory."

As he spoke, he grabbed my hand and kissed my wrist, sending waves of pleasure through me.

"Contain the Enchantment," Haedyn grumbled.

"Oops! Sorry!" said Jioladh, without the slightest bit of remorse. "I'm always forgetting about it."

"Well, keep on forgetting and risk the wrath of the King."

And carrying on in the same vein, we descended some stairs. I sniffed: I could smell something incredibly appetizing. I was practically drooling. "What do they make here?"

Jioladh had quit channeling Enchantments my way. He was still unbelievably alluring, but not perfection itself. In truth, he was the most gallant faery to cross my path thus far. For example, just now he'd helped me negotiate the stairs. Too bad I didn't trust faeries, though, not at all. All of them are hypocritical horrors.

"I don't think Doran would be too put out by just a minor Enchantment. They aren't capable of binding his adorable little toy to me. And look how she's blushing — it's adorable."

Blushing? Um, the last time I'd blushed was when I was being potty trained. Okay, and when I looked at Doran in bed.

"Just the same, don't cross the line," Haedyn warned. "Enough, got it? Have your fun, but be careful."

I glanced at Jioladh and, to my amazement, he winked at me. I wanted to ask him if he was crazy.

We turned a corner and entered a huge

room dominated by the smell of incredibly tantalizing food, and the clatter ubiquitous to any restaurant.

Without even thinking about it, I followed Haedyn and Jioladh while looking around me and enjoying the smells. It was an interesting place.

Clearly, it was carved into a cliff or something: the stone walls were amber-brown, with golden streaks, and roughly hewn. And the light: it was bright, like the rising sun. I had no idea where it emanated from.

The place wasn't very crowded. There were just a couple of tables with patrons. The tables themselves were carved out of a dark green translucent stone. Haedyn led us to one such table in a far corner. I carefully lowered myself onto a bright pillow that lay on a semicircular stone bench. And then I asked, "So is this a local cafeteria?"

"I prefer to call it a small dining hall," Haedyn grinned, opting to sit next to me, thereby forcing Jioladh to sit further down.

I didn't seem to be attracting too much notice, just a couple of faeries who glanced my way briefly and then were distracted by whatever they were talking about. Apparently, nobody wanted to stare too openly at the King's toy.

What ensued was simply wondrous. For example, I didn't see any waiters, yet there were dishes on the tables: bronze colored plates and elegant chalices. Plus utensils, and lots of them. I was glad that I'd been well-versed in etiquette as a girl and so knew how to conduct myself at a place like this.

But I wished Jioladh would keep away. I couldn't talk about things with Haedyn while he was here.

"Rory, what do you want?" Jioladh's question interrupted my thoughts. "I mean, to eat. Just tell me and I'll say it out loud. As you are human, it won't be heard if you say it."

"So they'll bring anything we want?"

"Absolutely," Haedyn said. He had already uttered an unfamiliar word, and presto! — An impressive hunk of meat surrounded by strange vegetables appeared on his plate. And the smell!

Almost drooling, I said, "Steak with corn and peas. And juice. Cherry." And then I added, impulsively, "And bird's nest soup."

Jioladh repeated all this, and a few seconds later I stared at my plate. There were two dishes, actually. One held the steak, and the other held a jelly-like mass in which I discerned what looked like webs. So this was the most expensive dish in Asian cuisine? This mucus-like substance?

I started with the steak, trying to avoid looking at the soup. I'm glad it didn't stink, at least.

"Aurora."

Wow, it was great hearing somebody call me by my full name! *Jioladh, you've grown in stature in my eyes.*

"How do you like it here?"

"I want to go home," I said candidly. Haedyn sighed, but said nothing, but Jioladh was evidently surprised.

"So you haven't fallen under the spell of our King? My, my..."

"I'm mesmerized. But I still want to go home."

"You're a strange one," Jioladh said thoughtfully, stirring a thick brown concoction. "Usually humans who find themselves among faeries forget about everything else. And they live as if in a beautiful dream. Although ... The Court of Shadows is here in Alfheim. Perhaps the proximity to Chaos disrupts our natural charm. What do you think, Haedyn?"

"Could be," the healer said curtly "It could be that after years of existing in isolation from us, humans have developed an immunity."

"But what difference does it make," the redheaded charmer said cheerfully. "Here's what I think, Aurora. Maybe I can buy you after Doran's tired of you? The Seelie Court has always been favorably disposed toward humans."

"You're no longer of the Seelie Court," I said.

"Nevertheless, I was born and raised there.

Haedyn, what do you think? Will Doran let me buy her once he's through with her?"

What a guy. Even as he was saying such unpleasant things, his eyes were sympathetic and, as if, trying to tell me something. I tried to remember what I'd heard or read about the Seelie Court. As I recall, they did treat people better.

Haedyn shrugged, and said something about not selling the skin of the bear until it's dead. Which offended me — I almost dumped my soup on him. It was hard, but I didn't, deciding that life was too short to waste time letting the faeries push my buttons. Anyway it was senseless. They were impervious to me, and I'd just end up getting all worked up over it.

And, anyway, I had better things to do, like feasting my eyes on the sights. I saw seven different faery species. Indeed, the most beautiful of all was without doubt the highest 'caste.' The rest looked ... intriguing.

For example, there were little faeries no taller than my waist. They'd be downright cute, except for their glittering red eyes and the spike-like teeth that were evident when they smiled. And then there were the two hulks over there, almost ten feet tall with huge eyes and noses to match them. Or that super thin woman in an unusual dress akin to artsy rags, with a pale, thin face and bright yellow eyes. She noticed me looking at her, and gave me a big smile, so broad that the corners of her lips touched her ears. I shuddered and switched my gaze to the fluttering lights playing tricks here and there. A thought suddenly occurred to me: there were all these species, yet only the upper echelons suffered from deformities. Others might be ugly, but this was naturally ugly, the way they were meant to be. None of them had mismatched ears, an exposed brain, or deformed limbs. Why not?

I fidgeted and mentally asked Jioladh to be a good boy and run along. Alas, my two companions were discussing some experiments related to treating particles from Chaos. Clearly my mental dispatches weren't registering with Jioladh. But I overheard enough to know that the treatment hadn't worked yet, and could even result in increasing the disfigurement.

And yet you refuse to even consider radiation? I almost spilled my juice. I pulled myself together and tried to regulate my breathing. Doran never did give me a straight answer when I asked him about it. And in all of the ensuing turmoil, I'd forgotten about it. This could explain my queasiness even. Had Haedyn somehow protected me and healed me with his magic?

Just thinking about it made me uneasy. What if radiation and Chaos were somehow linked? Why would only the higher faeries be impacted in terms of mutations? Is it that they're in closer contact with it? But Doran looks just fine. As do the healers...

I had all sorts of chaotic thoughts running through my head, and only Doran or Haedyn could help me restore order there. But the latter was occupied with his red-haired colleague, while the former was busy traipsing about on his royal duties. I needed to be patient. Luckily, I had plenty to occupy myself with.

Back at the lab, I lingered until late into the night, poring over books on faery anatomy. Fortunately, Haedyn was totally okay with this. He'd deposited me there, and then taken off somewhere. I suspected he was with Jioladh, talking about matters related to their healing activities.

And there was no sight of Doran. The kitten was nowhere to be seen, either. I immersed myself in my studies until just about midnight. By then, my head was spinning. Haedyn didn't come back to the lab, and so I was escorted to my chambers by two Hogmani. Once there, I undressed as if in a fog, readied myself for sleep, and dropped off into a deep slumber almost as soon as my head hit the pillow. But my sleep was interrupted.

It was a little after 2 a.m. when I jerked awake a. It was like someone had summoned me in the dark, empty room. Heart pounding, nerves on edge, my eyes snapped open. But the two night-lights in the floor revealed an empty room. No one had called my named. At least, not out loud.

But the kitten sat atop my chest. And its green eyes glowed like two magical embers. They didn't gleam in the dark like real cat eyes, rather, they glowed.

I gulped, and for some reason whispered, "What's up?"

The Shadow twitched its tail, just like a cat, and for some reason I said, "You know, I'm fully aware that you're a Shadow. But can I give you a name? It'd be a way of distinguishing you from the others. Can I call you Zephyr?"

M-r-r-r groused the "cat," as if to say "Why talk about this now? — whatever." But he didn't seem opposed to my naming him. Alright, then.

And then, suddenly, it was just like a 3D movie. I was still sitting in my bed, but I was also in Doran's quarters. Which was rather over the top in its gloomy splendor.

The King was there. But he wasn't alone. Hands clasped behind his head, he was all but lying on his huge bed. He was attired in light pants, nothing else, except for the ubiquitous silver pendant on his powerful chest. Shadows swirled around his head, touching his short black hair. Doran looked suspiciously happy.

"I demand that you return my subject!"

The voice of his companion was arresting, despite the angry tone. And she herself was so 'splendiferous' that I was not even jealous.

Meaning how can I be jealous of perfection itself? She had a fantastic figure encased in a sparkling, translucent gown, thick honey-colored hair, fastened with a golden hoop, huge almond-shaped amber eyes and flawless features. And her sexy, slightly raspy voice gave even me goose bumps. And all I was doing was watching her in 3D!

"Go ahead, demand it, Ornia, demand. I enjoy listening to you speak."

That's the King of the Court of Shadows for you. When dealing with his peers, Doran behaved quite differently, although I could discern a mocking note in his gaiety – very carefully disguised mockery. The stupendous lady, meanwhile, was definitely from the Seelie Court. I could feel it in my bones.

"Cut it out!"

"I'm not doing anything but listening patiently to your whining about my new subject."

"Do you know what that bastard did?" Ornia hissed like an agitated rattlesnake.

"Fucked your lady-in-waiting," Doran chuckled, and I started, making Zephyr blink disapprovingly. Although, who was this to him?

Merely the Queen of the Seelie Court!

"Is that what he told you? And did he forget to mention that he so enchanted two half-breeds that after he fled, they killed themselves? And another mortal is still in a coma. He played his flute, enchanting her, then he fucked her and fled."

I remembered the sounds of that flute, and shuddered. I must never forget that if I ever see that flute in his hands again, I'd best take off running and not look back.

"That's unfortunate," Doran said grimly. "I am, indeed, sorry to hear this, Ornia. But now Jioladh is a member of my Court. And here, he is guilty of no wrongdoing. Merely a few attempts to fool around with my toys, oh, and fuck my sister."

"What hasn't been with her, really? Doran, hand over my subject."

"He's *my* subject," the King said. "You should've done a better job keeping tabs on your favorite. The Court of Shadows does not betray those who come in peace and ask for haven. Do you simply want to prattle on about it for a bit?"

"I came to demand the judgment of the Wild Hunt. And I accuse Jioladh of deliberately harming those who are helpless before his magic!"

"I reject your request, because I do not see anything criminal in Jioladh's actions. Ornia, I understand how easy it is for you to let your guard down in front of me, but do not play the fool. What is it that you seek here? You know, of course, that the notion of a judgment is absurd."

The beauteous Queen of the Seelies stood there, biting her lip a little. She emitted a soft glowing aura, so alluring that I felt like basking in it. It wasn't overtly sexy or arousing in any way, rather it was bright, airy.

I felt a painful prick in my chest and screeched a little: Zephyr had taken it upon himself to scratch me, or did he bite me? In any case, it snapped me out of my little trance.

"Doran..."

Oh, that voice! So thrilling and insanely sexy, how could the King resist it?

"Yes, that's my name. Are you again set on seducing me? Chaos, this is, indeed, quite a performance!"

"Just think of what we could do if we were to unite our two Courts! Doran! My Court is stronger, more ancient, and more prosperous. And you can bring in all of the benefits of Chaos. Can't you see what this means? We could..."

What they could do was left hanging: The broadcast was suddenly interrupted.

"Hey, where's the sequel?"

But Zephyr had already jumped off of me, and, flailing his paws through the air like he was swimming underwater, he floated out of the bedroom.

"You can't trust any felines!" I hissed after him, and lay back on the pillow. And what was all that about? Why show me the two rulers together in conversation? So that I keep my distance from Jioladh? Or to let me know that the Seelie Queen yearns for a union with Doran?

I turned over and hugged one of the pillows. I needed more sleep, but a whirlwind of thoughts and feeling were spinning round in my head. And I was truly bewildered as to why Doran would reject such a seductive offer? What a gorgeous Queen, and a fabulous Court, to boot.

Like a green-eyed snake, I felt pangs of jealousy stir within me. A weak little snake, to be sure, but poisonous, just the same. Mentally, I tried to carefully stamp it out. Allowing myself to be jealous of faeries made as much sense as opting to throw myself from the top of the Eiffel Tower. Both were akin to suicide.

Somehow, I managed to fall asleep again. Two hours later. After tossing and turning, I was exhausted. I threw a couple of pillows onto the floor, scolded myself for giving a damn, and then I finally fell asleep. And I had a dream, so unexpected, so vivid, so realistic. I dreamed that I was still lying in bed, when, suddenly, Zephyr came back.

In the dream, I got up, somehow confident that I should follow the Shadow, which was circling around near the door flashing his eyes at me.

It's funny that the sensations I felt were just like real life: the cool stone floor under my bare feet, a light draft kissing my bare and for some reason flushed skin. In the dream, I didn't bother putting on clothes.

A pale lilac mist swirled in the corridor, in which Shadows were frolicking And I felt something...strange, extraordinary, welling up within me. I felt like I was on the verge of grasping something really important. Meanwhile, the space around me was breathing, changing, and as if alive. With every cell of my body, I felt the palace itself changing. In the daytime, I couldn't really see this, but in my dream, I understood this, and accepted it with complete equanimity.

I kept following Zephyr as we passed along a corridor filled with that animate mist and... then I realized that I was awake.

Sitting astride Doran. An absolutely delighted, aroused Doran, who was already holding me by the hips. I automatically tried to "dismount," but his steel grasp held me in place.

"I have one question. How?" the King asked. "I told the Shadows to let you into my chambers, but didn't think that you'd show up so quickly."

My response could win a prize for spontaneous banality, "I'd like to see if there's any radiation impacting the palace."

Good one, Aurora, just the thing to say whilst sitting on a naked man. Who is so excited already that he's about to enter you. I felt the tip of his rock-hard cock right *there*, about to move inside, and almost lost my train of thought. *What was it I wanted to talk about...?*

"Radioactivity?" Doran asked in a soft tone. "What, do you suspect something?"

He raised his hips a little, penetrating deeper I was flushed with heat mixed with a delicious kind of pain which only increased. Struggling to keep from moaning, I said in a ragged voice:

"I can't...oh!. can't talk about it... right now. I ... I need to check ..."

Just then Doran once again gave a slight thrust, generating a tiny flash of what felt like lightning inside me. Here I was, swimming in his arms again. What was up with that? Not to mention that I wanted to press every inch of my body into his.

"How are you going to do this check?"

I leaned over and licked the King's nipple, then nipped at his skin and felt such exultation as Doran's breathing audibly quickened. Awesome!

"I need...."

"What?"

I felt the heat build up in me, moving toward a crescendo. But somehow, I managed to hold on, not let it all out. Although by now I was so caught up in the ecstasy of the moment, any thoughts that entered my head were immediately banished.

"Counter, a... counter," I somehow remembered the word. "A counter...Geiger, m.-m-m."

Doran suddenly grabbed my face in his hands and stared at me for a couple of seconds with glowing eyes in which swirls of darkness merged with a greenish fog. It was like he was probing very deeply into me with his eyes. So deeply that it was a little creepy. What is it he's trying to see there? And why?

"If you have to, then so be it," the King said gruffly. What ensued was something so shamelessly sweet, yet fiery... Throughout it all, Doran kept holding my head so that I had to look into his eyes. Right into them, which made my head spin.

It was too good. So good that it seemed like anymore and I wouldn't be able to withstand the relentlessly powerful thrusts that made everything inside me explode. I felt him moving harder, harder, the force was almost unbearable. I was drowning in a pool of tenderness and unrelenting power, gasping for air and again and again felt myself imploding only to be reborn. In a new world.

After releasing his molten lightning, Doran sat up and started greedily kissing me. He reveled in my exclamations and protracted moaning. And shuddered from the aftermath of his orgasm. "My Rory," his hoarse voice penetrated my mind and remained there forever.

I fell on my side and closed my eyes, feeling the lingering orgasm gradually subside. So intensely insane. I heard Doran get up, and thought about taking a shower, but just didn't have the strength. I lay there, limp, as if I had no bones inside me anymore. I was devoid of thoughts, energy, left only with a lazy euphoria.

"My Rory."

I head these words he'd uttered echoing inside me. I just sighed. Guys were always saying things like that, things that made you want to smack yourself on the forehead. Although, actually, there was a certain logic to the King's words. As far as he was concerned, I did, in fact, currently belong to him. And this was signified by the bracelet-tattoo on my wrist. Ah, if I knew how to remove it, just watch me make tracks.

The bed groaned a little under the weight of the returning King. I felt everything inside me flutter again. I couldn't not respond to his presence, and he clearly had far too many pheromones.

I felt his hot body pressing into my back as he set about matter-of-factly spooning me, one hand completely covering my breast. Which immediately grew heavy as if it was filling with desire. Whoa! I was wiped out!

"Rory," his breath touched the back of my neck, "I propose peace."

I opened my eyes in surprise. Was I dreaming all of a sudden about how a certain Faery King was demonstrating humanity?

"Excuse me, what did you say?"

Doran nibbled my neck, giving me goose bumps, and purred into my hair. "You and I have the same goals. I'm not ordering you to agree, but I am proposing that we coexist in peace."

"*We* have the same goals?" I asked, dumbfounded.

"Exactly! I want you to help us regain the ability to procreate, and you want to help us so that you can return to your homeland. Moreover, we are drawn to each other. Maybe you shouldn't try to enrage me anymore?"

I couldn't stand it and rubbed my eyes: Was that really Doran in bed with me?

Well, yes, that's him. He lay there, his eyes now perfectly normal, with a silly grin on his face.

"What's behind such diplomacy?"

"If you're less tense your work would move along faster."

"Well, in that case...It would seem that you're also having sex with me to help me relax, right?"

"You are insolent for a mortal," Doran said. "I've never encountered a mortal like you before. And your insolence is not stupid, but very well thought out."

He rolled over and loomed over me, leaning on his fists. His ragged breathing mingled with mine.

"I want to make love to you because I love

to hear you cry out in ecstasy," he said in an even, low voice, "I love to hear you moaning beneath me. I love feeling how wet you are when I touch you."

He lowered himself a bit and pressed his firm lips on mine, swollen from kisses, whispering so that his soft-as-silk words penetrated my very being:

"Every time I see you, I want to take you, again and again. Until you're putty in my hands. And you beg me for more. Understand? But I do not take women by force, therefore I say to you now: stop making up problems, just relax and enjoy your time here at the Court of Shadows."

It was hard to think coherently, but I tried. "So when am I going to work?"

"Whenever you want to, except at night."

"So you're offering me hot, steamy sex and peace? But I haven't quarreled with you. We discussed the rules, and I accepted them."

"You hate it here, Rory. What I'm saying is, why not look at things differently?"

Doran's face — hard and stern — was very close. I could smell his body, and just wanted to snuggle into it like a cat and purr. But, clearly, the King wanted a response.

"Okay. I agree to give peace a chance," I said, choosing my words. "All the more so since I really should try to look at you from a new angle. Just take this off."

I held my hand out, indicating the wrist

with the "bracelet."

"Take it off," I said softly, "so that I don't feel like a possession."

The answer was short and nothing if not telling: "No."

"Why not?"

"First, I cannot remove the symbol of my ownership over you. Second, if I remove it, you'll try to escape."

"My word won't be enough for you?" I said, my eyes narrowed. The intimate atmosphere we'd been enjoying was quickly dissipating. And Doran's eyes grew colder and harder with every second.

"You are always striving toward this imaginary freedom of yours, Rory." His words hit me like a whip, "I understand. But with the future of my people at stake....no, I will not remove the bracelet. I don't want to reveal to all that you are my weakness. And I'm not going to let you go. Are we done with this, now?"

Despite the fact that it was warm, I felt a chill. Well, Aurora, got it yet? You get all relaxed, and oh-so-chill, and decide that the faery isn't so bad after all, right?

Wrong! You're not an autonomous creature here. You're just an educated animal. Although, indeed, he really does need my mind. My body is just a nice bonus.

"Yes, message received."

I got up and slipped out of bed, fighting

the urge to wrap myself in a sheet. The King's look was far too lusty, as if nothing had happened.

"There will be no truce," I said in a cold tone. "Don't worry, though. I'll do my job. Don't count on any more than that."

And I'll think up a special revenge. As soon as I'm finished dealing with your damn genes.

"Stop!" Doran's roar pinned me to the spot for a couple of seconds. His voice held too much power. So much so that it was only with great difficulty that I forced myself to make my way toward the exit.

Just then I was encircled by swirling Shadows. I could see the King's enraged face through them. "I didn't say you could go."

"I need to sleep," I said impassively, "And avoid stress. I have a lot of work to do tomorrow, and then there are your ceremonial games. I assume I'll be in attendance there?"

"Sleep here. I'm not asking you."

I shrugged and got back in bed. Great, here we are. The Shadows disappeared, no longer detaining me. But something cold and slippery lingered in my heart. I silently lay in the immense bed and turned away. I hugged myself and bit my lip when I felt Doran's hand sliding down my thigh.

I simply mentioned quietly, "Someone doesn't like to take women by force, isn't that right?"

"Your body is telling me ye'".

"My body — that's one thing," I said eloquently. Doran's not a fool, though, so he understood what I was saying. It was even rather interesting seeing what he'd do. Would he really go so far as to take me against my will?

He froze. I felt his hot, angry breathing behind me and involuntarily flinched and closed my eyes. Then a pause, during which my heart pounded in my ears. The seconds flowed by like honey dripping off a spoon.

What's your move, King?

And then, when I was about to scream from the stress of it all, it was over. Doran simply disappeared from the bedroom, exiting through the shadow portal. It was awful, cold...I felt like crying. I even sobbed a couple of times. But then I forced myself to calm down.

It wasn't like anything had changed. I was shown my place from the get-go here. I was a slave, even if a privileged one. So we work, and at the same time we develop a plan for exacting revenge and then escaping from here.

Great. It's just that inside, I felt an unpleasant drag. After all, all I wanted was to be able to feel like I was free, as opposed to feeling like a pet poodle. Because deep down I got it: Doran wasn't about to allow anything to impinge on his authority in the eyes of his subjects.

But let's start with the fact that he basically purchased me and brought me here against my will. Again I sobbed dryly, angrily. I could try putting myself in their shoes, seriously. But did the tragic situation the faeries were in really give them the right to treat me like a dog on a leash? Not to mention the other conditions of my "tenure" here. It was like, "help us, please, and also service the King. Otherwise, you're fated to forever be a whipping dog for the Wild Hunt."

I sensed I wasn't alone anymore, looked up and saw Zephyr. It seemed he'd grown some, and was now sitting on the pillow next to mine, his paws wrapped around his tail.

"Leave me alone."

The Shadow narrowed his green eyes, but stayed where he was.

"Why did you lead me here?" I asked angrily. "See what happened?"

Why couldn't they talk?

Zephyr seemed to arch it's back and fluff its fur. Which is strange, saying this foggy little entity had "fur".

"I'm the idiot here," I continued my monologue, "because I knew deep down that it was futile to ask. But I took a chance, I did ask. But now everything is clear. We'll go on working, smiling, waving."

Zephyr fluffed his fur even more, so that he was like furry little ball. And then from somewhere deep down inside him, a shaky voice issued from the Shadow, although it was more like the rustling of grass:

"It's-s-s f-f-fine."

I felt my eye widen in shock. "You're *talking*?!"

Zephyr spoke slowly, clearly with difficulty, not to mention that hissing sound. It was like two foreigners trying to communicate. One of whom had a really strong accent.

"N-n-not us-s-sed to s-s-sp-speech."

"You're not used to speaking?"

"Yes-s-s," responded Zephyr shortly.

"Why are you talking to me, then?"

Oh, we women. One second, I was just lying there wallowing in self-pity, and the next I wasn't, all because of the talking Shadow. How could my mood change so quickly?

But my clever little brain quickly gave me the answer. Clearly the world was full of jerks of the masculine variety. So beating myself up every time I came across one would kill me inside. But here I was, talking with a Shadow, and that's truly something unique and interesting. And, moreover, it beats thinking about Doran. Yeah, he was still there, at the edge of my mind. But still, this was better than lying here torturing myself over what had happened.

"You," the Shadow kneaded his "paws". "You...okay?"

"Me okay?!?"

"Feeelinkss-s-s. "You....and D-d-doran."

I snuggled under the covers, although I was already plenty warm. Especially due to the heat generated by the Shadow's words.

"So you deliberately led me here, right? Why? Did you want us to quarrel? Or do you get your kicks from sex? If so, you can lap it up at this Court to your heart's content."

"F-f-feelinks-s-s d-d-dif-f-ferent."

"Meaning? Feelings about sex?"

"F-f-feelinks-s-s b-b-between you and K-k-kink."

"Me and the King? Stop. Stop, stop, *stop*! What do you mean 'feelings different'?" What business is it what our 'feelings' are?"

"T-t-tas-s-sty."

Zephyr licked himself and added in his rustling tones, "Help, R-r-rory, b-b-rink f-f-f-eelinks b-back here. Or..."

"Or what?" I asked grimly, "Are you going to threaten me, too?"

"It ends-s-s... the Kinks-s-s agreement with us-s-s. Ends-s-s-s."

"What agreement?"

My head was already spinning what with all these secrets.

"Ours-s-s," Zephyr said cryptically, and sprung off the bed. I heard his sibilant hiss from the floor, "Ror-r-ry is-s-s s-s-o good. Tas-s-s-ty."

Oh wow! "If I'm so tasty, they why haven't you all pounced on me and eaten me?"

"Whaaat?" Zephyr was surprised, and flew

up above the bed, hovering above me. "Hush-sh-sh now.... we...r-r-reas-s-s-on-able. We l-l-like to know you l-long t-t-time and s-s-s-afe. N-n-n-ice and eas-s-s-y. We no k-k-k-ill nic-c-ce K-k-k-ink, nic-c-c-e R-r-rory, nic-c-ce f-f-aer-r-ies."

"So what's this got to do with the King?"

Zephyr was evidently thinking, and then he did a smart little pirouette and responded, "I s-s-show you. S-s-sp-eech s-s-still hard f-f-for m-m-me. But Chaos-s-s..."

This was turning out to be a really interesting chat. It had notes of surrealism, not to mention the prevailing situation.

"What about Chaos-s-s?" I bit my tongue – I didn't intend to tease him, but Zephyr didn't seem to mind. He didn't seem to care what kind of tone I adopted with him. What seemed to matter was the gist of the discussion.

"Chaos-s-s-s drives-s-s p-p-peop-p-ple c-c-craz-z-y."

"Yes, I've heard."

"B-b-better t-t-o sh-show you agreement. You no g-g-go craz-z-y."

"Why not?" I asked, warily. I figured he was about to tell me there was something different about me. Because I knew how it worked in the realm of fantasy fiction: Anyone who stands out is the one who gets hit the hardest.

Zephyr moved in so close to me that we were face to face, staring into each other's eyes.

To be honest, it was a bit creepy staring into them. There weren't any pupils in them, just two holes with a liquid green flame dancing in them. Incidentally, the Shadows that hung around Doran all had glowing red eyes. Just an even red light. Lanterns from hell.

"Your e-s-s-sence," again the rustling sibilants touched my ears, "i-s-s unknown." Hidden. B-b-but you are c-c-c-ap-p-pable."

"Stop right there," I raised my hands and warned him, "I don't know about my essence, but Haedyn checked me out. I am an ordinary person, honestly! I was brought up in an orphanage, then went to college, and devoted myself to science. I'm not one of your kind or anything unique."

"Not unique," agreed Zephyr. "Your es-s-s-enc-ce thought. I can't read it. F-f-f-aeries c-c-c-an't f-f-f-eel it. Ps-s-s-s."

He hissed just like a cat. And again he spoke more calmly:

"I s-s-show you s-s-something. Just in cas-s-se. L-l-look"

I involuntarily looked into the green eyes again. And in a flash, it was like I fell into their depths. I would have screamed in surprise, but my voice was gone.

Chapter Nine

I FELL FOR what felt like a split second. The green flame dissipated, and I found myself in a light purplish fog. I heard Zephyr's voice in my head.

"I am not s-sh-showing you the s-s-scenery. Jus-s-st in ca-s-se.."

For sure - what if he messed up and I were to go bonkers? What a shame to go through all this.

"Ex-x-xactly."

And I realized that somehow Zephyr could read my thoughts. Perhaps he'd been reading them all along.

Before me, the fog cleared, revealing Doran. I was startled to see him, but then I could tell that he didn't see me. If only because I was looking at the past. An archive. A memory.

And so I looked at him more closely.

This Doran looked just as imperious and stern, but more exhausted. I felt my heart ache a bit when I saw the King's chiseled cheekbones and the deep shadows under his eyes. There was also a deep vertical line etched between his eyebrows, and his fists were clenched. Doran seemed to be quarreling desperately, and now he was listening to the response. But I wasn't able to hear what they were saying. And then, suddenly, it was just like someone cranked up the volume, and I could hear the King speaking. His voice was ragged, exhausted but still unconquered.

"I'm willing to enter into a pact with you. But should it fail, only I shall suffer the consequences. I am the ruler, and it is incumbent on me, alone, to fulfill the terms and conditions. The rest of my subjects shall escape punishment."

The voice that now issued a response chilled me to my bones — and then some. It resonated in every cell of my body. And the feelings it provoked were very strange. It wasn't fear, it wasn't curiosity...no, I couldn't put my finger on it. It's kind of like when you were a kid and still believed in Santa Clause, so you decide to wait up for him by the fireplace. But then, you hear something coming down the chimney and it spooks you. So you try to run, but you can't.

"The faery doesn't understand what he's getting into."

"The faery understands," Doran said, his teeth clenched, still motionless. Or maybe he couldn't move?

"You cannot withstand the initiation, Faery. The Shadows will meld into you, becoming part of your essence. Even if you do withstand it, you shall always have the terms of the pact hanging over you. All sorts of emotions, be they obscure, be they dark, be they bright, from your Court. The Shadows shall possess the ability to feed off them without harming the fairies. They shall penetrate their dreams, thoughts, and feelings. To my Shadows, your subjects shall reveal all. But you, yourself, shall reveal the most. And if you fail to fulfill the terms of this pact, then you shall fall into my embrace, where you will suffer for centuries under the hands of those who preceded you in serving me."

"If this is what I must do to ensure the integrity of my Court and see it flourish, then I agree to the terms."

"Are you sure, Faery? The curse of the near-immortal is boredom, *ennui*. I know your people. You choose to end your lives when you tire of existence. You tire of gaiety, you tire of scholarship, you tire of the company of others.

Mortals are short-lived, but their emotions are always vibrant and tasty. What a pity that their world is out of our reach."

There was a brief silence, and then the bone-chilling voice continued, "I can make you the head of the Wild Hunt. This will be easy, once you are armed with your new power. With this power, and the help of the Shadows, you can open a portal to the world of humans, if only for a short while. In exchange for this, you'll allow them to enjoy the sensations of human emotions."

"You mean they'll kill them?"

"No, they'll feed off them, grow stronger."

"Agreed."

And in a flash, Doran doubled up in an excruciating spasm. I gasped and put my hand over my mouth as the King fell to the ground as hundreds of Shadows pierced him. Clearly the process was incredibly painful. And when Doran's eyes rolled back in his skull so that only the whites could be seen, I was so frightened that I stopped breathing. Could he stand it? *But of course he could, silly.*

Finally, it was over. Shaking, bathed in sweat, Doran slowly rose from the ground. He swayed, but managed to pull himself together and straighten up. I saw how black swirls now clouded his eyes. And there were Shadows scurrying around his feet. And I, too, wiped my forehead, which was damp. If that's what the

Shadows did to a faery like Doran, then it was probably horrific.

Right then I was jerked back into reality. I blinked in confusion when the lilac haze was replaced by my bedroom and all its trappings. And Zephyr was again sitting on the pillow next to me, his head slightly bowed.

"Well, what-t-t-t?"

"So the deal Doran struck with Chaos was that, in exchange for strength and power, he's supposed to ensure you get some tasty emotions to feed off of, and also let you into the world of humans now and then?"

"Yes-s-s."

"But now this isn't working out for you?" I asked. Meanwhile, I was dying for a drink. Fortunately, on the bedside table were various carafes, including a couple containing wine. I turned away from Zephyr and poured a glass of the standard greenish juice with a sour taste. I gulped it down while listening to the Shadow.

"Emotions-s-s-s s-s-s-scarce. Bor-r-ring. F-f-fear, l-lus-s-st, bor-r-ring. Degener-r-ation. Help Dor-r-ran."

"Help him? How?" I asked, setting the glass down. "Are you talking about children, or about sex with the King?"

"Children. Lots-s-s of children, lots-s-s of strong emotions-s-s. Fresh. Not bor-r-ring."

I had the feeling that someone was trying to pull one over on me. Why would the Shadows suddenly decide to throw in their lot with the faeries? Were they really so bad off living under Chaos in his realm?

"How did you live before Doran showed up?"

"Aw-w-w-ful," Zephyr wailed. "The world of people was-s-s clos-s-sed; no one here but s-s-subhumans-s-s and pr-r-rimitives. The Faery s-s-saved us-s-s from bor-r-redom."

"Doran abducted me by force," I said. "So it shouldn't surprise you that I don't really want to save him."

"No-o-o?"

Was that snickering I heard in that single syllable from Zephyr? I almost blushed. Really, if he could so easily read me, then he knew what an emotional mess I was inside.

Doran had really taken a huge gamble by making that pact with Chaos. But what he was doing was all for his subjects, first and foremost. And for that, he's to be respected. It's not his fault that the faeries had begun to slide into depravity. I suspected that the catalyst for this was the exodus to this world. Okay then, we'll see what the experiments reveal. I had high hopes for them.

"Okay. I'll do what I can to save Doran. But I want something in return."

"Ps-s-s?" Zephyr hissed inquisitively. I, too, could make a deal. Of mutual benefit.

"Find a way to get this thing off of me." I

lifted my wrist with the bracelet-tattoo, and continued, "No, I'm not going to swear to you that I won't try to escape. My plan is to look for a way to get back to Earth. And once I find it, you'll remove this bracelet. Deal?"

Zephyr sat there thinking for quite some time. A long, long time. I was already steeling myself for his rejection of my offer. But in fact, I was pleasantly surprised.

"Yes-s-s. I promis-s-s-se. I s-s-shall remove the br-r-rand of the K-k-king. When you want."

Then he looked at me and licked his lips. "Ye-s-s. G-g-good. You. Happ-p-py."

Indeed I was! I now knew that the Shadow could free me from the bracelet. Now I just had to find a way to get back to Earth. And I also had to help out the faeries, not just out of goodwill, not at all. I, myself, was intrigued by their problem. What was the source of it? And now that I knew I could, in fact, escape from this place, I really was curious.

What's going on with you, my Faeries?

Of course, I assiduously rooted out of my heart and head any sympathy for Doran. Why feel sorry for the one who dragged me here against my will and placed such chilling conditions on me?

"I have one more question. Why isn't Chaos able to open the portal to our world? Isn't he, like, all-powerful?"

"S-s-strong, yes-s-s. Not al-l-l-p-p-powerf-f-ful. P-p-ortal...two s-s-ides." Zephyr was clearly choosing what to say.

"You're definitely expressing yourself better."

"Pr-ractis-s-s-s."

"What do you mean, the portal has two sides?"

"Woman," hissed the Shadow, "Portal can open in and out: two s-s-s-s-s-sides. Not jus-s-st one. And this-s-s is-s-s dooms-s-sday. For-r-r you."

"So how does the Wild Hunt pass through it?"

"S-s-simbios-s-sis. But not enough for a lar-r-rge portal."

"Wait a minute!" I jumped in. "So you can open portals that are big enough for a couple of faeries, but not big enough for all of the Shadows to flood into the world of people. Or to let a lot of people come here. Right?"

Zephyr nodded, and I went on,

"And to open a really huge portal, you need someone on the other side. Someone who possesses magic. Right? But there isn't anyone like that on Earth. So there's no chance that a huge portal will be opening up anytime soon."

Zephyr nodded again, and sighed somewhat wistfully. I, too, sighed to myself, but with relief. At least Earth wasn't under any kind of threat right now. Which was just fine. But then something occurred to me.

"So how did the faeries find their way here?"

"As-sk them. S-s-sleeep now."

And Zephyr streamed toward the exit. But before he disappeared, I shouted after him, "Why are your eyes green? All of the other Shadows have red eyes."

In response, he threw me a green-eyed glance, and vanished. I sank into the pillow and stared at the faintly glowing ceiling. Sleep, of course, was out of the question. Not after what I'd just learned. That is, that Doran's life essentially was in my hands. I felt rather uneasy about this, to be honest. I don't like that kind of responsibility. Be it a human, an animal, or a faery, a life was not to be toyed with.

And Zephyr hadn't come out and said so, but he'd hinted that the Shadows were delighted with the thing between me and Doran. Well, what next? H-m-m-m-m.

Whatever am I to do about this?

Morning came, and still I had no answer to my predicament. First, because of the incredible night I'd had, I'd shamelessly slept almost until noon, and secondly, Haedyn finally roused me, and before I was even fully awake, said, "The tests are in. But you have to explain all the data. There's a lot of algorithms and calculations, not to mention charts and graphs."

"Lots of results, you say?" Still half-asleep, I sat up in the middle of the bed.

Haedyn rolled his eyes, which actually wasn't a good look for him: the whites of his eyeballs against his ash-colored hair was creepy. Not to mention his pointy teeth. But I was accustomed to his face, so to speak. I saw him as a truly good guy.

"The Hogmani have made it possible to transfer the results to a 3D image. Do you want to get going so we can see them, or would you rather sit here asking me about them?"

"I guess I'll get up," I mumbled, suddenly realizing that I was still in Doran's bedroom. There was no sight of the King himself. It was as if Haedyn knew what I was thinking, and said, "On the day of the games, Doran is busy right up until he makes his entrance at the Arena. He has to welcome guests from the other Courts."

"How do they get here?" I asked, climbing out of bed and looking around. I was thinking I'd have to go to my room for some clothes when I spied my pants and vest on a nearby lilac-colored settee. And there were shoes, as well. I'd picked up some bad habits here. I had no shame anymore, so could dress in front of whoever. Not that Haedyn gave a damn about my nakedness. What turned him on was my brain, in the scientific sense.

Haedyn impatiently tapped his hoof while I got dressed. Before I could even do anything with my hair, he grabbed my hand and dragged me to the nearest Misty Arch. On the way there, he told me about it, meanwhile paying his respects to the high-ranking faeries that passed by.

"They pass through the Central Arch, which is open for exactly one day. The Seelie and Unseelie Courts are also in Alfheim, but they exist on other planes which are protected from Chaos. And the faeries from those courts don't come here without protective amulets."

"What do you mean, other planes?"

We were nearing the Misty Arch. I noticed that there were a lot more faeries around today. And there was excitement in the air, as if this was a holiday. Lots of faeries were showing even more skin than usual. I saw one faery adorned in gems, and nothing more.

"If you divide a piece of paper into three parts, and then glue them together again, then it sort of looks like the piece is whole again, right? That's what Alfheim is like. Alfheim seems to be a single entity, but in fact, it has many levels, all existing in their own sphere. The Seelie and Unseelie Courts all shield themselves from the influence of Chaos since their magic is unrelated to Chaos."

"Why do they hide from Chaos, though?" I

asked, almost stumbling. If not for Haedyn's quick hand helping me, I'd have planted my face on the floor in front of everybody. But stumbling seemed to an appropriate reaction to seeing a 7-foot faery attired only in a broad metal belt with an intricately ornate engraving. He was holding hands with a tiny woman with glistening long hair wearing nothing but a glittering, transparent gown. And his double-pronged penis was fully erect, and so big it almost reached his navel. Add to this a greenish pallor and long white hair, framing a narrow, arrogant face with bright yellow eyes.

"Oh, did Dognat startle you? He's the head of Alfheim's mercenaries."

"Why aren't you considering radiation?" I abruptly changed the subject. Haedyn gave a short bow to a dark-haired faerie couple, dressed exactly the same, with a half-breed trailing behind on a leash. I looked away and gritted my teeth. Science...testing...think, think!

"It's not like that. We've taken care to shield ourselves from any sources of radiation. And there's the other Courts, as well. Chaos is just as harmful to them as radiation is to you. It almost killed us upon our arrival here. But Doran managed to strike a deal with Chaos. He had the foresight to see that such a union would force the other Courts to reckon with us."

It was becoming increasingly chaotic around us. But just then, Haedyn pushed me into the Arch, and just like that we tumbled into the laboratory. And a moment later, my joyful cries rang out around the room.

"Holy moly!"

It was a natural response to what I saw before me: the results of the tests were suspended mid-air. It was just like a sci-fi movie. It was awesome — the results were displayed in a greenish-gold light, and flickered a little.

"Incredible!"

"You can touch it. It's safe."

Cautiously, I barely touched the 3D image, and uttered a jubilant cry: the figures and images could be moved, extended, and stretched. I was speechless! I just stood there in awe.

It took a few minutes for the elation to subside. Then I got down to business. Haedyn propped himself on the edge of a table and asked, "Well, what's the prognosis? I'm a healer, not a scientist. Or, rather, not much of one."

"Alright," I muttered as I looked over the data. "Let's see..."

It was no easy task, really, piecing all of the results together. It took me almost three hours and a couple of glasses of some kind of juice that was a good substitute for coffee. At first, Haedyn was hovering over me, but then he took off somewhere. He showed up again as soon as I sat back in my chair, utterly exhausted. I still wasn't done checking over the figures, though.

"Well, what do you see there?"

"I told the instrument to start sequencing, identifying mutations and also initiate mitochondrial sequencing. My goal is to at least get to the bottom of what you are as a species."

"Did you find out?" Haedyn asked. He grabbed a chair and sat down next to me. In his hand I spied what looked like something to eat, but I was too excited about my findings. Food was the last thing on my mind.

"Your genes are a lot like ours. But they've undergone serious mutations. Humans would have perished from such mutations. But you're all doing just fine. It's as if some force took some human genes, shook them all up, twisted them around, and put them back in the DNA chain."

I paused, thinking. something troubling had been nagging at the corners of my mind for about an hour.

"Haedyn, It's *you* I've been studying here. I mean, all of you who live under the auspices of Chaos. What if that's what's behind the mutations?"

The healer thought about it, then shrugged, "It'd be easy to check, Rory. Today we'll get you plenty of samples for your research. What else have you learned?"

"That's it for now, but it's more than enough. So now what I need are, in fact, various samples, such as from half-breeds, faeries from the Seelie and Unseelie Courts, and also from the young and the old, meaning faeries who even remember our world. And we'll also sample my own blood, just to compare. And ... and ... and ..."

"It's time for you to get ready for the Games," I heard Doran's voice cutting into my thoughts. Again the King opted for a showy, shadowy entrance, this time exiting his portal in the middle of the laboratory. I forced myself to stay calm, although I felt myself freeze inside. For a single, unbearably long moment.

And then...

"Rory, get yourself together," he said curtly, cutting me to the quick, and then casually tossed a thin, brittle package wrapped in paper at me. I caught it, and with difficulty squelched a reply. It was unexpectedly heavy. And when I unwrapped it...

"What *is* this?!"

"This is what you'll be wearing at the festivities tonight," the King said impassively, looking over the data suspended in the air. As if he was utterly engrossed.

Silently, I lifted up a garment comprised of thin, silvery chains studded all over with a multitude of tiny gems. It was like it drew in the entire laboratory, so relentlessly dazzling was the effect.

Fragile chains and diamonds and nothing

else ....

I looked pointedly at the King, as if to say "You've got to be kidding.". But I knew perfectly well that I was wasting my time. He wanted me to don this glittering *bling* and trail behind him.

Still assiduously studying the data, Doran nevertheless threw looks my way. I felt my skin burn from the gleam in his eyes.

My first impulse was to reject this slutty chainmail, make a scene, throw it at the bastard. Would he punish me? After learning from Zephyr that he could remove the bracelet, I wasn't as worried about that. This was war.

But I hesitated. What if I were to, well, play along with the way things were done here? What did Doran expect me to do now? Blow up? Seethe with resentment? After all, he's no idiot. He knows full well that I'm not going to put on something like this. Did he simply want to revel in my humiliation after I rejected his attempts at a truce yesterday?

No. That wasn't it. I just didn't see the King as such a petty being, willing to degrade me for kicks. Did he want to show me my place? This was more likely, but probably still not quite right.

For some reason, I intuitively felt like he was simply testing me. Seeing how far he could go. I don't like that kind of thing, but I do like riddles.

"Is that what I'm supposed to wear?" I said

calmly, sliding the gently tinkling chains between my fingers. The dazzling diamonds actually made my eyes hurt.

"Yes."

"Okay, King. I'll get dressed, then. May I retire to my room?"

I struggled to keep myself from spitting out that request. *Let's do our best to keep it together.*

"No, you will change in the next room. Then, the Hogmani will escort you to Nuala and her girls. They'll finish putting you together for the Games."

"This way, Rory," Haedyn said, indicating a distant door. It's not that the healer was confused, rather, he looked a little upset. I felt like he understood what I was going through. Silently, I moved towards the door. Behind me I heard Doran's frigid tones,

"We have no time now, but tomorrow morning you'll report to me on your findings."

"Of course, King." My voice was even icier than his. But inside, I felt like lava was boiling in my veins, and I had a terrible foreboding.

The room in which I was to change was very small and cramped. Haedyn was quite the pack rat, it seems. The room was full of his clutter. A spacious bed piled with pillows dominated the space, which also housed plenty of shelves loaded with this and that, and a round table. I cleared away some room in front of a tall, oval mirror within which some strange symbols seemed to be suspended. I avoided looking in the mirror, and instead got busy. Fortunately, I quickly located plenty of knives and other sharp objects. Alright then. Right over there was a fine dagger. It was compact with a nice wooden handle. And it was also sharp.

I set to work. After ten minutes of intense focus and furious action, I was done. I donned the glittering chain mail, which dropped from a slender collar around my neck, seductively draping my chest and hips. It was like tinkling crystals with every movement I made. Too bad I didn't have stilettos to wear with this getup.

The conversation came to a halt upon my re-entry into the laboratory. But where I noted implicit approval in Haedyn's eyes, Doran's face froze when he saw me.

"What did you do?" he growled. And the Shadows at his broad shoulders seemed to be alarmed.

"What do you mean?" I said ingenuously, "I got dressed. King, you didn't tell me that I was to wear only these tinkling little chains."

"But you've wrecked the outfit," said Doran. It's strange, but he didn't look angry. In fact, if anything he looked like he was secretly glad. For a couple of seconds.

"I modified it," I said, although I don't know why. Using the knife, I'd transformed my pants into hot pants, sort of, and I'd cut my vest up to be sort of a bra. Along with the glittering chains, the effect was pretty good.

Doran ran his hand over his chin and smiled. Like a predator anticipating his prey. "Well done, Rory, you managed to pull one over on me. Unfortunately, I must now clarify what it is I expect. I expect, Darling, that you will remove the extraneous clothing and wear only what I brought you. I mean the chain-mail embedded with diamonds."

I shrugged and replied: "No problem. I'll be right back."

"No, I'll do it myself."

"Off I go to the Arena," Haedyn hastily cut in. "King, I'll take Jioladh with me. He's a seasoned healer and can help out."

"Take along whomever you want," Doran answered, not taking his eyes off me.

"So what's this performance about?" he asked, once we were alone.

"What's the point of yet again humiliating the person who's your greatest hope in terms of the survival of your species?"

"I can't leave you here. Our protocol requires that I display and take pride in what is," Doran actually floundered a bit, "er, mine. Especially when it's a human. Your kind is so very rarely among us anymore. Oh, and put this on, too."

He pulled out of the air a small silver chain on which a flaming orange 'flower' flickered. I flinched and heard him say

"Don't worry. This is a precious stone that is mined at the border of Ruadh. The Faeries from the other courts wear such stones to protect themselves from Chaos."

"So why do I need to wear it?"

"Let them think that you, too, require protection from Chaos. Just in case."

"But your subjects have already seen me. Without the stone."

"You can carry it in a pocket. So wear it. But no, wait."

He stretched out his hand and parted the jingling chains. Very slowly, one by one, he began to unfasten the remaining three buttons on my cut up vest. As he did so, he said, "Do not accuse me of deliberately humiliating you, Rory. Trust me. I am doing all I can to minimize your discomfort. But sometimes you must pretend that you are my toy."

One button ... another ... his fingers touched my skin. As if by chance. But that's all it took for my heart to jump through the roof. Which was crazy considering the outrage and anger I was feeling at the moment. Although, what am I thinking? My anger merely added a strange piquancy to it all.

I imagined the Shadows must be really enjoying it all.

"But I am angry with you, Rory," Doran went on calmly. "You stubbornly reject my offer.

And you try to wound me behind my back. It's odd...."

He pulled off my modified vest, and then started to remove my 'hot pants'. Which was easy to do. He simply undid the strap holding them up. True, by the time he was done, I felt a stirring down there from his touch. It was so unexpected, which made it even more exciting.

I wouldn't be surprised if we were to have an earthshaking event right then and there, in the laboratory. At any rate, I found it hard to breath. The air crackled with pregnant pauses and silent glances.

"You're too honest for a faery, too...logical."

He adjusted the chains and took a step back. Then he ran his hands down my torso, and nodded,

"You look great. I'll come by Nuala's in a couple of hours to get you."

And suddenly he reached out and pulled me towards him and literally crushed my lips in a hard, hot kiss. He grabbed my hair in his fist, clenching it. And I couldn't help it. I felt his tongue slide inside my mouth and leaned into him, responding to the kiss. I, too, was greedy and demanding. This, in spite of everything.

Was Zephyr hoping for some action? Well, here you go. Don't over-indulge, though.

"Now's not the time," Doran exhaled, pulling away. He again stepped back, clearly reluctant.

"Later, after the Games, I'll take you, Rory. You won't be getting any sleep tonight."

I felt a wave of anticipation and my knees started trembling. Judiciously silent, I followed after the three Hogmani who showed up to escort me. Actually, I saw this as a chance to talk to them. "Hey."

The trio looked at me expectedly.

"Do you know what radiation is?"

"If you tell us, we'll figure it out," one of them said hollowly, his bald head glistening in the brightly lit corridor.

I explained. By that time, we'd passed through two Misty Arches and found ourselves in a round hall with a domed ceiling under which tiny creatures with dragonfly wings were flitting about. They'd be rather cute, even, if they didn't sound like giant flies.

The Hogmani led me to double doors fashioned from lavender stone. The panes of the door had strange symbols etched into them which emitted a strange pale glow from time to time.

"We understand what you mean," said one of the Hogmani, his eyes gleaming with reddish flecks. "But why do you need this Geiger counter? We ourselves can tell you that there is radiation here. At the lowest tiers. That is where the creatures of the underground bask."

My mouth went dry. And even Doran's

kiss was vanquished from my mind. "So there *is* radiation, then?"

"Girl, compared to the radiation emitted by Chaos, your radiation is a joke."

I almost lost my balance and felt sick. Oh, how impressionable I was! "Wait a minute. But how... But I...

"The Shadows protect you from Chaos," the Hogman explained patiently. "They possess a special magic. Protective. They protect us all and we have gradually adapted. But the radiation is buried in the deepest depths. And there are slabs of stone covering it. And also the magic, which binds the creatures. We keep them for the Hunt, and also in case there's a war. But the King knows that people are fragile. Haedyn inspected you, but just the same, you need special safeguards. We've got to keep you alive, right? We need you."

Shaking his head as if to say "what a weakling," the Hogman then nodded to his buddies. The three of them pushed open the heavy doors and stepped aside, letting me through.

Docile now, I stepped inside, and immediately began to sneeze. It was the smell of the place. Sweet and spicy, fragrant, bracing and a little exciting. The different aromas attacked me from all sides, like bees attracted to a pot of honey. I froze, looking around.

"It's a human!" the dulcet tones dispelled

the dimness of the space. And suddenly a golden light illuminated the chamber.

"It's been so long since I've set eyes on a human! And I've never dressed one before!"

"Oh... uh..." I sputtered, quietly glad that I did not suffer from arachnophobia. Because the creature approaching me looked so strange that I was seriously taken aback. Imagine a tall, very slender woman with short cropped hair and a beautiful, bony face with huge, black eyes. Sounds attractive, right? Now imagine that she has four thin arms with long, agile fingers on each side. She reminded me of a granddaddy long legs. What she wore only reinforced this impression: a short, tight dress made of brown leather.

"What a darling girl!" the strange faery actually sounded like a burbling brook when she spoke. "Hurry, come with me!"

She grabbed my hand and dragged me along, telling me that her name was Nuala and she was extremely happy to see a human. After all, who hadn't she fixed up, including the King and Queen of the Unseelie Court? But she'd never done up a human – this was a first. As she spoke, Nuala gesticulated with all her hands, save the one dragging me along.

We ended up in a huge room with mirrored walls such that I saw endless reflections, making my head spin a bit. Above us was a high vaulted ceiling in red and gold, below

— a glossy burgundy floor and furniture of the same hue, all very gaudily carved with gold detailing. Compared with the somber lines and the black and lavender hues that prevailed throughout the rest of the palace, all this seemed rather garish and bright. Looking at the burgundy floor, it seemed to me to resemble blood. But it hardly mattered.

"How sweet!" Nuala sang in the meantime. She was already turning me this way and that, toying with my hair, my face, and for some reason peering into my ears. And she did all this simultaneously.

"What's so sweet," I asked, trying not to topple over.

"You are," Nuala cooed, done inspecting me. "Such a pretty, fresh mortal. I already know just what to do with you."

She pushed me into a generous armchair and shouted, "Girls, come here!"

Then, to my astonishment, I heard the rustle of wings and three girls flew into the room. There were no more than 3 feet tall, nimble and looked kind of like frantic dragonflies. At their backs were transparent, iridescent wings. They were attired only in a piece of lavender fabric wrapped around their torsos.

"So, then," Nuala said, beginning to assign duties. "Brianna, you take the hands, Kara — feet, Sayibh —the core."

"I hope you're not planning on dismembering me," I said, jokingly.

The 'dragonflies' all giggled and scattered in different directions, but Nuala patted my head and said, "It's good you have a sense of humor, and Doran clearly appreciates your temperament, Girl. My assistants will take care of your lovely limbs and nails, and also make up your face a little. Meanwhile, I'll do your hair. Great hair, so thick."

The dragonflies returned with a bunch of phials, tweezers, and some daunting miniature tools made from a reddish-golden stone. One of them knelt before me, the other bent over her hands, and the third very carefully began to feel my face with fragile delicate fingers.

Nuala continued to chat, while combing my hair with three brushes at once.

"Have you seen what Doran's opted to wear today? And this is the Games. He always goes about in black and purple, although he looks just great in green and gold. But of course 'we men know better and spit on such trifles'. Oh, he does not listen to Nuala, does not listen. I offered to change his wardrobe, image. After all, the King is the face of the Court. I remember the Unseelie Court when there was a feast. Their King and Queen started their preparations the day before. Oh, I had such good times there. Oh, it was crazy fun...."

"Don't you like it here?" I asked carefully. I

saw our entire retinue in the mirrors. Nuala's hands were all over the place, impossible to follow.

"I like it. Although Doran swears that my little nest here looks like a combination of all three Courts, he lets me be. He understands that I am a creative being who needs to follow her flights of fancy. And what to do if my thoughts take control of the situation? I am, after all, both of the Seelie and Unseelie Courts, and my father is a genuine Buggane."

"What's that?"

"A shapeshifter," Nuala responded, "He kidnapped my mum and held her captive for a month to ensure she wouldn't run off. Then I was born. But if someone is even distantly associated with the Seelies, then they can't stand anything else. So I was sent off to the Unseelies, where my daddy lived. Only by then he'd gone off somewhere. So I was raised by another Buggane couple. They were childless."

Continuing to do up my hair, she kept up her chatter. Even her assistants seemed to be listening attentively.

"The problem with those Courts, Dearie, is that they're so cliquish. In the worst sense of the word. Either you belong to them heart and soul, or else you get a lot of attitude. By the time I grew up, I'd had enough of both of them. I was too ugly for the Seelie Court, and too tainted for the Unseelie. And this was despite my great relations with the royal couple. In the end, I was raped a couple of times, almost killed for being too close to the Queen. I really didn't flourish in that environment. Then they started killing my helpers and stealing my tools. My magic isn't good for much more than aiding me in my work, dressing faeries —and whomever, up, making them look good."

"Do you use Enchantments?"

"Oh, no! Enchantments are wielded by the Seelie Courts. I am not endowed with the ability. But I can tweak appearances a little, so that they always look that way. I changed the appearance of one courtier so much that it deformed him for a year. Not even regeneration helped him after that."

"So how did you end up with Doran?" I asked during a rare pause.

"He was visiting the Unseelie Court and proposed I come back with him."

"And they just let you go?"

"No one is going to raise a fuss over a hairdresser, even if she's very talented. Doran swept me away and made me the Chief Stylist of Ruadh. All of us here were at one time outcasts and loners."

"But now you're all very grateful to him for his protection, and the Court of Shadows."

"Yes, and ..." Nuala stopped short, and asked in surprise: "What's going on?"

I listened, and heard what sounded like

hundreds of wings flapping behind the door leading to the short hallway.

The dragonflies also stopped what they were doing and exchanged curious glances.

"Those are Pixies," one chirped, "beating their wings. But we didn't summon them."

"No, we didn't," Nuala said, dropping her hands full of brushes and other styling implements. "So what are they doing here."

The doors flew open, as if an invisible giant was about to enter. And a stream of small creatures flooded into the room flapping their wings, producing an irritating rustling noise.

What followed was nightmarish. Emitting a nasty cheeping noise, the entire mob rushed at us. Because of the mirrors, it seemed like armies of them were attacking. I spied one of the Pixie's bulging eyes and small sharp teeth before I was thrown to the side. But before I could even get alarmed, the room was suddenly flooded with Shadows.

"This way, Girl!" Nuala barked, pushing me under a huge table. Two of the dragonflies were already huddling there. Sadly, the third was lying on the floor, as if lifeless, amidst the mob of Pixies. But they were quickly dealt with, and in no time, it was like the floor was littered with broken butterflies.

The Shadows hadn't been sleeping on the job, that's for sure. I spied Zephyr amongst them, grimly moving between the Pixies.

In a few minutes it was over. Any remaining Pixies suddenly froze in mid-air and fell to the floor in a *swoosh*. The Shadows paused, and all turned toward us huddling under the table.

"They're saying that they'll report to the King about what happened," Nuala said, still tightly gripping my hand. "They say to carry on with our work and that they'll stand guard."

"But what happ…"

"The Pixies went on a rampage. So now the Shadows and guards will try to figure out what happened."

"But where…."

"They'll take Brianna to a healer, don't worry. We're pretty hard to kill."

Nuala quickly got back down to business again. And she again started prattling. She brought out more devices to do my hair up as the Pixies were swiftly carted out of the room. Meanwhile, several Shadows remained behind. They were almost invisible, and completely silent.

"I don't understand it," Nuala said, as she quickly arranged my hair. "The Pixies are, of course, unusually mischievous little devils, but they aren't malicious. They alone can move freely between the Courts. Except for certain other loners. But to attack us like that….no, they might play a trick or two, nick something or the other, but to attack us, no."

I was silent, as I was thinking about the incident at the Tree. What if I was why the Pixies had rampaged like that?

"How do Pixies relate to mortals?"

"Just fine. When they lived on Earth, they even helped them sometimes. Do you think they were riled up by you? Why would that be, Girl? Did you do something to offend them?"

"All I did was catch a glimpse of them."

Two hours of non-stop chatter from Nuala, and the transformation was complete, i.e., I was now drop-dead gorgeous.

"Well?" asked Nuala, proudly adjusting one final lock of hair. "What do you think??"

I gasped, and silently looked at the multitude of reflections of me, trying to recognize "Aurora" in the stranger I saw from all angles. The "dragonflies" had applied some kind of lightly fragrant cream to my skin which gave it a shimmer, and my hair was arranged in a cascade of curls that fell down my back. It was like some strands of my hair were a silvery color. And the skin on my face was glowing. I had luxurious eyelashes and huge eyes, and even though I didn't look like I had any makeup on, I was much more beautiful and younger looking. *Like a virgin on her wedding night.* I thought. In fact, the dazzling chain mail looked just fine now. It was intriguing, even sexy, but not in a vulgar way.

"So now where do I go?" I asked, still

mesmerized by the "new and improved" me. No kidding, Nuala's a genius! Even my lips looked a bit fuller! And my eyes were, how to say, arresting.

"I and the Shadows will escort you."

And so I set off with Nuala and the silently vigilant Shadows toward the Arch, which exuded a dark purple mist now.

"This will take us to the Arena," Nuala said. "And once there, the King's guard will take you to his box. Bear in mind he might be in a foul mood."

"Because of the attack?"

"That's right," Nuala nodded, tapping her high-heeled shoes on the stone floor. "Also, Doran doesn't like hosting delegations from other Courts."

"Why not?"

"Because he knows that they are not coming here in friendship so much as looking for weaknesses. Although Chaos is not omnipotent, he is extremely powerful. However, only Doran was able to enter into a pact with him. And both the Seelie and Unseelie Courts are itching for a change. They know that we harbor here all those who were booted out by their Courts. To them, although we keep to ourselves, we are nonetheless a threat."

This time, the passage through the Arch was much longer. One....two...five...seven seconds went by. On the good side, I felt no discomfort save for that whining, mosquito-like noise.

We were ejected at the base of some unbelievably huge gates. Really big —I threw my head back to follow how they shot up into the slate-gray heavens. I was filled with a huge sense of dread. How was such a monstrous construction erected, and by whom? Meanwhile, the Arena was perfectly round with a translucent dome.

"My dear girl, I'll leave you now," Nuala said cheerfully. "Here is your escort to the King."

I looked around and saw approaching me the now-familiar, bald-headed greenish-gray faeries, all attired in their fine jumpsuits that fit so tightly that each muscle was revealed.

"Good luck!" she whispered, and ran to the gates, where she melded into the crowd, which was slowly advancing. Nobody in the line was upset by the wait, nor did they seem to even mind it. They all simply moved forward, steadily, animated. The dull rumble that sounded like crashing waves was just the roar of a multitude of voices.

"Mortal, come with us."

Apparently, I got to enter through the VIP zone. I obediently walked between the two guards, compared to whom I must have looked like a slender reed. I mean, their arms were as thick as my leg.

"Aren't you hot in that jumpsuit?" I asked,

noting that the thin, yet dense fabric covered every inch of their bodies, right up to their fingertips.

"In your place, I'd be glad that we were dressed thusly," he chuckled.

The second guard explained, screwing up his close-set dark eyes as he spoke,

"Our skin is deathly poisonous. But we are excellent bodyguards, so we wear this attire to ensure the safety of the King. If there's a sudden attack, we need only recite a spell, and - *poof!*- we're naked."

I gulped and, just in case, made sure I wouldn't inadvertently brush against either one of the guards,

"But how do you, er..."

"We are eunuchs," broke in the first, at which I checked myself, and asked no more questions. That being said, I was itching to ask for details. Had the other Courts made them into eunuchs, or was it Doran who'd had them castrated?

We didn't have to go far. The bodyguards approached a smooth segment of the wall, and one touched it with a green stone suspended from a chain, generating a portal. I was propelled through it, not especially politely, but not in a rude way, either. It was like I was an animal that needed herding.

I stepped out into a short, wide corridor leading to a thick lilac and silver canopy.

"This way," one of the bodyguards said. And all of a sudden, I felt my heart pounding and my palms grow sweaty. Just the same, it would truly be gratifying seeing Doran's reaction to my makeover.

I moved forward a few steps on a warm, springy floor, pushed aside a swathe of heavy fabric in front of me and found myself on a balcony. It was a huge balcony, in fact, with several luxurious seats and no railing whatsoever. Although...I did notice a sort of force field where the balcony dropped off.

Ensuring his fingers were covered, one of the bodyguards grabbed me by the elbow, and under the stares of the faeries all seated there, led me to the central chair.

There sat Doran. And as I looked at him, I got it: he could not reveal how he felt under the gaze of the Seelie and Unseelie Courts. Not even with a glance, as the faeries would surely notice. So I had to conduct myself like a toy. Therefore, I silently sank down onto a large silver pillow and pressed myself against the King's legs. I felt his hand drop carelessly onto my head, and casually stroke my hair, sending warm waves coursing through my body. Ah, no doubt Zephyr was in heavenly bliss right now.

But what about the other faeries? I carefully looked around, not wanting to attract too much attention. Ah, dream on! All eyes were trained on me. It's like they were all wildly curious. I was like an exotic specimen. Yikes! Lounging among them I saw the huge faery with the double-pronged penis. It was....most impressive, even when slack.

"What a dar-r-rling!" I heard a low, feminine voice. It was a dark-haired faerie with almond-shaped, dark gray eyes, high cheekbones and a generous mouth. She was a rare beauty, dangerous, snakelike. This impression was amplified by the slinky bronze dress she wore, which looked like glistening scales.

Sitting at her side was a dark-haired man, thin and agile. He looked like a panther. And his coal-black eyes slid over me as if he was undressing me with his eyes. Although why bother? The tinkling chains exposed all my "charms" to anyone who wanted to look.

"Doran," a rather dull, slightly quivering voice said, "a truly fine acquisition. Why not share her? In honor of the festivities?"

"I like that idea," the double-pronged faery said, and my heart sunk while my mouth went dry. I wanted to put on a brave face, but I felt like crawling under Doran's chair and staying there. So, where is the lady companion of this lustful guest able to handle all he had to offer? Didn't she burst during the throes of ecstasy?

Doran paused, as if considering, well, *sharing* me. All this time my skin was crawling and my hands were icy cold. And so when I heard the King start speaking in a lazy drawl, I started.

"Why would I share my dish with you if I myself am still not satiated? My appetite is still ripe for this tasty treat."

"Well, when you've had your fill, will you share the leftovers with us?" the brunette asked, suspiciously smoothly.

"Your rich imagination, Ita, undoubtedly pleases Sinid. It is not for nothing that you are the King and Queen of the Unseelies," Doran said in the same tone. I just sat there, working to regulate my breathing, while sweat trickled down my back. I didn't really think Doran would opt to share me, but you never know, after all.

"I understand Doran," broke in the faery that Haedyn called Dognat. "He's not going to share the secrets of Chaos with us, but this is just a mortal. However, if you are dying for something new, I'm happy to offer you my lovelies. They're half-breeds, fresh and sweet."

"Hush, Dognat. You're always going on about sex," Ita said.

"Not always. Sometimes I sleep."

Then he turned his huge frame toward me, stared at me point-blank and winked, saying, "Don't tremble, mortal, Doran is more than enough for you."

"Well, it would behoove us to gather together all of the powers that be to deal with disputes and divvy up the slaves," the mellifluous voice was like honey. I knew as I turned to look that this was the golden-haired, beauteous Queen of the Seelie Court. Who could ever forget that voice?

"Ornia, like usual you just have to draw attention to yourself, don't you?" Ita grumbled. All of the men, as if on cue, switched their gaze to the fair-haired queen. Meanwhile, my delight in seeing her was again mixed with suspicions. Can such beauty be for real?

"I have no need to resort to such tricks," Ornia replied, gracefully settling into the last empty chair. She wore a dress of glittering golden cobwebs that highlighted her flawless figure and full, high breasts, her hair piled high, and her enormous amber eyes accentuated by her lush lashes. She embodied the feminine ideal.

Ornia was accompanied by two muscular male faeries in snow-white uniforms, with short blond hair. Their faces stoic, they seated themselves on either side of the Queen.

Just then Zephyr appeared on my lap so unexpectedly that I almost started. Well, I'm not supposed to see any Shadows unless Doran allows it, right? Right. So let's not disavow anyone of that notion. And so I kept on idly looking around, meanwhile noticing how the King's fingers tightened slightly as he stroked the nape of my neck.

Outwardly, he remained calm, but he

said,

"Ornia, why are you using your Enchantments here? They are wasted in this company."

The Queen suddenly lost a bit of her luminous luster. And yet, I still had a hard time not staring at her.

"As we are all assembled here now," continued Doran, "I propose that we start the Games. Especially as we have many a number of combatants waiting their turn in the Arena."

Chapter Ten

WHAT I EXPECTED to see was some sort of gladiator-type fighting. In fact, I wasn't too far off the mark, although I fell far short of the scale of the Games.

Although, to be sure, the size of the Arena should have clued me in. I had a great view from up in the royal box. It was awesome in every sense of the word.

I won't describe everything that happened — it'd be impossible. It was a blur of blood and magic, exultation and excitement, that saturated the atmosphere. Doran had mentioned that, outside of the games, duels were forbidden at his Court. So it was only once a year that anyone with a beef could challenge his or her opponent. It was no surprise, then, that there were a lot of quarrels being settled at the Games. Faeries are vindictive creatures.

They fought two by two, or in groups. Often, entire families took part. I tried to see when magic was used, but the only signs of it were wounds appearing out of nowhere, or else one or another combatant unexpectedly turning tail and fleeing. Nope, no *abracadabra*, no poofs of smoke, nothing. That being said, it was clear that the faeries were using a lot of magic. In fact, it was used as much as any other weapon, be they daggers or long swords.

I didn't see anyone get killed, but there were plenty of wounded. And there was one individual who sustained what had to be mortal injuries. His chest was split open, exposing his lungs.

Then there were two families whose children had decided to couple, but then fell out. There was also the young faery who ganged up with his friends to brutally rape a former lover. When his hacked up body, *sans* his penis, was carted out of the Arena, I confess to feeling a grim sort of satisfaction. But Doran told me that he'd eventually grow a new one, over half a decade, or so.

The King of Shadows explained a lot to me during the Games. Apparently, it wasn't considered bad form to chat with your toy. Meanwhile, none of the other VIPs in the royal box paid any attention to us. Their eyes were fixed on the action – the subjects of the Court of Shadows were taking part in serious combat. And their bestial blood-lust and exultation was palpable —I literally felt it in my skin. Even the Queen of the Seelie Court was totally engrossed, leaning forward and clutching the armrests. Her mouth agape, cheeks flushed and eyes shining, Ornia was totally engrossed in the Games. The Unseelie couple was equally mesmerized. Alright, maybe they weren't pumping their fists in the air, or shouting, but their flashing eyes, quivering nostrils and parched lips spoke volumes.

As for Dognat, like Doran, he remained outwardly calm. Although this impression was belied by his double-pronged member, which again was standing at attention.

"Why is it just once a year?" I asked quietly as one group was removed from the Arena, while the victors proudly basked in the accolades of the spectators.

"It gives the Shadows a real feast," Doran replied, his eyes still fixed on the events in the Arena, where a new match-up was about to start. Two tall, agile faeries were brandishing wickedly long blades.

Indeed, there was a huge multitude of Shadows about. They flew beneath the dome, glided along the stands, and behind Doran, a whole flock of them was rummaging about. And judging by how the others were nervously eyeing them, I wasn't the only one to notice.

"So you see, today we give the Shadows what they want from us. The emotions are ripe, pungent, fresh, and there are hordes of guests."

"Wait," I said in a barely audible whisper, "This kind of sacrificial offering really works?"

Doran cast a quick glance at me. And I knew that I was spot on.

And right then, Zephyr, who was still sitting on my lap, suddenly swelled to the size of a huge watermelon, and then he froze. I almost doubled over trying to look as if I didn't notice. It was hard, though. Zephyr looked ridiculous, like a fluffy ball with legs. Doran was even a bit bemused, and threw me another look. *No, King. I have no idea there's a round kitten right there on my lap.*

After a couple of minutes, Zephyr reverted back to his normal shape. He sat as before, as if nothing had happened. Meanwhile, I was dying to ask him what that had all been about. But I couldn't. Something inside me kept on telling me not to show all my cards — not yet.

Meanwhile, the games went on....and on....and on.

Broken arms and legs, bloody scalps, disembowelments, and ... not a single corpse. But screams and adrenaline saturated the air. It seeped into the blood of the spectators. I could tell this by their inflamed eyes. Doran's eyes swirled with darkness — the Shadows behind him were furiously dancing.

Even I felt the effects of the adrenaline. I felt a strange tension rising up with me, rather like unrelenting desire. I can't even explain what was going on inside my head right then. What is it that made me bite my lips and dig my nails into the flesh of my palms? Although I disliked what was transpiring in the Arena, I couldn't help but look.

And this strange fascination stayed with me until I felt myself suddenly being jerked upwards.

"Come!" Doran said curtly, dragging me behind him. He pushed aside the thick cloth and stepped into the short corridor. It was dark, and there were some small coves in the wall. I was pushed into one of them, not roughly, but also not exactly with tenderness. My chains jangled somewhat plaintively, crushed by masculine hands. One of them planted itself at the base of my spine, but I didn't even squirm. How could I? I was sandwiched between the stone wall and the equally stone-like King.

There was no tenderness, no warmth, and no need for either right then. This was bestial passion, indomitable and alive, but no tenderness. Not now... not today.

The chains dug into me, and the cold wall pressed into my spine, and it all was mixed with the insane pleasure that shot through me as

Doran entered me. Grabbing me by my hips and lifting me, he pounded me with sharp, hard thrusts. Then he stopped, shuddered, and groaning loudly, he came.

What the..?!?! I froze, pressing my forehead against Doran's hot, rock hard shoulder. I could feel him breathing, his heart beating against mine. Then I stirred, and gasped at a sudden pain spreading through my body.

"Sorry."

Was he apologizing?

Yes, apparently, and that's not all. With extraordinary tenderness, Doran picked me up and carried me back to the box.

"So it's okay to be so display such tenderness to your toys in front of everybody?"

"Of course. You are very fragile, and these Games — they hearken back to our bestial origins."

"I could tell," I muttered, feeling how raw my tender lady parts were. This, then, is the price for his pleasure.

"I'll ask Haedyn to take a look at you and make sure you're okay."

"No need to. I'm fine. I was also swept up in the atmosphere. So people feel it, too?"

"It's a kind of magic. Perhaps you can feel the echoes of what's happening."

When we got back to the box, no one seemed to notice us. Why not? Well, it could be they were all glued to the slaughter going on between two clans in the Arena. Only Ornia cast a filmy glance at the King of Shadows.

I lost track of the Games after that. After the sudden, harsh sex, I couldn't keep my eyes open. When I opened them, the Games were finally ending. I heard the hum of voices all around me in the box. It was the usual chatter, talking about the Games. Boring. I raised my head and realized that, in fact, I had curled up on my pillow. How precious! Just like a good little doggy.

"Rory," Doran's voice brought me out of my stupor, "go with my guard. They'll escort you to the healer. You really should get looked at. I'll be by later tonight."

Was he actually still counting on getting some more? *Um, I don't think so, King.* I didn't need to see any more naked men for a week, at least.

As I followed one of the bodyguards, I glanced back and say how Ornia stood up and was starting to glide towards Doran. And then the heavy curtain hid the box from my view.

"Let's move along faster," the bodyguard said, turning towards me. "Even without you, the healers are plenty busy."

Indeed. Haedyn needed to collect a lot of blood samples. And he had to be stealthy about it, so that nobody noticed.

"So no one dies during the Games?"

I didn't really count on a response, but

apparently the bodyguard didn't mind chatting a bit.

"It's unusual. And as the Judge of Alfheim, the King intervenes."

"Uh-huh," I said, puzzled. "So what does that mean?"

"He acts if he feels that the offense is serious enough to warrant more than blood and degradation."

"He kills them, then?"

"Not quite," the bodyguard grinned. "He gives them to the Shadows of the Hunt to play with. Let me tell you, that's something to see. Alright, this way."

Haedyn and Jioladh were in a spacious room lined with stone benches. They glided between those bloodied by the Games, quietly talking with them and treating them.

To me, the wounds looked just terrible, and definitely mortal. Both male and female alike, all of them beautiful, and yet almost all had some kind of deformity. It might be an extra breast, or it might be no neck — the range was great. I had to ask Haedyn if they'd always suffered from this kind of thing.

And the issue of the radiation ... it really weighed on me. It was a real burden.

Haedyn noticed me and waved Jioladh over, who was bent over a girl whose arms were almost totally severed.

Pretty beastly, all in all.

How can this be considered okay? I asked myself this and then suddenly recalled how I'd been swept up in the thrill of it all whilst at the Arena. I guess I, too, had an inner beast.

And that sex ... crazy, bestial.

What was happening to me?

I asked Jioladh for an answer to this when he was scanning me, and he shrugged.

"Aurora, you seem just fine to me. Any light chafing during sex will heal on its own. Although, okay, I'll see what I can do."

He pressed his hand on my lower abdomen, while looking intently into my eyes with his bright green gaze. They were almost gleaming from his inner faery power. And his red hair was as if waving in an invisible breeze.

Oh, yeah – his fingers were already brazenly stroking my stomach, moving down, down.

"That's enough," I said, stepping back. I mean, all I was wearing were those chains, and he was starting to get a little personal, I thought.

"What a shame," he murmured, but he withdrew his hand and stood up. "You're really healthy, Aurora, even, well, too healthy."

"What do you mean?"

Jioladh shrugged, as if to say, "figure it out" and then added,

"You should leave now. This isn't the kind of thing you should see, is it?"

"You've never seen a horror movie, have

you?"

"A what?"

I sighed and tried to explain, "We like to watch movies on Earth. Do you know what movies are?"

Jioladh silently shook his head. *Great. Let's teach him all about Earth culture.*

"They're moving illustrations. Stories. People act out different roles, and it's captured on special equipment, and then shown to other people. Some of them are horror movies, scary, bloody stories featuring monsters and such. Is that enough? Do you understand?"

"Yes, I think so. You enjoyed these moving pictures, then? That's what you like to watch instead of Games? It's safe, but still scary."

"Exactly!"

"Go now, Aurora, before I decide to challenge the King, which would be my death sentence."

"Faeries have much more to offer than movies do."

"You are far more mysterious," the red-headed charmer whispered, looking into my eyes. "And I love mysteries."

I almost drowned in his gaze, which was chock full of Enchantments. But my mind was screaming at me, telling me to wake up. Somehow, I broke the spell and looked beyond Jioladh... and spied one of the wounded sit up and for some reason stretch out his hand toward Jioladh.

And then everything became blurry. I clearly saw the hand of the wounded man barely noticeably begin to pulsate. It looked very strange. As if hot air was sort of emanating around the hand.

Then, instinctively, I pushed Jioladh to the side, and suddenly, we were both thrown back. It was a strong, yet invisible force. After flying through the air we landed on the floor with a crash, Jioladh beneath me. I screamed from a sharp pain in my ankle, and froze, afraid to move, because just then, all hell broke loose.

"Just lie still," Jioladh whispered, turning over and shielding me with his body. "Fool!" he added, angrily.

"Back at you!" I snapped before asking, "Why am I a fool?!"

Really, I was offended!

Still covering me with his body, Jioladh propped himself on his elbows and carefully surveyed the scene. I peeped out from under him and saw that the Shadows had stationed themselves around us. Meanwhile, the perpetrator was being dragged away. He was limp, and so he looked like a big rag being dragged across the floor. The bodyguard who'd accompanied me here and had been about to leave yelled at Haedyn, who was shouting back at him.

"What happened?" I whispered. "I thought

that someone was trying to cast some magic your way."

"Whatever you were thinking," Jioladh hissed rather harshly, "why did you jump in to save me? Don't you know that if anything happens to you, Doran will have my head? Seriously. I'm always the most likely suspect to him."

True enough. I hadn't thought of that.

"You healers are greatly valued here."

"That's right. So first he'll rip me apart, and then he'll reconstruct me. Who knows what I'd end up looking like after that."

As a scientist, I was intrigued. "Is that really possible with you faeries?"

Finally we were separated. What happened was two grim palace guards surrounded Jioladh, while Haedyn threw his arms around me. He looked incredibly panicked as he scanned me with trembling hands.

"Don't worry, Haedyn. I feel fine!" I tried to calm him down, but he spat out,

"Quiet!"

And it was only after he'd identified and healed a slightly dislocated shoulder that he relaxed a little. Just the same, I could see that he was still rather agitated.

"So tell me what happened?"

"One of the patients tried to injure Jioladh with some kind of magic force. And it was so concentrated, I don't think he'd have survived.

Or else it would have been a slow recovery for him."

"So even wounded he tried to attack?"

"Exactly. So, now he'll face an interrogation, and we'll find out all there is to know."

I looked at Jioladh, who was still explaining something to the guards, and then he nodded and left with them.

"Where is he off to?"

"I assume they'll take him to the King. Meanwhile, you should go to the laboratory and wait there. Don't leave, got it?"

Of course I got it. Over the past few hours I'd almost been ripped apart by Pixies, and then I'd barely escaped being blasted by magic. If it was deadly enough to kill Jioladh, I guess that all that would have been left of me was a pile of *bling*.

"Who's going to escort me? Surely you have to stay here."

"Don't worry. We found someone to take you."

And when Aerona sailed into the room a couple of minutes later, I was hardly surprised. It only made sense to Haedyn to turn to Doran's sister for help. I was, after all, Aerona's last hope for attaining motherhood. It was in her interest to ensure my safety.

"Let's be off then," she said curtly. "Move it."

Aerona was clearly uptight. Her pallor seemed even more pronounced, emphasized by her form-fitting black and purple gown. She more or less relaxed once we got to the laboratory, but only after she did a careful check of the premises.

"Alright, have a seat," she said — her first words since leaving Haedyn. "Doran is most likely still with the royal lowlifes from the other Courts. And Haedyn won't be free for quite some time."

Then she looked at the genetic analyzer and asked, "Any progress?"

"Not much," I said candidly, sinking into a chair. "But I can tell you that there don't seem to be any issues at the genetic level. We're awaiting a more wide-ranging sample. And I have a question. Aerona, are you aware of the radiation deep underground here? We humans consider it to be extremely dangerous."

"Are you talking about the underground hearth?

"Yes, why?"

"Well...have you used it as a heat source for very long?"

"We've always used it," Aerona shrugged. "According to legend, the first Faery Hills were spewed out by the underground hearth. It's convenient, safe, and warm. And our creature-combatants thrive down there."

"But how do people..."

"Oh, do you mean the people we carried off to the Hills?" Aerona gave a thin smile. "Don't worry. We shielded them with our magic. True, our shield only covers our lands. Beyond our borders, though..."

"They've always been exposed to radiation," I muttered. "All your magic did was stop them from getting sick. But as soon as anyone left, the radiation poisoning took effect...My God!"

"Yes, that's why we've rarely abducted people. Only the prettiest and most talented. And we've done our best to keep them here. But we were fertile when we lived on Earth, Rory. Don't seek out answers to our problem in this radiation."

But this was news to me. I'd read about the underground hearth in Haedyn's books — the ones that I was able to understand. Before, though, I hadn't associated it with the radiation.

So it turns out the radiation wasn't the issue. I had to look elsewhere for answers. Sheesh! I'd love to get my hands on some really ancient faery blood. I'd have to ask Doran.

I got up and started pacing back and forth under Aerona's intrigued gaze. The problem... yes, it was of the utmost urgency. Right now, the faeries had seriously mutated genes. And yet, they were alive and healthy, and essentially immortal. They weren't sterile — not the men, anyway. But they couldn't produce offspring.

And this world was where they stopped giving birth altogether.

It didn't have anything to do with Chaos, since this infertility curse extended to all three Courts. Two of which were not impacted by Chaos.

"Aerona, how will Haedyn get blood from faeries from the other Courts? Faeries that don't live here?"

"He's not the one assigned to do that. I am," Aerona said wickedly. "Today I'll be throwing a party and all of my 'admirers' will be there. Not even the snobs of the Seelie and Unseelie Courts can refuse the sister of the King of Shadows. Come tomorrow morning, you'll have samples of their blood."

I tried not to think about how she planned on acquiring the blood. Results come first, right?

Aerona lingered for a little while longer, and then left, after assuring me that I was safe with the ever-vigilant Shadows.

And I remained there, alone.

But I certainly wasn't bored. I still couldn't get thoughts of radiation out of my head. Was I really right to discard it as the potential source of the problem?

I hurried over to the stack of books I'd

piled up and grabbed one. It was about living on Earth. And it contained lots of images. Great pictures, bright, clear, and different angles. I started leafing through the book, just seeing what hit me. Then I slammed the book shut, and let out a curse.

What I needed was more blood. And yes, I knew I was going to get more, but only toward dawn.

So I decided to stay put. I'd lie in wait for Haedyn's arrival. And then I'd get the samples and start checking them out right away. The sooner, the better. But until then, what could I do?

I starting reading. I explored everything related to faerie diseases, how they developed, and also about their lives in general. Now that I was aware of the underground hearth, I read about it once more. And I shook my head. Radiation was not fatal to fairies. But just the same, I had to be careful.

Chaos and radiation ... radiation and Chaos. It just seemed like the issue was the one, or the other. I felt like I was really on the verge of a breakthrough. I started feeling it out and ....suddenly I drifted off to sleep. The day had been far too eventful.

I dreamed of the sea. I drifted in the warm surf and gazed at the heavens above me. I heard seagulls cawing, people laughing...I was relaxed and happy. The warm waves gently rocked me, soothing me, calming me. I felt incredibly blissful. I felt like stretching out like a cat and purring. *How about a daiquiri, waiter? And where's that good-looking guy I'd been flirting with?*

Then, I saw a slate gray sky through my half-closed eyes. Were those clouds gathering? What happened to the sun? What's that green haze rising on the horizon?

"Ror-r-r-r-ry!" The thundering bass flooded over me. I opened my eyes and saw an enormous cat's head rising over the horizon. "Ror-r-r-r-ry! S-s-ooo yum-m-my!"

I screamed and ... woke up. The sea, the beach and the giant head of Zephyr vanished, and I had no idea how I'd been transferred from the laboratory to Doran's chambers. The King himself was standing nearby discarding his shirt, which fell like a dark cloudlet, dissolving in the air. In the play of darkness and glow of the pale lilac lighting cast as if from frost-covered trees, Doran look particularly sexy and dangerous. I noted the cut of his muscled body, his chiseled lips, and the darkness in his eyes.

"You brought me here," I noted, not bothering to ask. "Why? I wanted to read some more until Haedyn showed up."

"You read enough," Doran nodded, discarding his trousers, which also dissipated in a cloud of fog. "That's quite a talent you have, reading with your eyes closed and your face planted in a book. Haedyn will do fine without you."

"He doesn't know what to do..."

"I meant that he'll store the blood samples until you get back to the laboratory. Get some sleep, Rory."

Right, get some sleep, Rory, next to a naked man with yet another hard-on. Although it didn't seem like the King was in any hurry to do anything about it. He lay on the bed, hands behind his head, and stretched himself out.

"Doran," I coughed, parched. "What happened in the infirmary?"

A crease appeared between the King's brows. A couple of seconds went by, and then, reluctantly, he said,

"It was an attempt to hurt Jioladh."

"But why?"

"An incredibly stupid move to make. A former Seelie saw Ornia and lost his mind. It's no secret that our red-haired healer used to be her favorite. That Seelie fled here, having fallen out of her graces."

"Wait, but no one who comes *here* from the Seelie Court has any reason to stay there. What good would attacking Jioladh do?" I bit my tongue. I was worried that Doran would take offense, as I was essentially calling the Court of Shadows a scrap yard for refugees.

But Doran didn't mind and merely said, "The Queen's Enchantments have a powerful effect on her subjects. It can take years for them to wear off. This former subject decided to court her favor by finishing off Jioladh. Even he couldn't really explain why. He mumbled something about beauty, innocence and honor. Before he was killed."

"You mean he was executed?"

"He tried to kill a healer," Doran said coldly. "There is one punishment for this. But what were you doing there?"

I had to be very careful about what I said. "Jioladh was examining me, and I simply pushed him out of the way."

"How did you know he was in danger?"

"Well, I saw how the patient's hand was pulsating. Isn't it normal to see something like that?"

"Yes, it's normal. Rory, don't do things like that anymore. Right now your life is priceless."

"So what about those Pixies? Doran, you seem to have lots of would-be assassins running around."

"Yes," the King nodded, "too many. Usually there are one or two a year, but now, it's a frenzy. The Pixies were under a spell."

"How did the Shadows miss it?"

"There are two possibilities: the opponent was strong and unknown, so they didn't want to intervene."

"But shouldn't they follow your orders?"

"Yes, they should. The problem is that they

are cagey. Even when they're following my orders, they still look after themselves."

"And their logic is not human, or even like yours," I added slowly, "Right? And so you're okay with it, because what matters most is their obedience. But their goals...as long as you walk the line, it's all good."

Doran gave me a long look and then sighed, "You're too perceptive."

"Is that a bad thing?"

"No, but I'd better not forget about it. You look far too innocent. It can throw me off-balance."

"We women can be wily, I guess. Can I get some sleep now?"

"You can," the King smiled slyly, "but then you'll miss what I was going to show you."

Curiosity has always been my downfall. So I raised my head and smiled in anticipation. I imagined various steamy possibilities. "So is this something that I can only see at night?"

"No, why do you ask? It's just that you won't have time for anything tomorrow. You're stubborn. And I'll need an army to tear you away from work."

"So what did you want to show me?"

"You wanted to sleep," Doran recalled, his eyes triumphant now.

"I already got some sleep. I feel great. So what is it?"

"Well, if you ask me really nicely..."

"Please!"

Doran jumped up and held out his hand. I obediently took it, got up and only now I realized that the annoying, tinkling chains were gone. Someone had removed them. I didn't have to guess who.

The King waved his hand slightly, and I caught my breath. The wall with the two arched windows simply vanished, and an ethereal silver light spilled into the room.

I found myself at the edge of the floor, like standing on a cliff.

"Don't be afraid," Doran whispered, wrapping his arms around my waist and pulling me back against his chest. "You won't fall. I won't let you."

Ruadh sprawled below us in all her nocturnal glory. It was night, but the city wasn't sleeping. I realized I hadn't been breathing, and inhaled sharply.

The opulent statues that had made such an indelible impression on me were now moving. The white lines etched in them emitted an even glow, and their heads were rotating three hundred and sixty degrees. The tall, peaked towers that dotted the landscaped pulsed in time with the pale, heavenly glow, while the roads were in a state of constant transformation. As was the city itself. Like that park over there... suddenly it was bigger, and one of the lanes abruptly buckled up and became a dead end.

And shimmering on the horizon was a pale green luminescence. It was as if the sun had just set.

"Is that Chaos?"

"That's the border with Alfheim. Essentially, that's where two worlds meet and merge: the land of the faeries, and the realm of Chaos."

"The city is unstable."

"Stability and Chaos are incompatible. But that's rather fun, even. And it's not dangerous."

Still awestruck, I continued to look out over the city at night. What a sight! There were Shadows flying over the rooftops, lanterns spilling rainbows of color, and a cluster of golden crystals in the center of one of the squares. From so high up, I couldn't make out any faeries moving about. But I had the feeling that the city was wide awake.

I was no long sick when I saw the city, no longer shivering. Quite the reverse, in fact. Ruadh's beauty was strange, alien, and a little insane, even, but it was absolutely fascinating. I wanted to simply stand there, drinking in the ethereal glow, the pulsating towers and statues, the emerald 'sunset'...

"Do you like what you see, Rory?"

"It's fantastic," my whisper flew into the night air. "Do the other Courts look like this?"

"Of course not. The Unseelie Court is dominated by darkness and silver, while the

Seelie Court is all unicorns and butterflies and gold. But I have my Shadows and forever changing landscape."

I felt his arms tightening around my waist as he went on thoughtfully, "I love this city. It reflects our nature, which is dark and changeable. We arrived here like a band of castoffs, unwanted by the other Courts. And now the Court of Shadows can challenge anyone. There's only one thing missing."

"Children."

"Exactly. We have no future. There are those who cross over the border into Chaos, and simply disappear. After centuries of living, life loses its luster. It can happen that boredom, *ennui* can overwhelm you and make life unbearable."

"That's a sign of weakness," I said, watching the Shadows dance around one of the statues. "What a long life should give you is the opportunity to learn as much as possible. Make a slew of discoveries, grow, flourish, expand in all kinds of ways."

"That's the way a mortal thinks."

"No, it's the way someone who doesn't want to indulge in self-flagellation thinks."

Doran's hands slid upward, embracing my chest, tenderly, gently. And I felt silk ribbons softly brushing against my belly and legs. It was cool and soothing and also exciting. I looked down and saw them – silky shadows. Dark and translucent, they slid around me, softly touching me, teasing me.

"Are they sentient?"

"They're a part of me," Doran purred. His fingers played with my nipples, which immediately grew hard.

"Meaning?"

"My magic, Rory. Look."

And I did look. In fact, the Shadows seemed to stream out of him and stretch out towards me. They encircled my legs, hips, wrists. One gently stroked my cheek and slid down my stomach. Another slid between my legs, making me shudder a little. I felt a barely perceptible touch, and caught my breath.

"Look at the city, Rory."

I couldn't tear my eyes away. Meanwhile, every inch of my skin was tingling from desire as I felt the gentle touches of the Shadows: my breasts, my hips, my stomach, my....

"Feel the life of the city..."

I felt Doran's hand on my neck, moving toward my face. His fingers were now on my lips, forcing them open. Doran took his time now, unlike before. He was obviously trying to prolong my pleasure, and the caresses soon melded into a kind of agonizingly sweet torture. My desire was soon so heightened that with the slightest touch I was gasping.

I felt like I now fully understood why after being with a faery no mere mortal would do. No other lover could light a silken flame within me that warmed me to my core, and nobody else's kisses consumed me like this.

I felt myself opening up now under the veil of caresses, as if I was getting to know my own body all over again. I was raw with passion. I felt like I was ready to explode into a myriad of fragments.

But Doran held back. He continued to tantalize me, and knew exactly where to touch me, exactly how to touch me — I wanted to beg him to take me. I was ready to beg him, and had to bite my lip to stop.

"Do you want me now?" I heard him whisper. I could sense the urgency in his voice, and knew that he, too, was more than ready.

"Yes," I gasped, exhaling.

"Are you sure?"

I felt like killing him right then. Doran was toying with me. Toying with his "toy" — that's right. He bit my earlobe,

"Then say it, Rory."

"I want you inside me. Now. NOW! Or...or...."

Doran laughed so heartily that my knees buckled. I would've fallen if he hadn't been holding me.

"How can I refuse when you say it like that?"

And he entered me. Slowly, letting me feel every inch, until I couldn't take it anymore.

This time it was different.

It was painfully slow and inexpressibly delicious.

His strong hands kept me from falling...

His hot, hard body behind me moved in time with me...

Our breathing was ragged and interspersed with moans: both his and mine. And I couldn't tell whose heart was beating faster. And the Shadows slid between me and the King, while the tension inside steadily increased until I wanted to explode and was ready to cry out.

Our hearts were beating ever stronger, I no longer knew where I ended and Doran began. We were melded into a single, sparkling whole.

And what transpired between us was remarkably strange and simply wonderful. It grew until it was unbearable and then it burst. And then the tension subsided, and I shuddered, lost in orgasmic bliss, feeling Doran shuddering as well. He pushed his fingers into me and nibbled the skin on my neck.

I collapsed in his arms. Ruadh was still shimmering at our feet, her lights winking at us while the silver light flooded the bedroom. Everything seemed a bit unreal.

Doran was silent, I was in no hurry to speak. I just relaxed in his arms, listening to our heartbeats gradually slow down to normal, my thoughts empty as I gazed out at the city. Ah, that green haze rising on the horizon. It looked a little bit like Zephyr's emerald eyes. I shuddered, remembering my dream, and heard Doran say, "Try to stay in the laboratory. Something's going on in my Court."

"Like what?"

"The Shadows and I are trying to figure out what it is. Although... sometimes I have a feeling that they simply want to know how everything will turn out."

"What do you mean?" I didn't understand. "They might not tell you everything they know?"

"I'm not sure. Anything's possible."

"But you can order them to tell you!"

"They might not tell me if what's afoot isn't a threat to the Court of Shadows, its subjects, or to me, personally."

"What a strange pact."

"Believe me, this is the best deal I could make with them. At least they shield us from any threats."

"But I don't belong to your Court," I said slowly, rolling the words off my tongue, realizing I felt uneasy.

"No, you don't," the King agreed, and I felt his hands tighten as he held me, "but they know that much depends on you. And if it all works out..."

"*There will be children, new emotions and a feast for the Shadows,*" I mentally finished his sentence. Oh, how I wanted to talk to Zephyr now — I had questions! But the kitten was off on his own pursuits.

Meanwhile, I was carried off to the bath chamber, from whence we headed straight to bed.

"I didn't understand my father when he became attached to a mortal," Doran said. He settled back, holding me tightly against him. Feeling his warm palm against my stomach, I felt like I was melting in a tranquil pool of happiness. And had no thoughts about what lay beyond this moment.

"And you've never been with any mortal women before?"

"I had no time for preying on girls and abducting them. And then we came here, to this world. And, as you can see, there are few mortals that can adapt to Ruadh. Our guests from Earth never survived past a day."

"You can say this so calmly?"

"Rory, you still have problems with our norms?"

Really, why bother? Here we were, feeling great, tired, talking. I paused, got a grip on myself, and then said quietly, "How are mortals supposed to come to terms with your norms?"

"You could at least try to understand."

"Sorry, but no, I really can't. For us, life is a priceless gift. What if I hadn't survived?"

In response, Doran shuddered and sighed.

"I'd rather not think about it."

"By the way, I still wonder why I was able to adjust to this place."

"You're unusually strong, perhaps. No one knows why some can adapt, while most perish."

"So your father had a mortal lover?" I decided to move on to something safer and less troubling.

"He did. It must have been the eighteenth century. I don't remember it well. She was a red-haired, green-eyed beauty, and was nearly burned at the stake – they thought she was a witch. To destroy such a beauty would be a real crime. My father used some Enchantments and stole her. I don't even remember her name. He brought her to the Hills where she lived for almost a hundred years. He even pushed my mother aside for her. He would have loved it if she'd borne him a half-breed. But then, the girl decided to run off. She must have been tired of being a toy. Even if she was beloved. We know the end of this story."

I imagined the beautiful young woman with auburn hair returning to her kind after a hundred years away, and literally turning into a pile of dust.

"I'll bet your father missed her a lot, right?"

"Indeed he did. He managed to become attached to her."

"Grow accustomed to," "become attached to," "desire," — that's how they described it here.

Never did I hear talk of "love", though.

I needed blood samples to complete my research and discover the cause of the faerie's inability to have children. The sooner I did this, the better. For my own sake. Get the job done, secure my freedom, and get back to my own world, pronto-fasto.

Because, unlike the fairies, I knew what love was. And right now, I was afraid of my ability to love. Yes, I was.

Then I drifted off to sleep, warmed by the King's embrace and overwhelmed by fatigue. But I was clearly aware that I was sleeping. Because in reality I could not sit on the edge of the still wall-less bedroom, my legs dangling into the abyss below me. Meanwhile, there was Zephyr pacing nearby, his long tail twitching, hitting my bare legs now and then.

"So what's going on?" I asked gloomily. "Who is it that's out to get me?"

"Don't wor-r-ry."

Well, he'd made some progress with his speaking skills. I squelched a desire to kick the cat and see how far he'd fly before coming back.

"They've made two attempts against me, but you tell me not to worry. Listen, seriously, what's going on? Who am I bothering so much?"

"Many are bother-r-red."

"Thanks. I feel better now. Lots better." I clutched the edge of floor under me and hissed,

"Can you be more specific?"

"Do you want to go home?"

"Of course I do!"

"Then s-s-stay calm, R-r-r-rory. We guard you at the behes-s-st of the King. We guard you becaus-s-se we need you."

"Me?!"

"It s-s-seems-s-s s-s-so, yes-s-s. R-r-right now it's-s-s not all clear-r-r."

"Not to me, either," I admitted. "I always thought of Chaos as an omnipotent entity."

"Chaos-s-s is-s-s powerful," Zephyr agreed, "but not omnipotent. He is primordial, limitles-s-s-s, but mus-s-st follow the laws-s-s that created Light, Darknes-s-s, Life and Death. Otherwise he will again rule and he will be . . . bor-r-red. As he was for time immemorial. S-s-s-o bor-r-ring. Hor-r-r-ible. Tor-r-tur-r-rous."

"Is that why you're waiting for something now?"

"Yes."

"For what?"

Instead of responding, Zephyr levitated in the air opposite my face. He patted my cheek with a translucent paw and emitted a soothing hiss:

"R.r.r-oy mus-s-st focus-s-s on her wor-r-rk, and the S-s-shadows-s-s on theirs-s-s, All for the good of Chaos-s-s and R-r-uadh."

CHAPTER ELEVEN

"ALL FOR THE GOOD of Chaos and Ruadh."
For some reason, Zephyr's parting words
were etched in my memory. I would
ponder them more than once in the ensuing
days. And, as it turned out, there was good
reason to.

Haedyn and Aerona provided me with
plenty of blood samples. Really, lots and lots of
them. I felt like purring when I gazed upon row
after row of test tubes. And I was glad that the
Hogmani had the foresight to create two genetic
analyzers. Both were operating non-stop.

First, I conducted hormone tests, and in
this context I mentioned to Doran that he might
have been better off abducting a fertility

specialist instead of yours truly. After all, that's who would know the most about such issues.

"Do you think I don't know that, Rory?" the King responded. "I tried. But none of them could survive here. And their backgrounds really weren't comparable to yours — they lacked the knowledge we need."

"Well," I said wearily, "sometimes I feel like I must've done something wrong to end up here."

"Rory, there are many women who would love to be in your place."

"Really?"

Doran remained haughtily silent, as if to say my disbelief didn't merit a response. That's a faery for you. It's all about the sex, isn't it? Who cares about minor matters, such as the fact that just being here in "faeryland" was a threat to my wellbeing?

The days raced by at a frantic gallop. Every morning, the Shadows would awaken me; I'd quickly throw myself together and be off to the laboratory. After the assassination attempts Doran didn't let me stray too far.

"We don't need to put you in jeopardy," he'd growl every time I told him I needed to get out sometimes or that I wanted to look around. "I do take you with me when we have feasts to attend."

"But then I'm your favorite toy, a dog on a leash!"

"Forgive me, but I cannot announce to all that you're actually a great scientist!"

"This particular great scientist is sick of these four walls."

"Rory, I can't risk losing you. Right now we don't know who is trying to harm you, and why."

That was, in fact, true. The investigation turned up one dead end after another, greatly frustrating Doran. Apparently, a powerful, rare spell was influencing the Shadows, so that in response to any questions we posed, all they'd say was that neither the King nor Ruadh was in any danger. And Zephyr deftly evaded all of my attempts to question him. So I buried myself in my work and tried to focus solely on matters related to it.

Haedyn did his best to help me out, sometimes at the expense of his medical practice. I complained about having to get by without the Internet, or my beloved research journals and articles. Although...

"Haedyn, I'm an idiot."

"Really?" the healer grunted, busy doing something at the tables next to a long, narrow window.

"You can visit our world! You could get me some scientific articles in addition to what you've already brought back for me."

"Rory, we've already lugged ten thick volumes back here. What a shame that the Hunt isn't a delivery service. Bear in mind that it's not a good idea to open the portal too often."

"But I need the latest research," I said, looking up from a microscope. "Seriously. We're going to get the results from the samples soon. And I can't store everything in my head."

"Alright, then. Soon, Doran's going to call the Wild Hunt together. I think we can get you what you need."

I bent over the microscope again, trying not to grin. I couldn't help thinking about the Wild Hunt bursting into our research library, grabbing our collection of journals, and sauntering out of there with them.

"And I still need samples from your Tree. I have the feeling they're important."

'You'll get them."

True to form, it was Doran who just then showed up out of nowhere. Although I'd seen how he did it quite a few times now, I still was taken aback when he stepped out of a cluster of shadows in his cool, arrogant manner. At both the first and second glance, I could tell that his eyes were swirling with darkness— I expected lightning to flash out of them any second now.

"Is everything okay?" I asked cautiously, mentally checking over what I might've done to set him off. *Nope, nothing.*

"There are those who want only what is not theirs," said Doran, approaching me and then swiftly pulling me toward him and almost forcibly kissing me. A greedy kiss, lusty, biting, making me moan.

"Ahem," Haedyn coughed delicately. "Did someone have designs on Rory?"

"The Unseelies wanted to acquire her for their prince."

I started coughing.

"You've got to be kidding!"

"This isn't anything unusual," the healer said in a soft voice. "Humans are such a rarity these days, you see. And for some reason, all faeries are attracted to them. You're beautiful, carry yourself well, and so it's no surprise they decided to try their luck."

Now I saw a green glow in the King's eyes, reminding me of Ruadh's nocturnal horizon.

"You turned them down, though, didn't you, Doran?" I asked, mildly alarmed, feeling his hands around my waist like a vise.

"Indeed I did, most diplomatically."

"You told them that there wasn't enough of me even for you?" I asked, squinting, remembering what he'd said in the box during the Games. "That I was your catch, and that was that?"

"You don't know Prince Aodhan. I wouldn't wish him upon any mortal," Haedyn jumped in. He'd served the Unseelie Court before joining Doran. "Yes, he's far too degenerate in his sexual proclivities. We should keep mortals away from him."

"Too 'degenerate' even for you?" I was

taken aback. "Seems to me you faeries are pretty brutal when it comes to sex!"

"Our kind of fun is a far cry from out and out sadism," Doran said. "And here, we frown upon rape. Who needs rape when the willing are at your beck and call? But what turns Aodhan on is forcibly taking women to his chambers."

"And then it takes weeks to bring them back to where they can function again," Haedyn added. "Rory, let's waste no time wrapping up this research, saving the faeries, and sending you back home."

Sure thing. Sounds great. Although yes, my heart sank a bit when I imagined how I'd get by without the King of Shadows in my life. But yes, I wanted to go home! Away from this madness!

Doran looked into my eyes and frowned a little, as if reading my thoughts. What did he expect? Did he really think I'd give up my freedom in exchange for sex, no matter how awesome? Hello! Maybe I don't want to spend the rest of my life with a bracelet encircling my wrist!

I'm sure he was astonished that I wasn't hanging off of him, or swooning at his feet. *Sorry, Doran, I guess your faery dust doesn't work so well on me.* Whatever the case – maybe it was my scientific orientation, my cynicism– his charms had no effect on me when it came to my freedom. Although, yes, when Doran wasn't around, I would think of him, and yes, I noticed that I would wonder when I'd next see him.

Lately, we'd been spending a lot of time talking. The Hogmani would escort me right to his chambers after I was done at the lab. Sometimes Doran wouldn't show up until very late. Then he'd crawl into bed and draw me close, waking me up in the process. Other times he'd arrive earlier, in the evening. And then we'd more often than not make love – hard and furious, or soft and gentle. After that we'd talk about whatever. I wouldn't probe too deeply, but did a lot of listening. I heard tales of his childhood, and about the bloody path he took to create the Court of Shadows. And the more he told me, the worse I felt. Because, yes, conversations like these brought us closer together than did the most passionate lovemaking. Sex would awaken my body, but his words crept into my heart and soul.

"So when can we go to the Tree?" I asked, snapping myself out of it.

"Right now," Doran answered. "But I must accompany you. There's no other option. I and my guard shall escort you."

"The only reason I wanted to enter alone last time was that spell."

"Yes, I know, but do heed me when I say that you must stay by my side."

I, too, didn't want to take any risks. But after that incredible night when Doran and I made love overlooking the city at night, I really wanted to get a better look at the place. Sadly, my work kept me imprisoned in the lab. Maybe, maybe when my work was done....

Did you forget what fate awaits you should you fail?

I shook my head, trying to dispel that inner voice.

I remembered the way to the Tree of Life from our last attempt to get there. The corridors, the Arch and the huge round hall with elaborate walls. But this time, I didn't have to worry about a trap, nor did I have an overwhelming urge to approach the Tree alone.

"Will it bite me?"

Doran was a little ahead of me, and he turned a bit to reply, "No one's had that happen for 2000 years or more," he responded with a straight face. He pushed open the massive doors with surprising ease. I guess some kind of magic was in play here, too.

The guards closed ranks behind us, ready to repel any enemy.

But no such enemy was in sight. All I saw was a room flooded with daylight, and without thinking, I clutched Doran's arm. It was like stepping from the kingdom of darkness and silver into the kingdom of exhilarating light.

For the first time in ages, I smelled freshly cut grass and flowers, and before me I saw what looked like a glade. My eyes were a little blinded by the light, and I blinked, suddenly realizing that all of a sudden it was both softer and dimmer.

The glade was picture perfect, with bright flowers, thick, lush grass and insects gently buzzing. Here was a piece of nature, hidden from the world. I couldn't see beyond the glade. My view was obscured by a golden haze.

My eyes were drawn to the silhouette of the Tree. Slowly, still hand in hand with Doran, we approached it. The Tree seemed to exude a soothing, yet vital ambiance. It was like looking through the windows of your home as you approach it on a cold winter's night, knowing that its homely warmth and light await you. I don't have personal experience with such cozy domesticity, but I think I know what it feels like. Soft and warm.

So how was I supposed to get a sample of this Tree? I couldn't get myself to simply tear a sample off of such a perfect entity.

"Leaves," I whispered when we got very close. "Some of them are yellow."

Doran looked at the Tree sadly, wistfully.

"This is our fault, Rory. The Tree has ceased to unite couples. So we have stopped approaching it, and when magic is neglected, it starts to wither away."

Something in what he said seemed very important to me. But I didn't have time to ponder it, because just then I heard a soft rustling sound. A gentle wind swept through the branches, causing the yellow leaves to drift to the ground where they disappeared, only to be replaced by fresh, bright green leaves.

The guards froze, and I heard a sharp intake of breath at my back.

Meanwhile, the Tree continued to undergo a transformation: tender pink flowers, like miniature roses, blossomed amidst the vibrant green leaves— a multitude of flowers, all exuding a delicate aroma.

Doran grasped my hand and squeezed it so tightly that I cried out and tried to pull away.

"That hurts..."

I stopped short and stared, wide-eyed. Our wrists were encircled by a vine comprised of the same pink roses.

Judging by the expressions on both Doran's face and those of his guards, we'd just seen a miracle.

"The Tree..." they sighed, still behind us.

I silently looked into Doran's face, where for the first time since I'd met him, I saw a panoply of emotions playing: from out and out astonishment, to naked fear. Should I be starting to worry about something?

"The Tree..." Doran sputtered, hoarse, as if he didn't know how to speak well. "We've been ... united by the Tree."

Before I could process this, he added,

"We shall bear children."

Children? Utterly stupefied, I stared at the

King, unable to take in what he was saying: Whose children? Mine? Ours?

The vine continued to wrap itself around our wrists, the petals of the flowers tickled a bit. The fragrance made my head spin a little, making it difficult to think clearly.

And at our backs, I heard one of the guards whisper reverently, "The Tree has come back to life!"

"But it's a mortal..." another guard began, stopping short when Doran turned a darkened look upon him.

"You know what awaits you if anyone finds out what happened here? Yes, the Tree came to life, but the circumstances have yet to be explained."

"Yes, King," the guards responded in unison, "We understand and will tell no one."

"Our lips are sealed," added one of them. "Why upset anyone? After all, this is the only mortal the Tree has ever united with anyone."

"Exactly," Doran nodded. "First, we must ensure that the Tree itself is in order."

"Doran," I said. "What's going on?"

"We must get back to the lab, Rory," he said, hastily. "The vine will drop off in a moment and then we must get back!"

Something really strange had just happened. And I wasn't happy about it.

Soon, the vine dissolved into the air, and the King and I left, with him practically dragging me along. The guards hurried after us and left us at the doors of the laboratory. Judging by their faces, they were still deeply shocked.

"Haedyn!" Doran's roar shook the palace almost to the dungeons. "Haedyn!"

Haedyn flew like a bullet from his cubbyhole. Judging from his appearance, he'd been sleeping.

"What happened?"

"Is she a human?"

Haedyn looked a little dumbfounded, so I jumped in, "The Tree reacted to me in a strange manner."

I watched as the last vestiges of sleep in Haedyn's face were replaced by comprehension that something big was up.

"The Tree united us," Doran growled. "We are destined to bear children."

The healer stumbled and clutched a table, almost toppling a stack of books in the process.

"This can't be," he whispered, astonished. "The Tree cannot respond to mortals!"

"You're telling me!"

"Could it have made a mistake?" I asked cautiously. "I mean, if it's impossible, then...? Especially since the Tree has been dormant for so very long. Maybe it was sort of groggy, and so it was like a knee-jerk kind of thing."

They looked at me like I was an idiot.

"The Tree never errs," Haedyn said patiently. "It is the fulcrum of Life, Fertility. But only among the fairies. It has nothing to do with mortals. Nothing. At all."

He bit his lip and looked at me with an unreadable expression. And that's when it hit me, what he was getting at. I almost fainted, even.

"Wait a minute. Doran, wait, I'm a human!"

"Yes, a human," Haedyn agreed, looking off into space. "But the Tree tied you to Doran."

"But if the Tree doesn't unite humans, then either this is an anomaly, or...no, this is some kind of anomaly. Doran, you don't believe this is for real, do you? Especially regarding having children. Listen, all I want is to help you out and get back to my homeland. I don't need any kind of 'uniting' with anyone!"

"Shut up, Rory," Doran said, continuing to squeeze my hand. "Haedyn, what are your thoughts?"

"Well...it's already evening, and we can't do anything in the laboratory right now. Take Rory to her room and talk. Meanwhile, I need to think. I will visit the Tree and try to figure out what happened."

"It's an anomaly," I insisted. "Just an anomaly. Let's just ignore it and move on."

In lieu of a response, Doran dragged me from the lab straight to his room. As for me, for some reason his silence and demeanor made me highly uncomfortable. I read so many emotions on his face.

"Doran..."

He was silent, looking out the window, then with a wave of his hand, he made the wall transparent, again "wowing" me with the view of Ruadh at night.

"Doran." I said, almost pleading.

"What do you want to hear from me, Rory?"

"Tell me this is all a mistake!"

"The Tree doesn't make mistakes."

"But I'm mortal!"

"It has united us, Rory. You are mine and I am yours. What else can I say?"

"Just say you'll let me go when my work here is done," I said and waited with bated breath for his response. In my heart of hearts, I hoped that the King wouldn't refuse me. After all, he gave me his word! He promised! I had to leave this place lest my heart be broken.

"If you are the one for me, Rory," Doran said, sighing and shaking his head. "Then no, I cannot let you go. Henceforward, this shall be your home."

So there you have it. The words struck me to the core, momentarily stunning me.

"You'll hold me captive?" This was all I could get out. "What about your word, King? Yours to give and yours to take back? Is that how it goes?"

"Let's not talk about this right now," Doran

said wearily. "I don't have all the answers, Rory. Nothing like this has ever happened, ever. So you have no memories of your parents?"

For a second, I was puzzled by such a sudden change of topic, and then I got it.

"None whatsoever. I was two months old when they found me. I was rescued from a huge accident on the freeway. I guess there were several trucks and lots of cars involved. Many people were hurt, and I was taken to the hospital along with the other victims. They never did find my parents. I ended up in an orphanage. Later, they told me it was a miracle that I wasn't hurt. Doran, I know where you're going with this, but you're on the wrong track, I assure you! I have no faery blood in my veins! None! I am human! I feel cold, I experience fear, I know what love is, after all!"

The King silently looked at me, as if trying to glimpse what was hiding behind my eyes. What, really, was I hiding? I don't know.

"We'll figure things out," he finally said rather abruptly and headed for the door. "I'm sending Haedyn over. I want him to examine you again."

He froze, as if he'd stumbled, and suddenly he was at my side. He wrapped his hands around my face and spoke in a manner that made my heart stop and then sink:

"Rory, just give me time to figure it all out."

"Figure what out? Doran, I … damn it, try to understand where I'm coming from. How can we be united? We are from different worlds."

"That doesn't matter."

"But you're the one who told me that mortals cannot be coupled with Faeries."

"I just told you I'd figure out what's going on."

"At least get this bracelet off of me!"

"No!" Doran said, backing away. "Don't even think about it. Not now. Enough. Relax and wait for Haedyn."

"So that's how couples united by your Tree treat each other?" I snapped at him as he was leaving. Doran paused, then answered without turning around: "Only when one of the two wants to flee."

And he flicked his hand in the air, squeezing my branded wrist and jerking me forward a bit — I almost fell out of my chair, even.

"As long as you're wearing that bracelet, I can find you no matter where you are. You're safer with it on."

And then he left, leaving me sitting there, seething with rage. I was angry at myself, at him, at this entire idiotic situation.

I didn't care what he had to say to me. Right then all I wanted was to get as far away from there as I could.

To me, a couple was two people who chose

to be together, not a union comprised of a master and a slave. No, to be forced into a union was flat out unacceptable! How did that saying go? "If you love someone, set them free. If they come back, they're yours; if they don't, they never were."

Clearly Doran had other thoughts about this. "Should I sabotage his research, maybe?"

The thought flashed through my head, but I quickly discarded it. I was already up to my neck in the investigation and deeply interested in it. And yes, deep down I still held out the hope that once I succeeded, Doran would keep his word. I was even willing to stay with him for a while longer, as long as I could go home whenever I wanted.

Under those terms, I might enjoy living in Ruadh for a while. I wouldn't be choking with rage from being led around on a leash anymore.

Literally, by the way. Doran had done a beautiful job of illustrating this by jerking that invisible chain on his way out the door just now.

Before long, Haedyn showed up. He literally flew into the room

"Are you going to do an autopsy now?" I asked sardonically.

Wow. I still had a sense of humor. True, it was of the black variety.

"That's not funny, Rory. Come here."

I stayed put. With a heavy sigh, Haedyn walked up to me. The blue eyes in the handsome face were anxious and slightly wary. I tried then to calm him down.

"I'm not going to raise a fuss. And I'll carry on with the research."

I heard the healer breathe a sigh of relief. "Okay. Let's take a look, then. This won't hurt."

Again, just like on my first day at the Court of Shadows, Haedyn stood opposite me and slowly scanned me with his hands along my body. This time, he clearly had his magic on full blast: drops of sweat appeared on his forehead, his eyes shone with a pale blue light, and he himself turned a bluish hue that almost matched his radiant eyes.

"I can't," he gasped hoarsely, dropping his hands and collapsing into the nearest chair.

I carefully leaned over him and asked, "Am I human?"

"All indications suggest you are, and yet there's something else. I can't tell you what it is. You are too ... human."

"What does that mean?"

"I wish I knew," Haedyn smiled crookedly. "I do see humanity in you, Rory. But the Tree does not unite humans and fairies. It's like mating monkeys with humans."

"Please don't tell me we're like monkeys to you."

"No, you're not, sorry. I was just trying to illustrate what I meant."

"So, what now? The Tree made a mistake.

It's simply been dormant for so very long."

"Rory, the Tree is the embodiment of our life force. It cannot make a mistake. And so we have to look elsewhere, toward you."

"But you just told me that I'm a human!" And then I froze. "Wait a minute! "Let me check my blood! I've had checks done at home, but these were just of a general nature. Nothing unusual has ever turned up. But in the lab, we can check my genetic makeup."

"That's an idea," Haedyn said. "But let's get to it in the morning, okay? In fact, it's good timing since we're finishing up the final phases of the tests. We'll load your blood into the analyzer and you can watch what happens yourself.

I processed this, deciding how I felt. Nope, I wasn't up to dealing with this at the lab right now. I was an emotional mess, really.

"Okay. But... Haedyn, can you take me to my chambers?"

I saw a cruel interplay of emotions sweep across the healer's face, and then he waved and grumbled,

"Okay, let's go. I'll tell Doran that you threatened me."

"Great. That's perfect."

Everything was just like I'd left it in "my" room. I guess the bedding was different. It was now a dark lilac and the material was smooth, cool. I didn't really like it, but I wrapped a blanket around myself and closed my eyes. Okay, so where was Zephyr?

"Ror-r-ry..."

Speak of the devil... I opened my eyes. And yes, sitting right next to my face was my ghostly cat. His green eyes glowed eerily in the darkness.

"So," I said, tired, looking at him, "what's going on?"

"I'm s-s-satiated," the feline purred.

"Congratulations. How'd you like all that stuff about the union?"

The kitten's mug became so distorted so that I was alarmed. It was like the mask of a cute little kitten had slipped off for a second, revealing something extremely dangerous and very ancient.

"I don't know, R-r-rory. I do not like the Tree. It is alien. But the King was blazing with feelings."

"He said he wouldn't let me go."

"R-r-r-ory, t-r-r-us-s-st me."

"Everybody tells me to trust them," I said, complaining, "but no one will tell me what's going on!"

Suddenly Zephyr looked at something behind us and vanished in a stream of smoke. Then, the door to the bedroom opened and Doran walked in. He was stripped to the waist, with the amulet gleaming on his chest.

"Why are you here?" he asked coldly.

"Because I felt like being by myself. Might I be left alone?"

"I don't want you to be by yourself. Your place is next to me."

"And was I ever asked if I wanted to be next to you? On a pillow? On a leash?"

I turned away from him. I had no desire to talk anymore. I heard the sheets rustle and the bed creaked just a bit as a warm male form climbed in next to me. I felt my throat constrict from resentment. Was this how it was? I couldn't even be left alone to simply ruminate?

The King lay close to me, also silent. He, too, seemed to want some "quiet time."

And then, before I knew it, I drifted off.

CHAPTER TWELVE

I JOLTED AWAKE, and when I sat up, I realized that Doran had already risen. He stood in front of a group of Shadows, his back to me. Something like pale gray tentacles streamed from his hands. It encircled him and the Shadows.

My scientific brain was dumbfounded at witnessing yet another manifestation of pure, unadulterated magic. The physical laws I was used to applying to everything in my life were worthless when it came to stuff like this.

Pale morning light streamed through the narrow windows, making Doran look a little bit like a silver statue. A beautiful statue with tightly-etched muscles. I froze like a statue myself, even catching my breath.

What was going on? Despite the icy core of resentment inside me, I wasn't going to start a cold war. My fate would be resolved. It was just a matter of time.

I sat there, clasping my knees, and followed what was transpiring between Doran and the Shadows. They didn't move at all except for their waving "tentacles," reminding me of an octopus. Were they talking to each other? What were they were doing?

But then, it was like a breeze swept through the room. Doran stirred, and the Shadows vanished.

"Rory," he turned toward me with a sliver of a smile. "Good morning."

"To you, as well," I nodded. "What was that you were doing?"

"I was surveying events at the palace," the King responded. "What took place last night, and what's going on right now. What are your plans at the lab today?"

"I'll check out the test results, and also load my blood into the analyzer for testing. Why, what's up?"

Doran gave a crooked smile — it was odd.

"Well, then you're in for a shock. Just like I was."

"What are you talking about?!"

"Perhaps you'd like to eat first?"

But I was already looking around for my

clothes. Ah, there they were, hanging over the chair.

"First I want to know what you're talking about. And since you won't tell me, well..."

"Words fail me," Doran said, looking at me as I dressed. Meanwhile, I saw in his gaze the now-familiar lustful impatience that made me stir inside, that made me want to walk up to him and snuggle in his arms, feel his fingers touching me. Gentle, then a little rough.

I shook my head, and almost angrily pulled my vest off of a clothes tree that really did look like a tree. I cursed my hormones.

Hormones...

Oh, those hormones...

Oh, and that stuff about forgotten magic. Which doesn't let you get any sleep.

"Rory, you haven't even combed your hair."

"Well, you're still naked," I retorted, hastily winding my hair into a bun. "And who cares?"

Doran looked down at himself, then scooped what looked like a bundle of darkness out of the air, and brought it close to his chest. He was instantly attired in black pants and a loose dark purple shirt.

"Well then, if you're ready, let's be off."

I was ready alright. Unwashed, uncombed, in rumpled clothing, but ready to go. What was going on at the lab? Doran looked suspiciously calm, as if he'd already been there and had come to some conclusions about whatever it was.

I was glad that there weren't many faeries about yet. No one had to witness the sight of the unkempt mortal hurrying over to the Arch. Doran, meanwhile, neither hustled to keep up with me, nor did he lag behind.

Ah, yes, the familiar Arch. I was the first to jump through it to the other side, and rush to the laboratory. Since Doran didn't try to hold me back, I knew it was safe.

The doors were ajar, I flew inside and ... froze.

"My god," I whispered, as I viewed the scene before me.

The two genetic analyzers were now misshapen, with lots of missing parts. These were strewn on the floor throughout the laboratory. And my microscopes were also on the floor, or what was left of them.

"Wha...what..." I gasped, unable to speak. Behind me stood Doran, also silent. He was either keeping his rage pent up inside, or he'd already expended it somewhere and now he was pondering how to get his hands on whoever it was who'd caused such destruction.

"Haedyn!" I found my voice and immediately exercised my vocal cords.

The healer shot out of his cubbyhole. He looked weary, as if all the years of his long life were suddenly imprinted on his former eternally-youthful faery face.

"Ah," he said, dejectedly, "So you see what's happened, Rory."

Then I spun around toward Doran so quickly that I felt dizzy.

"Who did this?"

"I don't know."

"But you said that the Shadows were your eyes!"

"That's true. But somebody used an amulet to take possession of the Shadows."

I silently stared at him, my look demanding an explanation. The King sighed,

"The Shadows can be fooled Such an amulet is difficult to make, and it can only be done outside of the range of Chaos. Do you understand what this means?"

"Somebody brought it in during the Games?"

Doran nodded and added, "The main attribute of this amulet is that it cannot be detected. Extremely powerful magicians had to create it, using incredibly rare materials. Which leads to an intriguing question: Who is it who knew about your research, Rory, and who would be bothered by it? Of course, anybody might be upset by it, but whoever did this opted to act covertly instead of openly voicing an objection to me."

"Unseelies, maybe?" asked Haedyn.

"No," Doran shook his head. "In fact,

they'd strike openly."

"Chaos himself?" I asked. "He's capable."

"Chaos has no time for such trifles. How interested are you in ants building an anthill? Not much, unless they're like your cows that provide you with milk and beef.

"But someone did this..."

"Rory," Haedyn interrupted me, "Understand that Chaos can do whatever Chaos wants, threaten the Court of Shadows itself. More likely he simply pursues what's in his own interest."

Like everything else, this was complicated.

"I thought you were in control here," I said to Doran. He frowned and replied that yes, everything was under control, but not everything could be foreseen.

"In any event," he continued, "Haedyn said that no damage was done to the test results."

"That's right," nodded the healer, "All that was damaged was our ability to process new samples in the analyzers, along with the main components.

"So we can ask the Hogmani for help."

"We'll do that," the King nodded, "but it will take them days to restore them. Magic was used to contaminate these parts, and so they must be thoroughly cleansed. Okay, Haedyn. Can we see the results, then?"

"Yes. Rory, come here."

Haedyn rummaged around in the base of

the analyzers and pulled out a sphere that was overflowing with that golden-green energy. I walked over to him a little leery, as it reminded me of sci-fi movies I'd seen where people were accidentally exposed to alien poisons, or worse.

"It's safe," said Haedyn, clearly understanding why I was hesitant. "I'll extract the results, and you can interpret them."

A few minutes later a hologram with numbers and graphs was suspended in the air. It was a detailed genetic analysis, in addition to hormonal tests. If only I'd had something like this back at the Institute!

Just the same, I had to say "You're too calm about this, Doran."

"I don't see what good ranting and raving would do," he responded. "We need to find out who did this. That's all there is to it. It's someone from the inside, our inner circle, as there are few who know what we're up to here and what your role in all this is. And the amulet was hard to hide."

"Why is that?" asked Haedyn.

Doran smiled grimly, like a predator who was thinking about the best way to strike. Someone would pay.

"Because I once caught a bastard with such an amulet. Do you remember? A hundred years ago."

"I remember that you took the amulet and didn't let anyone into your chambers for three days."

"I studied how it was constructed, and took it apart," Doran nodded. "It's an extremely powerful amulet. But it does have a weakness. After it's been activated, a couple of days later, the energy starts to flow back to the source. The creators have foreseen this and disguised this process."

"And?" I asked.

"But they don't possess the magic of Chaos," said Doran cheerfully, "while I do. And so do the Shadows. So, after analyzing the amulet, I understood the essence of how it was disguised, and gave it to the Shadows. Now they will feel it. And lead us to whoever launched this attack."

Haedyn and I stared at the King in silence. I was rather overwhelmed by all this magic, while Haedyn was obviously mentally applauding the King. Doran basked in our silent response, and said, "Rory, what about our genes?"

"Well, personally, I have no complaints about them," I recovered my bearings, "but let's see now. I also ran tests on your hormones. So we'll see what's there and what's missing."

"I have to leave for a while," Haedyn said. "I have to do some healing. My King, with your permission."

"Can Rory get by without you?"

"Rory will be just fine," I responded, "But

this is going to take awhile. There's a lot to get through here. After all, you need some real findings here, right? King, I need a few hours to read the results and draw conclusions and so forth."

"Get to it, then," Doran nodded. "The Shadows will be here, so you'll be safe. I've ordered them to protect you."

"Can I see them?" I asked. Of course, I already did see them, sliding along the walls like semi-transparent beetles.

"No, but they'll be here."

"Alright then," I nodded in acquiescence. "I guess I don't need to see them."

"Rory ..."

The King's voice changed, and he took a step toward me, making my foolish heart quiver. Why was my heart so fickle? Despite how offended I still was, I could not squelch the feelings that were growing inside me.

"Everything will be fine," he said, with such certainty that I immediately believed him. I leaned forward, lips parted, as he gave me a kiss. A head-spinning, crushing kiss that made me melt.

"Yes," I whispered when the King pulled back a little. "Everything will be fine. And you'll let me go once I've completed my part of the deal. Otherwise...they won't be fine at all."

"Very funny, Rory."

Well, I warned him, anyway. I gently

caressed the King's cheek, turned to the results suspended in the air, and lost myself in my work.

After a few hours, I was glad that I'd insisted on acquiring a few essential books. I was also glad that I'd trained my nerves here in Ruadh. I almost had them under control.

I'd never encountered anything like this before. But to be fair, I've never studied beings like this before.

Shock, interest, amazement, and scientific ecstasy – this and more was what I experienced while analyzing the results. At one point I frowned and pondered something, even poring over one of my books to investigate. And then I nodded, satisfied.

I was putting everything together, but one piece of the puzzle was missing. And try as I might, I could find it.

"Rory ..."

I jumped, and almost fell off my chair.

"Sorry." Haedyn walked in, and then he whistled in amazement. "Wait, have you been sitting there all this time?"

"Yes," I nodded and, groaning, I rubbed my neck. "But I shouldn't have."

"That's right!" Haedyn said, frowning. "You haven't even eaten!"

"I drank something. Ah, water."

"Are all mortal scientists like this?"

"No," I replied modestly, "only geniuses. At

your service."

The healer snorted and looked at the Shadows.

"Get Aurora some lunch. This is integral to her safety."

Two Shadows dissolved in the air. I respectfully raised an eyebrow: If it's a need, then they obeyed. But based on what Doran had said, I knew that the Shadows didn't heed just anybody.

The fact was, though, that I really did need to eat something. And the Shadows brought me some kind of tender meat with rolls, and a salad of unfamiliar, but very tasty veggies. For dessert there were small pastries with a syrupy sauce.

"While you eat, I'll tell you something," Haedyn said, sitting down next to me. He pushed aside a couple of my books and continued, looking at the research results glowing in the air.

"On the border of Ruadh is a faery named Komina. She is very old, ancient even. In Earth years, she was born at the turn of the eleventh century. She is a loner and possesses tremendous healing and visionary powers. But she's nasty in terms of her temperament, and so none of the Courts will have her."

"Why did she choose to settle down near Ruadh?"

"Because she's curious," Haedyn shrugged. "She does not interact with the Court of Shadows, but sometimes Doran goes to see her. I don't know what they talk about. I just know that sometimes when the King comes back, he's very irritated and refers to her only as 'that old fool.'"

I asked, while chewing, "So what are you getting at here?"

"I think Komina can tell us who you are."

"I'm a human!"

"Are you sure?" Haedyn asked, lowering his voice all of a sudden. And I was about to shout that yes, I was sure. I opened my mouth and...closed it. I picked at my salad and thought about it.

No, I was definitely a human. I thought like one, and I felt like one. And faery morals and psyches were alien and repulsive to me.

But I understood them. It's not that I accepted them, but I could easily understand them.

Like pulling rabbits out of a hat, I plucked up one thought after another.

I never got sick. Almost never.

I'd easily adapted to Ruadh.

I could see things I wasn't supposed to see.

And there was that cat with green eyes that communicated with me.

I started to feel a little woozy.

For the most part, I was impervious to the attractions of the faeries, although, yes, their

Enchantments could affect me some.

"Maybe I'm Doran's granddaughter?" I suggested thoughtfully, enjoying the expression on Haedyn's face. I wasn't being serious, of course. But my brain was masking uncomfortable realizations with humor.

"Are you done eating?" Haedyn decided to ignore my speculations about an ancestral relationship with Doran.

"I'm not hungry anymore," I muttered, pushing aside the leftover food.

"Then tell me about your findings."

Yes, let's move on from this. Especially because I myself didn't want to focus on my potential origins anymore.

Because I was what I was — human. A *human being*, got it?!

"Haedyn, before I tell you, can you summon Aerona? I wanted to ask her a couple of questions."

The healer nodded and turned back to the Shadows. Twenty minutes later, Aerona was there, as always beautiful and extremely seductive in an iridescent dress with lilac sparks.

"What's happened," she asked capriciously. "Rory, did you come up with a cure? I'm first in line for it!"

"When I do find a cure," I sighed, "then we'll have to check for side effects and ..."

"So let's create a homunculus and test it,"

Haedyn broke in. "Moreover, Rory, you can easily test for side effects on any of us. We faeries are difficult to really hurt."

Wow. Willing test subjects. Impressive.

"Aerona, I have some rather odd questions for you. Tell me, when faeries give birth, are they in pain?"

"Well," the sultry temptress thought, "while we still lived on Earth, one of my maids-in-waiting gave birth to a child. She said it didn't hurt. But then, as I recall, once we relocated to this world, that changed. The birthing process became longer, and more and more often we had to resort to surgery to get the child out, and it was very painful. Very, very painful."

"Yes," Haedyn confirmed, "Think of what you call cesarean sections."

"One more question. Aerona, were you and your husband united by the Tree on Earth?"

"Yes."

"What were your feelings for him then?"

The King's sister's eyes clouded over. As if she was trying to remember something forgotten and could not.

"I don't remember," she finally whispered. "I want to remember, but I can't. It's like it was a dream. But....why do you ask me this?"

"Doran said that for you, love is a weakness."

"Yes," Haedyn nodded. "We are incapable of love. And there is no need for it. Respect, trust, attraction. But to love is to expose yourself. We arrived here in bleak times, Rory. And love often turned out to be a cruel joke, and dangerous."

I nodded, drawing conclusions for myself. And again I asked Aerona, who stood immobile in the middle of the laboratory:

"Why do you want a baby??

The princess was even taken aback for a few moments.

"Well ... it's a baby. Children for us ..."

"They're happiness," I finished her sentence for her. "I get it. I've studied your history. You faeries have a very reverent attitude towards children. Sincere and deep love, not just responsibility."

I sighed and went on, choosing my words as carefully as possible. My theory ... I was not completely sure I was on the right track. But it seemed logical enough.

"I've run a careful, thorough analysis. Understand that I might not be right because this is the first time I've conducted research on anyone other than humans."

"I believe in you," a deep voice came from the lab door. Doran showed up just at the right time, or maybe Haedyn had summoned him. In any case, the King calmly approached the table, sat down on the edge and looked at me expectantly.

"Go on," he said quietly. I swallowed and

tried not to look at him, because the King's gaze seemed to burn through me.

"At first, I erred when I assumed your genes were deformed. It's more like they...um, evolved with a mutation. You have magic, we don't. Most likely, its presence can be explained by the structure of your genes. But! I found a gene that we don't have."

Ugh, my palms were sweating. I was never so nervous, even during my board exams. Not even when I was carrying out my first major studies.

A new gene... yes, many scientists would give an arm to make such a discovery. But this was one great finding I would never get to share with the world. Because there were no such things as faeries on Earth anymore. They're the stuff of myths and legends.

"So, this gene produces a hormone I've never encountered. And here's where the story takes an interesting turn. A hormonal analysis has shown me that there are minor differences from humans in your genetic makeup. But! You don't produce oxytocin. You have it, but this unknown hormone suppresses it, almost totally.

"I know what hormones are," Doran said, "but what does this oxytocin do? If it's suppressed, then this must be because it should be suppressed."

"Perhaps," I nodded. "Oxytocin is called the hormone of tenderness and joy, the 'love drug,' the 'cuddle hormone.' At the physiological level, oxytocin triggers an attachment mechanism: It helps a mother or father develop an attachment to his or her child, binds a woman to her sexual partner, and generates in a man a romantic mood and the willingness to be faithful. By and large, oxytocin is also the hormone of fidelity.

"So, oxytocin also helps the uterus to contract, initiates labor. Haedyn, I've delved into your books. I've read that, in fact, it used to be much easier for faeries to give birth than for humans. Also, I read that faeries were overwhelmed with waves of happiness and boundless love for their babies, and this occurred during the birthing process."

As I spoke, my hypothesis sharpened in my mind. "So, based on all this, I can assume that you once had oxytocin. And then you stopped producing it. Why? It's a mystery. So then, our main goal here is to see to it that oxytocin is no longer suppressed."

Silence fell upon the lab as soon as I quit speaking. And in that silence, Aerona looked a little puzzled, and Haedyn was clearly thinking about what I was saying and nodding his head, then the King was looking increasingly stormy.

Soon I expected to see flashes of lightning.

What was it that I'd said? Or did he really expect a different explanation? Whatever, I didn't like it. Right away I recalled that I'd be reduced to serving as a hound for the Wild Hunt if I were to fail.

"Find a cure," the King said grimly.

Gee, that's helpful. I guess I'd never have thought of that myself.

"The main problem is that even if I were to give you massive doses of oxytocin, right away the new hormone would suppress it. I don't know, it ... it looks like some kind of defense mechanism. But from what? And why was it here that it kicked into action?"

"So the plan is to somehow disable whatever produces that hormone," said Haedyn.

"What are you saying, really?" asked Aerona. "Does this mean, then, that we'll be able to bear children?"

"Yes," I said, "All we have to do is find out how to activate what you need to have them. Not long ago there was one incident. It was when a faery was impregnated by a man."

"Poor thing," Aerona sighed. "It's good that her husband was punished. Think about it, a half-breed, they'd have gotten over it, raised him."

"Yes," I said slowly, looking in front of me, "a half-breed... Haedyn, can half-breeds give birth?"

"They used to. But not anymore."

"So the gene is dominant," I grumbled. "You know what, let's be honest here."

"Honesty is good," Doran said. I glanced at

him and slowly said:

"I've determined the cause, but it won't be easy to find the cure."

"Rory," said Haedyn, "you've accomplished a great deal already."

"But not enough," Doran's cold voice instantly brought down the temperature, so to speak. "You can do this, right?"

"As long as you don't threaten me!" I snapped. The King was silent, but his silence spoke volumes, and I had to bite my tongue to force myself to speak civilly. "I'll seek out a solution. But! I can't say how long it will take. And I will need more literature. Oh, and tonight I'll be sleeping here."

"Why?" Doran asked, raising an eyebrow a notch.

"Because when I'm hot on the research trail, I find it's easier for me to think. Tomorrow I'll catch up on sleep. And, Haedyn, for the experiments, we'll need some of your, er, homunculi. Are you sure they'll be usable?"

"Short-lived clones of faeries with no mind."

"Rory will test everything on me," Aerona suddenly said, frowning and looking at everyone in turn. At first, I wasn't sure what she was talking about. Then I got it, and speaking gently, I said to her as she stood there with fists clenched,

"Aerona, hormones are serious business. If

something goes wrong, it's no joke."

But the princess didn't even hesitate. "I'm not a fool, mortal. I know what the risks are. But this will help you find a cure as soon as possible. Homunculi may not be good enough. Haedyn lies. They aren't so pristine. But a purebred faery of the highest ranks is."

"I'm not lying!" the healer was incensed. "Rory, the homunculi would work just great in your experiments."

"I want to be part of the search for a cure!" Aerona was adamant. "And even you, brother, cannot forbid me from doing this! Do you know why? You do!"

I turned a dazed look on Doran. He nodded and said, "Aerona's desire for a child has reached a crescendo. Give her a chance to show her worth."

"Or I'll cross the border into Chaos," whispered the princess. She suddenly slumped over, like she was wilting.

"Rory, you don't know what it's like to live knowing that you're never going to see that little baby girl of yours, or that little boy. They come to you in your dreams. You're ready to bed whoever could, in theory, help you. Let me help you help me."

"Alright," I murmured, at the same time telling myself that I wasn't about to use any untested treatments on Aerona. I didn't want her mania to come back to bite me down the road.

And there was something really bothering me.

Aerona left, and Haedyn soon followed suit, flashing a glum look at me as he exited. Doran was the last out the door, after giving me a greedy kiss in parting and briefly pressing his forehead to mine. What was I to make of him? His cold demeanor earlier, and now this sudden rush of tenderness. Lately he'd been acting a little strange, I thought.

A little...

I passed the night in something of a frenzy. I went over the results again and again until I felt like my eyes were bleeding. I pored over all the books at my disposal. I talked to myself under my breath, and asked and answered my own questions. I sat down right on the stone floor surrounded by papers, and then got up and paced back and forth.

Finally, I realized that for the time being I was at a dead end because there was one thing I didn't understand yet: What the hell was the deal with the oxytocin? What was suppressing it? And most of all — why? If it used to be a normal hormone that was naturally produced, why then was it suddenly blocked?

I froze in the middle of the laboratory and clutched my head. I clutched it so hard that it hurt a little.

I'd somehow erred. Or else I'd missed

something — who knows what?

And what bothered me most of all was the Tree.

Finally, early in the morning, I couldn't take anymore. I shut down, curled up on the floor with the softest book under my head, and crashed.

Surprisingly, I got pretty good sleep. And I was even dreaming something or the other, when I felt someone gently shaking my shoulder.

"I thought you would fall asleep here." A fresh, alert Haedyn leaned over me and added, "I have some good news. While you were sleeping the Hogmani came and got the analyzers and promised they'd restore them within a couple of days."

I sat up and rubbed my aching temples. My head was rejecting my attempts to think, and my psyche was insisting on another five or so hours of shuteye.

"Where's Doran?" my voice was sleepy and slurred. I imagined what I must look like right now. I probably had the book imprinted on my cheek.

"He's dealing with things," Haedyn smiled. "The Queen of the Seelies has sent an official ambassador demanding the return of Jioladh. They say that if he is not handed over, she will be offended and will show all the wrath of a woman who has been wronged."

"That's quite the threat," I muttered. "Okay

then, I'll just take a nap and then get back to work."

"Doran has granted my request to take you to Komina. It's also an opportunity to get you out of the palace for a bit. It seems that the King is suspicious about the Seelies and their motives for being here."

"Oh ..." I still couldn't put my sleepy thoughts together. "Right now?"

"Well, you can wash and put yourself together, and I brought you some breakfast."

CHAPTER THIRTEEN

I ATE BREAKFAST in a kind of fog. Honestly, I
felt rather shaky. I still didn't think I had any
faery in me, but my brain was still processing
all that I'd encountered here in Ruadh. So my
hands shook a little, and I had that feeling you
get sitting in the waiting room at the dentist's. I
even felt my stomach churning a bit.

Haedyn also maintained a silence after
saying, "The Shadows will accompany us, but
you, of course, won't be able to see them."

"I don't see them even now," I said,
speaking the truth. No Shadows were about.

"There aren't any around right now. I'm
here with you, you see."

"So Doran has that much faith in you?"

"Here inside the laboratory he does, yes. You're done eating? Let's be off then."

Unconsciously dragging my feet a bit, I paused to drink the last drops of my juice. And I asked, "Have you ever been to see this Komina before?"

"Once. We managed to connect since we are both healers. It's been some time now since she's used her gift, though. She says she's tired, so let others do the work. But I do know that there are those who go to her. More often than not for her predictions."

I shuddered: I wouldn't opt to know what lay before me. What if they were to say "You're going to roll your car on Friday — that's it, your life is finished." That's all you'd think about until it happened.

As we were leaving, Haedyn looked at me and shook his head, "You should sleep more, Rory. You have circles under your eyes, and you're really pale."

"I'll get over it. I'll sleep eight hours and be just fine."

After exiting the palace, we went through the Misty Arch and proceeded past the Arena. As soon as we were in the city, I eagerly look around.

The buildings were pretty far from each other here. The Arena was in the midst of a perfect circle paved in a smoky black stone. I felt like the pavement was a little sticky, so that you couldn't slip on it. Above us stretched the now-familiar pale gray sky in which floated the sun, like a dull silver coin.

"Rory, our ride."

While I was checking out the scenery, Haedyn had procured a huge horse from somewhere. It was jet black, but with a silver mane and tail. The white eyes of the beast were slightly luminous, creating an eerie impression, to put it mildly.

"Where did you get such a beauty?"

"There's a stable near the Arena. This is my killi. His name is Eriox."

"It's not a horse?"

Haedyn easily grabbed me under my arms and swung me up to sit on the killi. The killi roared like a lion and loudly snorted.

"The killies have lived here since before our arrival. Since then, we've tamed them. But they'll only accept one master. And they'll be devoted to whomever that is. The only reason he'll allow you to sit atop him is because I am near. If I wasn't, he'd throw you off in no time and eat you."

"Interesting. I guess these killies aren't grass-eaters."

Haedyn grunted in affirmation and then easily hopped onto Eriox, behind me. Suddenly, I saw Zephyr not far away. He was moving across the black stones and then disappeared, as if he'd been sucked into them.

Pale lanterns shaped like stone pillars were situated here and there, while all the edifices were faintly glimmering. Squinting, I looked at the statue at the entrance to the Arena. Now, it had three arms. Before, it didn't. Really, though, what did it matter?

"Ready?"

"Yes."

"We'll take our time so that you're not blown away. But just the same, hold on tight and keep close to me."

Haedyn took the reins while I clung to a knob-like thing protruding from the strange saddle obediently sunk back against the healer's chest.

So this was what they called taking our time? The killi dashed along so fast that it took my breath away. Everything was a blur, and my heart was pounding in sheer terror. No way could I hang on! I was going to fly off the saddle and end up smeared across the pavement!

I felt a little bit like this when I was 16 and my friends and I took a ride on a roller coaster. A big, big roller coaster. Just like now, I clung to the handlebar and I also screamed incessantly. This time, though, I couldn't even squeak, the wind hammered any vocalizations back down my throat.

I have no idea how far we thundered along. I was focused solely on keeping my cold, sweaty palms from slipping off the saddle horn. And hoping that the killi wouldn't suddenly stumble.

But then Eriox began to gradually slow down. I could even lift my head after awhile. Slower and slower....and now he stopped. I groaned and went totally limp, almost falling away from Haedyn.

"Are you okay?"

"I'm never going to be a street racer."

"A what? Forget it. Collect yourself now and let's go."

For some reason, I'd pictured Komina as a hermit living in a hollow or something, far from inquisitive eyes. And there'd be a forest surrounding her abode with bare, twisted trees, and a prevailing gloom.

In fact, Komina lived at the base of a huge, dark, craggy cliff. One look at it and my head began to spin.

The crags were rusty red with black and greenish streaks, and they seemed to pierce the dense, pale gray sky. It was only when we drew near that I noticed the dwelling made of stone boulders. And it was only after I smelled the smoke that I saw it streaming from a short, thick chimney. The windows were small, with dark glass panes, and around the dwelling stretched a rocky valley.

"It that the border with Chaos?"

"That's the border between Ruadh and the Wild Lands. The King is exploring them over time, but it's slow-going. And from the Wild

Lands you can make it to the Seelie and Unseelie Courts. Shall we go in?"

I looked at the house. If not for the smoke from the chimney, one would think it was abandoned. There was no landscaping whatsoever, nor any other domestic touches, like figurines, not to mention a gate or fence.

"Um, I..." I had to cough. "Haedyn, did she, well, agree to this?"

"Komina is a very curious being. She also is endowed with pride and a strong ego. To her, I've always been an upstart. And this is a great opportunity for her to reinforce what a great healer she is."

"And that's enough for you?"

"Rory," grinned Haedyn, jumping off the killi and assisting me down, "I know how things stand, as do you, and as does Doran. Let the old hag do something for Ruadh and make us happy."

"So she won't harm me?"

"No, all the more so because I'll be right there."

That wasn't exactly the thing to say to calm my fears. Clearly Haedyn couldn't deny that Komina might have some unknown motives.

The healer politely knocked on the low door and shouted, "Komina, it is I, Haedyn, the right hand of the King of Shadows. I've come to you on business."

I narrowed my eyes and saw what looked like a very faint ripple emanate from the door. Then a sonorous female voice said, "Enter."

I felt my head and fingertips prickle as I ducked and stepped over the threshold.

The interior of the house was much more spacious and lighter than I had expected. We walked right into a large room, and I saw a spiral staircase leading to a second floor. The room was obviously not only a parlor of sorts, but also a kitchen, judging by the table with vegetables spread over it at the far end. There was also a huge fireplace, where flames peacefully crackled, and dusty green skins on the floor and stone walls. I had no idea what kind of animal they'd belonged to. The furniture was dark, with three wide tables piled with books, crystals, some kind of test tubes and — here I frowned — with the opened carcasses of strange animals.

"Why did you bring a mortal here? Although ... it's a treat. It's been a long time since I've had a look at their anatomy."

"No autopsies today, please," I blurted out, trying to make out the owner of the house.

Meanwhile, Haedyn sighed and said in an upbeat voice, "Komina, why do you want to scare the girl? One would think you don't know who she is."

"It's amusing to scare the mortals. And I enjoy the sweet smell of their adrenaline when they're frightened. Are you aware that it surpasses the aroma of lust in its headiness?"

Komina descended from the second floor. And I saw for myself what it means to be ancient in "faeryland."

Yes, she looked like a woman in her prime with flowing, snow-white hair, but in her light gray eyes, what I was there was wisdom and...profound age. But not a serene kind of agedness, rather, she exuded energy and strength. At first, I didn't discern any flaws in the stately, slim figure dressed in a dark silver gown. And then I saw it.

She was normal except for the huge eye in the middle of her high forehead that burned with a lilac light. The eye had a cat-like pupil which was in constant motion.

"So why did you bring Doran's skank here to see me?"

Gee thanks. Now I know where I stand here. I bit my tongue to hold back my knee-jerk response. But apparently my feelings showed in my eyes. Because Komina walked up to me, grabbed my chin rather roughly and looked into my eyes.

"Just look," she laughed heartily. "She doesn't like being called a skank!"

"Komina, Doran values this girl."

"She's a talented fuck then?"

Haedyn again silently ordered me to bite my tongue. I tried my best.

"It's not that."

Komina released her grip and went to examine the carcass of what looked like a massive rat on one of the tables. She idly played around with some of the intestines, and asked, "So what is it, then?"

She was clearly trying to get under my skin. Did she really think that her little show would make me swoon or something? She could think again! I straightened up and stared with obvious interest at what the ancient healer was doing. She continued to examine the entrails of the animal, continually glancing at me.

Haedyn didn't feel like beating around the bush, and came right out with it: "The Tree united Doran with this girl."

Dropping the entrails on the table with a splat, Komina spun around towards us. "That's impossible!"

"Alas..."

"This cannot be so," Komina was adamant, "Only faeries can be united by the Tree. It will not shine upon half-breeds or mortals. You evidently misinterpreted what was happening."

"It blossomed and entwined the flowering vine around their wrists."

Komina looked at me in silence. Her eerie, piercing look gave me the creeps. It was like I was physically sensing the woman's thought processes.

"And next there'll be chil-l-l-dren...," she

dragged out the word in a strange exaggerated fashion. And the pupil in her third eye was flickering like crazy.

"Maybe you can figure out what's going on," I said politely, "Because what I want is to somehow get back home."

The healer blinked. "You're planning on going back to your home?" she asked, as if surprised and amused.

"Yes, I am. That's where I belong."

"I'm just telling you, it's strange," Haedyn coughed.

Komina raised her hand up to silence him. "Girl, you do understand that then you will no longer see the King, nor will you feel his caresses, his presence?"

I felt my heart pounding, it was almost painful, but I simply shrugged and said, "We've developed a good thing, yes, but I'm drawn to my homeland."

Komina's sparse eyebrows quivered a bit. "How ve-r-ry char-r-rming," she practically sang, moving towards me. I glanced at her hands, bloodied by the entrails, and took a step back.

"Stay right there!" the old healer suddenly barked. "Haedyn, what made you think she was a human?"

"Because that is what all the scans of her have revealed."

"Idiot! No mortal can resist a faery's charms. Especially those of one of the highest faeries!"

"That's why I brought her here. At the behest of the King. You are wise, Komina. Your knowledge far surpasses my own. I am sure that you will bring to light the secret of this girl. Her origin."

Perfect. Komina was no stranger to vanity. She smirked, smug now, and nodded, keeping her piercing gaze fixed on me. It really made my skin crawl.

"Yes, this I can do. But what shall be my reward, then?"

"I assume you and Doran will work something out."

"Oh yes-s-s," Komina drawled in anticipation. "There will indeed be grounds for a generous 'thank you.' Doran is one of the most honest rulers of all I've encountered. And I've met quite a number of them. So let's see what we can make of you, Dearie!"

Komina moved in closer — I could smell tar and dusty leaves exuding from her. She raised a bloodied palm in front of my face and smiled in anticipation, revealing her snow-white teeth. Surprisingly normal teeth, in fact. "I sense that we're in store for something quite interesting."

That's right. I felt it, too. And deep in my solar plexus, I felt a strange tension. It wasn't painful; rather, it was like something inside me was about to burst. Probably I should've skipped breakfast. All I needed was gastritis right now.

Unlike Haedyn, Komina didn't pass her hands alongside my body, rather, she reached right out and touched me. I immediately felt a fierce heat from her palms penetrating me. The healer's eyes glowed with a barely detectable radiance, just like her skin. And her hands felt ever warmer. They were really radiant now, on the verge of too hot. But I bit my lip and stayed stock still.

"That's funny..." Komina muttered, "How funn...hmmmm....what's this now? Uh-huh, uh-huh...."

When someone scanning you says stuff like that, it's rather excruciating. I didn't know what to think. Haedyn stood at Komina's back, trying to signal to me that things would be okay. He even made faces that were meant, it seems, to buck me up.

"I don't understand ..." the ancient healer again muttered. "Oh, this is..."

Just then I saw how, suddenly, the pupils in all three of her eyes widened. And then the healer jerked aside with a strange hiss. At the same time she raised her hands with her fingers curved toward me.

"Filth!"

My seventh sense kicked in then, and it told me that I was about to be killed. I managed to glimpse how something translucent was building up around Komina's wrists, and I threw up my arms in the vain hope of defending myself.

Suddenly there was a blast all around me, and I was momentarily blinded. My body felt such an overwhelming heat that I had to cry out. I felt that anymore and I would burn to ashes. The fiery heat burst from inside me, along with tears and screams. Again I waved my hands, and through a veil of tears I saw Komina raise her hands to shield herself. And with difficulty, she deflected an invisible blow. Whose? Was it really mine?!

"Ha!" her harsh laughter sounded in the room as I writhed in the corner of the room in utter agony — my entire body was in pain. "Did you think you could stop me with that blast?"

Her laughter turned into a scream, and then into a rattle, and a narrow, long dagger emerged from the general location of her heart. She froze momentarily, then collapsed onto the floor, but even then she didn't die. Coughing blood, she tried to turn over.

I gasped, my breath hot, and watched as Haedyn walked up to the ancient healer and extracted the dagger from her back. And then he started severing her neck and kept at it until Komina's head was no longer attached to her body.

Not even a faery can survive without a head. That's not to say that you couldn't reattach it if you were fast enough. But it was clear that Haedyn wasn't about to do that. He tossed the head, which was still alive, to the side, and rushed toward me. But he was careful not to touch me, and stopped at a safe distance.

"Rory..."

All I could do was sob a bit, because my throat was burning, just like the rest of me. I felt like I was burning in an invisible fire that burst out from inside of me, and I felt incredibly weak. I couldn't even raise my hand. It seemed that Haedyn understood how I felt.

"It's okay, Rory, after a power surge this is what happens. For three days you will be very weak. All you can do then is sleep and eat. There's nothing strange going on."

"Nothing strange?!" I was outraged. "What's with the red-hot peppers inside me, then?!"

I coughed and was surprised no flames shot out of my mouth.

"Rory, you are a miracle," Haedyn went on. "I wasn't mistaken. Komina managed to awaken you. True, the old fool decided to play the heroine and kill such a treasure. What an idiot!"

"Who?" the words scratched my throat, "Me?"

"I'll tell you everything when the time comes. Now you are one of us. Frankly, it was only after the incident with the Tree that I began to suspect it."

"Doran ..."

Haedyn shook his head.

"No, Rory, forget about Doran. We'll take you where you'll thrive. Where your true essence will be manifested in all its glory. You are our brilliant creation. Jioladh?"

"In person," I heard Jioladh's voice. Where had he come from? He appeared out of the air and looked at me as if he was a little frightened.

"Haedyn, are you sure we're not in danger here?"

"For three days to a week, she'll be weak as a baby. Her body needs to adjust to her new state."

Body? Who were they talking about? Me, really? I couldn't collect my thoughts. Instead, they flowed from whatever it was that was unfolding inside me. I bent over, wracked with pain and coughed again.

"Haedyn, she's in pain!"

"Of course she is. She has to be. How many years now has her essence been blocked? And now it's bursting out of those confines. How fortunate that we suspected that she was a Sayphora before they killed her."

"I don't understand why they wanted to kill her at all."

"Don't you know anything?" Haedyn asked. "Rory's discovery was to profoundly change our world and return to faeries their fertility. But the King of Shadows was not deemed worthy of such a secret, was he? She had to be killed so that no one else would find out about the secret."

I could hardly keep my eyes open, and my mind clouded over. The voices around me grew fainter and fainter until they were like a buzz and then a gentle hum above me. And that excruciating pain...as if my internal organs were on the verge of melting.

Meanwhile, Haedyn carefully approached me and said, "But Rory, you don't have to worry anymore. No one's going to kill you. Not right away, at least. Please understand why we had to stage assassination attempts a couple of times. We had to. We had to ensure that Doran would insist that you needed to stay in the laboratory for your own safety. And I apologize, but I had to damage the analyzers. We didn't want to reveal any anomalies in your blood."

"But where are you...." I croaked.

"Where are we taking you? Oh, to a wonderful place! Lovely. You'll see for yourself. And once there, as soon as you've adapted to your new state, we'll fill you in on all the details."   "Jioladh, carry her outside while I get Eriox. The main thing is that we must make it to the crossing. It's too bad about Komina, but her fate was of her own making. You see, she was part of the plan back then, as well, but it seems that over the past few years she felt that she had to correct a mistake."

"Haedyn, she's wearing a brand."

"Oh, Chaos!" Haedyn cursed, smacking his forehead with his palm. "I forgot about that! Not a problem. Just saw off her wrist."

Even in my semi-conscious state, I comprehended what they were saying. And I tried to crawl away, although there was nowhere to go. I was up against a wall.

"Why are you hesitating?" asked Haedyn, "She won't die from the shock —I'll stop the bleeding, and it'll grow back over a couple of weeks. Hurry up and do it, or else I'll..."

He broke off then, and his countenance changed. As did Jioladh's. I knew why, too. Nothing like a coal-black Shadow in the form of huge panther with glowing green eyes springing into the room to make one lose their train of thought.

"Zephyr," I murmured, sliding more and more into unconsciousness. Yet my outer awareness was still afraid to cede full control over the situation. And there was much more to come!

On the heels of Zephyr the rest of the Shadows, all red-eyed, began flooding into the room, mouths agape in silent howls. Jioladh looked as white as snow, while Haedyn froze in place. Then he rapidly flicked his hands. He was evidently casting some kind of spell.

"What a pleas-s-sur-r-e!" the hissing voice filled the room. Then the door fell in, nearly bowling Jioladh over. And then in the doorway I saw....I saw...

"God," was all I could say. The spectacle of Doran in the guise of the Leader of the Hunt did me in. And then, thankfully, my consciousness left my body. The last thing I saw was how Haedyn hurled a desperate spell at the King, and the two Shadows in his path simply evaporated.

Chapter Fourteen

UNFORTUNATELY, I wasn't totally oblivious. In my delirium, fragments of what was transpiring seeped into my inflamed consciousness. I'd feel soothing, cool caresses, and I'd try to say something, but all that I could do was moan

I'm trying to regulate her magical currents, King, but they're too strong.

Yes, physically she'll pull through, but I'm not sure about her psyche.

Doran, what's wrong with her?

The prognosis is...

I don't know what she is.

Finally, I simply opened my eyes and realized that I was almost completely fine. My insides were no longer burning up, my skull didn't feel like it was being cleaved in two anymore, and although I felt a little groggy, my thoughts were nevertheless sharp enough.

"Rory!"

I recognized that tinkling voice right away. "Nuala!" I responded in kind. Or, rather, I tried to. Instead, I sounded rather weak and plaintive. The multi-armed faery then appeared, brandishing some kind of translucent bandages.

"Lie back down!" she ordered me in a stern voice. Well, anyway I couldn't talk. I was so weak, I couldn't lift a finger. And I could hardly turn my head.

"I'm alive."

"But of course you are!" Nuala said, surprised. She sat on the edge of the bed. And it was only then that I realized I was in the King's chambers. I saw a grayish noonday outside the narrow windows. But inside, the lamps cast a pleasant, golden light. The soft covers on the bed were also a golden hue. Underneath them, I was totally naked.

"How long," I swallowed as my mouth was dry, "have I lain here?"

"A week. Doran stormed and thundered, rounded up all of the healers. They told him you were fine, but that your body was adapting."

"To what?"

"To your true essence. Oh, let me show you what you've become!"

Well, that worried me. What did she mean? Did I have horns now, or something? Maybe I had a tail, or a couple of more legs?

Nuala momentarily disappeared, and came back with a silver hand mirror, which she thrust in front of me.

"Look!"

Worried, I looked at my image, and then I breathed a sigh of relief. I looked like "me," except that my skin was smoother, and the fine lines were gone. Oh, and there was an intriguing brilliance in my eyes now. But that was it. The same Aurora, with a size B bust and a tiny scar on the bridge of her nose. Wait, I guess the scar was gone.

"And what ... who am I now?"

Nuala set the mirror down and settled near me again. Good going Doran, for leaving her to tend to me. The royal stylist had a soothing, uplifting effect on me.

"Nuala?"

"I don't know what to tell you, Rory. They only told me to watch over you and see when you awaken. And then I was to alert Doran through the Shadows."

"And what about..."

"Haedyn?" Nuala hissed, spitting out his name as if it was a curse word. "The lucky bastard perished before we could interrogate him. It was some sort of magic block that basically consumed his brain. Totally."

"And Jioladh?"

"Well, he survived, at any rate. The hounds really had a go at him, though. As soon as he recovers, he'll be treated to all of the delights of our torture chamber. Our Master Slayer just loves his work."

It was strange, but I suddenly felt sorry for the red-headed charmer. He clearly was loathe to saw my wrist off back there at the old crone's house. But just the same, he was in cahoots with Haedyn.

As for the latter, I really felt no rancor toward him. I was simply utterly bewildered. How did we fail to see what he was about? And most importantly, who had he been working for?"

"Did you find out why he wanted to kidnap me?"

Nuala spread all eight hands out and shook her head. "Maybe we'll get some info out of Jioladh. But right now we're in the dark. What we do know is that they were planning on absconding with all your work, and with you, as well. Where to is still a mystery. Oh, I see that someone wants to talk to you."

Nuala stood up and quickly left, avoiding exchanging glances with Zephyr, who blew in just then. No longer a kitten, he now appeared as a mighty panther, moving smoothly around the room until he was next to the bed. He positioned himself so that he was facing me. His face was completely dark save for the almond-shaped eyes that burned with a bright green light.

"Well?" I asked quietly. "What do you have to say? What are Sayphoras?"

"I have no idea, my child."

I gaped at him. The Shadow had never called me that before. Why now?

"But, that's what Haedyn called me, a Sayphora."

"I know nothing of Sayphoras," Zephyr repeated, "I've never even heard of them. But a part of me is within you now, and I distinctly feel it. They were great magicians — I mean, whoever it was who enchanted you. And now you should be able to understand me."

I was stunned, and simply stared at Zephyr. I had part of a Shadow in me? Surely he was joking, right?

"No, I'm not joking," the smoky panther said. "You have a sliver of Chaos within you, in your genes. I can't fathom how this came to be. But now we know why the Tree responded to you. You are faery. You are Chaos. And you are human. I've never encountered anyone like you. It's great fun. And you will give to Doran the child that was prophesied."

Say what?!

'What's this about a child?" I looked at Zephyr, eking out the words in a weak, yet firm voice. "Well, tell me, and I mean *now*. What's this stuff about a child? And if Chaos is in my genes, then you ... um...".

"I'm his eyes."

And Zephyr slightly bowed his smoky head, which I felt like whopping. Instead, somehow, I extended my hand and touched the Shadow. I felt a pleasant warmth, and quietly asked him,

"So all this time I've been arguing with Chaos, then?"

"I've never had a problem with it. All the more so because I sensed something different about you, and I was curious."

"I can't wrap my mind around it. Who am I now? Where am I from? What the hell is going on here?!"

I buried my face in my hands, trying to grapple with the wave of feelings that threatened to overwhelm me. Then I heard Zephyr speak.

"I think you need to talk with the King."

And right then I sensed that Doran was near. I felt his presence with every cell of my body and soul, or whatever it was I had now. I raised my head and turned toward the door.

Zephyr was such a traitor! He'd already vanished from sight.

And there was Doran, slowly approaching the bed. And his eyes communicated so much, all of which made me all mixed up inside. Were faeries really unable to feel love? I had a hard time believing that right then.

Doran sat carefully on the edge of the bed and leaned over me. His feather-light kiss grew more and more intense with every second. I felt utterly intoxicated in no time.

"You're still weak," the King said, reluctantly pulling away. "We have to stop, before I'm unable to."

Actually, I felt the same way. Despite how feeble I felt, I was yearning to at least feel his arms around me.

"Did Zephyr tell you where I was?"

"Calling the essence of Chaos 'Zephyr,' — now that's bold," Doran said, chuckling. He reached out and stroked my cheek. It was as if he wanted to make sure I was really safe. "Well, I was being a little sly," he went on.

"Meaning?"

"I said in a 'couple of days,' but I didn't say it'd be *exactly* two days. In fact, the amulet would lead us to the source of the spell in a couple of days plus or minus a day."

I coughed and managed to say: "So even though faeries don't lie, they also don't say everything they mean, right?"

"Right. And we noticed the energy rollback when the Seelie ambassador was talking about a pact, about what to do about defectors and so on."

"And so you immediately sprang into action?"

"The future of the faeries was at stake,"

Doran said, shrugging. "And the Seelies probably aged a century or two when right there in the throne room I summoned the Wild Hunt. You were easy to find. First, there was the rollback, then there's the bracelet, and thirdly, Haedyn is one of the Hunters. So the hounds could easily smell his scent."

I recalled how Doran had appeared in Komina's house. He was all Shadows with streaks of green, and he had huge green wings with gaps of swirling Darkness, and his eyes were flashing — red and green. It was a terrifying, yet fascinating spectacle.

"Doran, what are these Sayphoras?"

"I have no idea."

Why wasn't I at all surprised at hearing this? "That's what Haedyn called me. And he also said that Komina tried to kill me because she felt terribly guilty about something. You faeries do have consciences, right?"

The King politely ignored my query. But when he heard about Komina, he frowned: "I cannot fathom why she tried to kill you. It was she who, many years ago, predicted I'd have a child. A child who was destined to change the lives of both humans and faeries. Who would restore to us our former power."

Ah, now I was beginning to piece it all together. Apparently, Komina wasn't able to see who would bear the King's child. And once she found out who was united to the King by the

Tree, for some reason, she was terribly frightened.

When a faery is frightened, people beware! But now what could I do? With Haedyn and Komina out of the picture, who could tell me who or what I was? Wait, Jioladh knows something.

"Doran, what about Jioladh, the traitor?"

"Well, the hounds seriously thrashed him, ripped out his throat, so for the time being he cannot talk. The healers are pouring additional energy into him to restore him, but it will take two or three days before he's back."

The King smiled and ran his hand through my hair, which was no doubt a mess. "We'll find out everything, Rory. Who you are, who thought all this up. And you'll provide me with the mightiest faery, and he'll have inside him a sliver of Chaos."

"I don't want to pop your soap bubble, but what's this child you're waxing poetic about? Don't you want to know my stand on this?"

"Rory, you're my mate. The issue of bearing a child doesn't even merit discussion."

"But it does. I'd have to carry it. And I thought I'd wait a number of years before planning on children. Right now we have a lot to deal with, don't we? First we've got to resolve all these issues and then we can think about having a child."

"I'll be the one handling the issues. Your

business is motherhood."

"You've got to be kidding."

"Who's kidding, Rory? I almost lost you. I'm not about to let that happen again. But you will continue your work, of course. I understand that you cannot do without it."

Wow, how very noble. Shall I kiss your feet to show my gratitude?

"And get this thing off of me. It's high time. It's maddening," I said. And, looking as innocent as possible, I extended my hand toward him. As before, it displayed to the world my status as a slave. Surely now he'd remove it, right?

The King glanced at my wrist and stood up.

"Let's wait until you get your health back."

"Doran!"

"Get well, Rory, I'll be back soon. You've got the Shadows here to ensure your safety."

"I've heard that one before," I said, somewhat snidely. I saw the King's eyes darken, but he immediately pulled himself together and said, "You're not yet ready to adequately perceive what's going on, Rory."

Oh yeah? In fact I totally adequately perceived what was happening, and what I saw was that his attitude toward me had changed, but in a most unexpected direction. Now, I wasn't just a prisoner. I was a prisoner who could bear him a child.

So tell me, then, what's love got to do with

that? I've always believed that when two people love each other, they're willing to meet each other halfway. No way do people in love hit each other over the head with sentiments such as "*You will do as I say and give birth to the Chosen One.*"

My best course of action was to get well ASAP, and then see what I could do about my lifestyle choices. And, most importantly, I'd better not forget to take my pills. I'd already gone off my regimen while lying here unconscious.

There was no point in crying over my situation. I'd come to see that here in 'faeryland', tears were as wasted as love. And anyway, I didn't feel like crying. But I did feel like throwing things around. That seemed like a fine idea. What stopped me was the futility of acting out like that. It'd be wasted on Doran.

Moreover, I was still weak, and I really did need to rest.

And that's just what I did. For the first three days, Nuala was essentially the only one to break my solitude with her rapid-fire conversation. In no time I was up on the latest goings on at the Court. Apparently, I was the talk of the town among the faeries:

Have you ever heard of such a thing? She's royalty, endowed with a sliver of Chaos, and on top of that, she's got some human genes in her.

Oh, and she's the future Queen.

When I heard that, I just about choked on the broth I was sipping and asked Nuala, "The Queen?"

The faery froze in mid-sentence, then rather helplessly asked, "Did I say too much? Nobody told you?"

I realized my fingers were itching to throttle a certain King. "Apparently not."

"Well, he'll tell you soon enough," Nuala shrugged. "Doran's extremely busy right now, you know."

No kidding. His right-hand man turned out to be a traitor. So yes, I knew full well that Doran was shaking up his inner circle. He was being cruel and methodical. On the good side, thus far no more traitors had crawled out of the woodwork. It seemed the Court of Shadows truly valued its King. As for Haedyn, well, it seemed he had a compelling reason to act as he did. Which, for the time being, was unknown. And while Jioladh could shed light on the situation, he wasn't back to normal yet, despite the efforts of two healers.

"How much longer will it be?" I grumbled, crushing the edge of the blanket in my hand. "We haven't heard a thing for three days now."

"The healers have been advising him."

"What about?"

"You need to rest, recuperate. Moreover, the magic within you is still boiling and might burst out all of a sudden."

"In other words, I should keep away from your King so that I don't accidentally incinerate him?"

"Well, that'd be hard to do," Nuala responded, not at all upset. "But you're doing much better now, and so I expect that Doran will come by."

"Yes, I'm much stronger today."

"I'm not talking about that, girl. It's just that tonight you've yet to fly above the bed and you didn't glow in that greenish color. And the Shadows didn't fly in a frenzy around you. You don't feel how you call out to them?"

I said nothing, digesting what I heard. Then, with a nervous laugh, I said, "Well, when I'm dreaming what I see are dancing ponies. And Earth."

"Well, that's the only place you'll see Earth now – in a dream," sighed Nuala. "Surely you understand."

"No, I don't understand! I don't understand, and it's because I've spent my entire life there. What's happening?"

"Ssshh! Quiet!" Nuala nipped my tantrum in the bud. "Let's get you ready for Doran, then, and you two can have a nice chat. Believe me when I say the King doesn't have it easy, either.

Every night he comes by when you're asleep. He's been tracking your changes. He's worried, Rory. But you know ..."

No, I didn't, but I decided to drop it. Lately, I couldn't shake the feeling that this was simply the calm before the storm. Nuala looked at me like I was a freak. And when Aerona had dropped by to see me, she almost fell to her knees when the Shadows slid around the bed now and then. I'd forced myself to smile and always did my best to act normal.

But there was no such thing as 'normal' anymore. Nor would there ever again be. Inside, I was still the same, but my old life was gone forever. Sure, I could do my best to maintain a state of denial, but the fact was that none of the roads before me led me back to Earth. My cozy one-bedroom apartment, my friends, work — all were now relegated to my past. And this filled me with a deep bitterness.

Yes, there was a sliver of hope that I could work something out with Doran. After all, he'd given me his word. Maybe he'd let me go back on a 'vacation'? It wouldn't be a prisoner asking anymore, but the future Queen, right? And as soon as I'm strong enough, the bracelet would be removed. Maybe even this very day.

I meekly allowed Nuala's assistants to help me to the bathroom, where I spent almost an hour. As I washed up, I wondered where Doran was. It wasn't just that I wanted to talk to him, I was also bored to death. Yes, I was drawn to the King despite all the frustrations, the misunderstandings.

He's smart, after all. I realized this long ago. That's why I found it so easy to converse with him. That's why I so often admired how he conducted himself. Nobody's perfect, of course, but Doran's strengths seriously outweighed any weaknesses. It means a lot when someone opts to sacrifice himself for his people.

And as for this business about bearing his child, well, we'll work something out. After all, it would have to be a joint decision.

This was my train of thought as they massaged me with some light oils that exuded a delicate aroma. Then they brushed my hair until it was perfectly straight and shiny. After which I was attired in something sheer and light.

"You don't need any makeup," Nuala said, examining my face. "You're already flawless, my dear. Look at how your eyes are sparkling! Are you missing him?"

I nodded. We had so much we really needed to talk over. And yes, I really did miss him, even though I was still upset. My feelings were so profound that my head was spinning and my heart was beating fast. God, my hands were even shaking, as if I was getting ready for a first date.

Then Nuala and her girls left after ensuring that the setting was just right: I lay in a pile of golden robes on bluish-black bedclothes. The lighting, of course, was intimate. Perfect!

With no Nuala around anymore, the room was dead quiet. A kind of anticipatory quiet, portentous. Even the Shadows were gone, including Zephyr. Actually, I hadn't seen him for days now.

"I wonder if I could conjure something up now?" I muttered, just to break the silence. In fact, I'd heard everybody talking about what I was capable of, but I couldn't even make sparks fly when I snapped my fingers.

"You'll learn over time."

Doran was clearly used to making a splash by showing up at just the right time. In fact, I was snapping my fingers as he entered the room, and he'd arched his eyebrows, seeing what I was up to.

"What will I learn?" was all I could ask as I drank him in with my eyes. He was doing likewise, staring at me with a wealth of feeling in his eyes.

"How to wield your magical abilities. It's a slow process, learning how, but you'll be impressed with what you'll be able to do."

"But who, what am I?" The words burst out of me.

Really, who?

Doran came over to me, and leaning over, he gently took my face in his hands and said softly, "You are my Rory, and that's what matters the most. We'll figure out the rest later. Together. I'll do whatever it takes. Whatever."

And he kissed me. With such tenderness, that I was surprised. It took my breath away and my arms wrapped themselves around his neck of their own volition. It's like they wanted to strangle him, they held him so tightly.

And we looked into each other's eyes. It was like a challenge, and an act of submission. A plea and a command.

"You are mine."

"And you, Doran, are mine."

His eyes swirled with darkness mixed with green flecks, while mine probably revealed unadulterated blinding desire. Not just a sexual longing. That was far too primitive, too shallow. Something far greater was welling up from inside me in a huge warm wave, and it was ready to sweep over both of us.

My magic was reaching out toward his magic.

The force of the resulting collision was profound.

Magic and kisses. Furious kisses that crushed everything in their path, exposing the soul.

I arched, clawing at Doran's shoulders as he lightly bit my nipple. I gasped from the sharp, painful stab of pleasure.

He bit me very lightly and then licked the

wound with his hot tongue. By now I was trembling all over.

"I won't let you go," Doran's low roar seemed to answer my incomprehensible sounds. "Never, understand?"

No. Right then, I didn't understand anything. The world had closed in on us, on him and on me, and the beating of our hearts and a new, magical pulsation. Our hearts beat as one. Gentle and feverish, maddening.

I melted as Doran slowly covered me with kisses, moving from the curves of my chest, down to my navel. Lower and lower, until I was squirming and shouting his name out loud. Because it wasn't possible to be burning up like this without being incinerated.

The magic in me silently roared and burst out.

"Your eyes," Doran rumbled, looming over me. Hard and hot, his steel muscles taut, and darkness in his eyes.

I just looked at him, not sure I could say a word.

"Gold and green flecks are in them, and darkness," the King said, and then he pressed his lips to mine and he said no more. As he painfully slowly moved inside me, I screamed in pleasure even as we kissed, while I responded to the urgency of his rhythm.

This was greater than sex.

This was greater than our magical

vortexes, which were now intertwined.

This was both too short-lived and yet centuries old.

I felt his warm skin as I held him close, and his searing kisses were almost painfully probing. It felt so good that it hurt.

It hurt so good that suddenly, I couldn't stand it anymore. And I cried out. And kept on crying out as I shattered into myriad sparks of pleasure. Only to come together again.

Finally, I was exhausted. And also devoid of thoughts. I simply lay in Doran's arms and slowly returned to my senses. What just happened? Sex? No. The word could not describe what had just transpired.

The King was also silent. He simply pulled me in closer. Again, it was like he was afraid of losing me.

Silence can be nice, I decided. Sometimes more is expressed in silence than in the deepest disclosures.

I found myself slowly drifting into a light slumber. But I was still feeling a little aroused. And Doran could tell. He lifted himself up, gave me a light kiss on the temple, and whispered:

"Get some rest, Rory. I'll be back soon."

"We'll talk then," I mumbled sleepily. I opened my eyes for a second and saw that the King was smiling. It was just a little smile, but quite sincere.

"Of course we will."

And take this thing off me. I wanted to remind him of the bracelet. But I was so tired, that I decided to let go of it for now, and said nothing.

Doran left then. And as I sank deeper into sleep, I lazily wondered what he was busy with right now. Perhaps he was inquiring about Jioladh, and when he could start interrogating him? It could well be another of the many matters that required his attention.

And suddenly, it was like a blindfold fell off. You know, as if you were slowly wiping the soot off of a dirty window. First, one clean spot emerges, and then it grows larger and larger. Until I saw the corridor beyond the bedroom door. I recognized the lilac walls with silver hieroglyphs that pulsated a little due to the magic forces within them. Now I clearly saw it.

It was a really odd feeling: like watching a computer game with 3D glasses. Then the dream simply dissipated. And I realized that what I'd been looking through the eyes of a Shadow. The Shadow evidently didn't care.

It was hurrying off somewhere. And I politely asked it to stop and take a look around. Something to the left was attracting it. It drew the Shadow in, and transferred to it a massive amount of energy. It was immense, and infinitely calm.

Chaos...

I conducted a mental sweep of the area. In

addition to Chaos, there was Doran. The Shadow saw him as a cluster of Darkness and chaotic magic. To the Shadow, all faeries were blobs of energy. Just out of curiosity, I asked her what I looked like to her. The Shadow showed me a silhouette shot with gold, smoke-colored, and green threads. So then, even in 'Shadowland' I was different.

I mentally asked the Shadow to head towards Chaos and Doran. I wanted to check out the entity that had sent me the kitten. Or who'd manifested itself before me as a kitten.

Just in case, at the threshold to the chamber, I had the Shadow pause and just take a peek.

Doran and Chaos were talking in a room with a wall comprised of a transparent power curtain. Beyond the wall, Ruadh was spread out in her nightly splendor.

The room seemed to be a study. There was a large table hewn from a milky stone, and lots of shelves carved into the walls and loaded with books. The books were clearly very old, so old that the only thing keeping them from crumbling was magic.

The furniture was carved out of the very same stone. It emitted a barely detectable, yet soothing radiance. And Doran was sitting right on the shiny dark floor in the middle of the room. He was shrouded in Shadows, as if they were robes. Next to him, and I blinked to make sure I was seeing right, lounged a huge green octopus. He was totally green, from his glowing green eyes to the tips of his tentacles, which were replete with suckers.

The octopus unfurled and rolled up his tentacles as he lay there, and also lazily said, "The Shadows are pleased, King, your Court is once again coming to life"

"You promised it would be the strongest of them all."

"It already is the strongest," Chaos replied. "Even should the Unseelies join forces with the Seelies, it is unlikely that they could triumph over you. I and all of my magic are behind you. They are powerless against us. And soon you will come to be known not as the Dog of the Hunt, but as the Conqueror."

"Komina predicted that I would have a child, and yet she was unable to foresee her own death," Doran said. "What a pity. She was a good counselor".

"Soothsayers cannot see their own future."

Doran nodded. Then a glass filled with a thick, burgundy beverage appeared in his hand. As he gazed at the rich liquid, the King said, "Today I went through all of my books and had all my scholars look through them. But we were unable to find any mention of Sayphoras. They did not exist among the faeries, it seems"

"Everything that exists had yet to emerge at some point. Long ago, there were no faeries."

"There's a sliver of you in her. And yet you speak so calmly about this?"

"A piece of me also resides in you, even if not from birth. And Aurora is a mystery, King. I love solving mysteries."

"And so you're not so interested in how she came to be?"

"Yes, I'm interested. But I'm not in any kind of hurry. I simply want to investigate, study."

The glowing green eyes slid around the room, and I suspected that Chaos noticed us.

"Tell me, King, did you tell Rory about her future son?"

"A powerful magician."

"Is that so?" Chaos almost purred. "I'm talking about the small matters, such as the prediction that he shall be the one to open the portal to Earth and lead the faeries there. Have you decided, then, to withhold that minor detail? By the way, I perceive new feelings in you. Likewise with Aurora. I believe that if she were to take another sample of your blood, she would see some interesting changes."

"What do you mean?"

"I mean that our theory, King, has turned out to be true. The analysis will likely show that the gene that suppresses the oxytocin is once again dormant. You've fallen in love, Doran. And now the feelings raging inside of you are so powerful that you won't be able to contain them.

But this is good, in fact. My Shadows shall have their fill."

Clearly, Doran was stunned... I could see him stiffen up, as if he'd turned to stone. Then, speaking slowly, he said, "You're saying that we used to love, and we could also bear children, when we lived among humans. As long as they remembered us. And now, we and our magic are forgotten?"

Doran fell silent, and then seemed to answer his own question with a bitter laugh, which made my heart ache. *What is it like to feel forgotten?*

"We used to regard humans as rather quaint, lesser beings. They do not possess our strength, our magic, our power to regenerate. They lack the wisdom, when all is said and done. So what has become of us?"

"What has become of you is need them. You need them to remember you," Chaos responded. I felt like he was actually gloating. But why?

"So we'll make them remember us."

"But what will you tell Aurora, King?"

"For now, we'll keep on telling her that she's here to return to our people the ability to bear children. In fact, I do believe she can create a serum that will temporarily activate our ability to produce oxytocin. Perhaps this will require human genes."

"You cannot keep her reined in for much

longer."

"By then, she'll have had a taste of magic and power," Doran responded, rather smug. "She doesn't have much human in her. And she's no fool."

"That's right! She's nobody's fool. And she will not permit anyone to rein her in."

And again, Chaos cast a strange glance in the direction of where 'my' Shadow was lingering. "You did not know, King, that you and she would be united by the Tree."

"A human? How could I know? I merely sought a human who had the brains to confirm what I thought was happening, using the tools of science. And who could also find a solution to our fertility dilemma. However, now the strongest of the courts shall be ours — the Court of Shadows. And my child shall lead all the of the Courts back to Earth. And he shall appoint governors to rule in all three Courts."

Alright! Enough already! With an effort, I interrupted my silent spying, and sat there, my head spinning a bit from returning to the here and now.

I felt a strange bitterness within me that I wished I could spit out. It's no surprise why I loathed anything to do with politics. It's all lies, lies, and more lies. Faeries could boast about their honesty all they wanted. But they were liars, just like everybody else.

I ran my fingers through my hair and tried

to steady my breathing. So, they'd lied to me. About everything, including the real reason I was here.

Lies, lies everywhere. I was surrounded by them. And this would continue as long as I was here. Or until I could have a talk with Doran.

And again, like bile, it welled up inside me: Why did I ever expect him to be honest with me? His eyes were on the prize, meaning he was going to be the biggest, baddest ruler and 'daddy' to the most powerful of all the faeries.

I tried to calm down and think things through, but there was no way. Maybe the magic in me was impacting my ability to reason, or maybe it was something else, but I was trembling and couldn't stop. My questions about Doran were multiplying, as were my concerns.

I took a long, cold shower to calm down before he returned to the room. I'd hoped it would help me get a grip, but I just got very cold, and so I wrapped myself in a blanket.

That's when Doran came in with a smile. And I smiled back, then cooed, "Dearest, what was it you were saying about a baby? That he'll be strong?"

"Very strong."

"But what if it's a girl? Just a normal girl devoid of magic? This is, after all, a possibility. My human genes may be dominant."

Doran laughed softly and, seating himself on the edge of the bed, he took my hands.

"Rory, what difference does it make if it's a girl or a boy? The baby will be the strongest of the fairies, understand? Komina said so and she knew. Any child of ours is destined for greatness. Already the magic you possess boggles the mind, even though you are still rudimentary at employing it. Just imagine how powerful you'll be once you learn how to properly wield it!"

"Oh, speaking of, it turns out that I can use the Shadows to see. Why did Chaos manifest as an Octopus on his visit tonight?"

I spoke innocuously, but could not prevent a tinge of anger from seeping in. Then I watched with interest at the interplay of emotions on his face. It was like *'Holy hell, she's in the know already!* But hey, you're supposed to be completely open with your 'significant other', aren't you?

"Don't you know that it's not nice to eavesdrop?" he finally said. He scowled and his eyes, now a luminescent green, seemed to glitter.

"And don't you know it's not nice to lie about a child to the would-be mother?"

"I was waiting for the right time to tell you."

I freed my hands from Doran's grasp and said nothing. I wanted to see if he would attempt to expound on that.

"Rory, do you realize how your life has

changed? Telling you everything all at once wouldn't be good for you right now."

"I wasn't seeking a major life change. And my name is Aurora!"

"The life you had was not truly your life," there was distant thunder in Doran's voice. "Someone or something hid you. And we'll find out what their motive was. But you lived a false life. You belong with us. With me."

"Am I not the one who should decide which of my lives is genuine? You don't even know what I am!"

"I know that you and I are united. And I will do all in my power to give you the answers you seek."

"What I've seen thus far is simply your desire to seal the deal when it comes to a child."

Doran's response was a long, patient sigh. Rory, you need two to bear a child and..."

"A straightforward task, right?" I said bitterly. "If we get right to it, we can spit one out in no time! In my world, a couple first decides if they both even *want* a child. After that, they go about planning for it. Sometimes the pregnancy is unexpected. Even then, there are a few options."

"*This* is your world! You should accept this, Rory, and learn to love Ruadh."

"Of course, Sire!" I was shaking with anger, but could still speak. "That's an order, right? I'm talking about loving Ruadh."

Doran clenched his fists so tightly I heard the joints crack, and his eyes momentarily blackened. And I fell silent, afraid I'd blurt out more bile.

"Rory, I'll do whatever I can for you. Do you believe me?"

"I'll believe you if you let me go."

"Where?" Doran asked grimly.

"To Earth. I miss my friends and my apartment. I miss normalcy, a life with no flying cats and frenzied Pixies. I'm tired of feeling like an incubator for some kick-ass magician. I'm tired of being everyone's go-to girl for some kind of miracle. All I want is to stroll down the street, sit in a cafe, chat with my friend, chill out."

Doran was silent, thinking, and my heart sank. *C'mon, let me go! Give me freedom and then I'll return of my own volition! I'll come back to you! I really was a little in love already with this strange, rather crazy place. Please, though, let me have a little taste of my past life.*

"No."

The single syllable fell like lead on my head. But Doran went on, gazing out the window.

"No, Rory. I simply can't take the risk when it comes to you. Right now especially. You're unstable, you need to learn how to wield your magical abilities. The last thing you need is to go back to Earth."

And although there seemed to be some

truth in what he said, it was a bitter, bitter pill to swallow. I couldn't accept it. And I couldn't shake the feeling that he was keeping something back.

"Doran, you do realize that, according to the prediction, our child is slated to conquer Earth?"

"No, not conquer, rather return the faeries to their homeland, that is all."

"And you think that won't be a problem for the human race? Look, everybody! The living legends have come back! No big deal. Let's go about our business. What you're talking about is a war, plain and simple! I don't even want to contemplate what the consequences will be."

"Were I human, I wouldn't deign to put up a struggle."

"Were I faery, I wouldn't want to contend with a nuclear bomb."

"What human would want to fight against Chaos and his magic? Chaos would pulverize such a bomb and eat it for breakfast."

We stared at each other, and I felt like a raging dragon. It is amazing flames weren't shooting from my nostrils yet. Meanwhile, Doran maintained an icy calm. At least on the outside. "I refuse to bear your child until you tell me in detail what the consequences will be for my world," the fire-breathing dragon said.

And what is it about faeries not lying? Okay then, here's some truth for you.

He's not going to kill me, after all. And I didn't have much to lose. If we're supposed to share a future, then I needed to be respected as a person rather than a mere vessel for producing offspring.

And I felt like I was starting to burn up inside, as if hot bubbles were floating up from my abdomen to my head. For a moment, everything grew dim and I shook my head and dug my nails into my palm. All I needed was to start shooting out fireballs, or whatever was about to erupt out of me. But then it seemed to pass. I felt like my hair began to sizzle a bit, even.

The silence in the room was deafening. It smelled sharp and clean. It smelled like rancor. The Shadows had gathered around Doran in a thick, agitated mass. But I felt like they'd do anything for me, if I so desired. And so I just watched Doran and waited.

"You seem to have forgotten something, Rory."

Really, that "pet" name. He *deliberately* used it!

Doran's tone was nothing if not icy. I felt goose bumps on my skin, and my fingers suddenly felt frigid.

"I am the King, Dear. And my first concern is my subjects. If a better life is to be found on Earth, then that is our destiny. Will there be war? We will rise to the challenge, although I prefer a diplomatic approach. Did I mislead you? No, I didn't give you the full story, knowing as I did that for the time being, you were better off not knowing it. And yes, I believed and I still do believe that you would find a solution to our problem before our return to Earth, even if a temporary solution."

"But *my* first concern is for those who live on Earth. You cannot force me to bear a child."

Darkness flooded into Doran's eyes. And for a moment, he seemed beside himself. I'd never seen this before. He seemed to be rather enraged, even.

"This shall come to be — I will not have it otherwise!" his roar echoed through the room, nearly blowing the lamps out. And then, to my horror, my familiar box of pills suddenly appeared in his hand.

"And to ensure that you know that I mean what I'm saying..."

In a flash, my birth control pills turned to dust and were gone.

One telling moment in which my heart slowly crumbled. As did my hopes for living happily ever after. All that was left was bitterness, and there was plenty of that. So much so that I felt like I had to let some of it out.

I looked into Doran's dark eyes and said, "You won't even notice the drone that will fly over you and turn all of the faeries into embers.

You left six centuries ago because you feared iron and the march of progress. What do you expect has happened since then? You're dying out, it's like you're going extinct. It's like you're dinosaurs, like petrified rock!"

And, indeed, Doran's face was rather like a stone mask now. And all of a sudden, I expected the bracelet to sear me with pain, and I clutched my wrist. The king noticed the gesture and said impassively, "I wouldn't stoop so low as to inflict pain on my mate."

And he left without another word.

"Get this thing off of me!" I shouted after him. His response was the sound of his retreating footsteps and a string of alien expletives.

I lost track of the passage of time. Time stood still whilst a tempest raged within me. I felt like it wanted to break me apart. Magic, magic and more magic! It had an impact on how I spoke — I wanted to say too much.

And what a shame that was, such a shame. Even if we put aside everything we'd just said, what we had together was still in question. I'd gotten the message loud and clear: I was to give birth. Sooner or later.

I wasn't opposed to someday having a child, except that, according to Doran, that child was destined to conquer Earth. What else could I call the return of the faeries to their so-called homeland? There's no way they'd be greeted with flowers, followed by peace treaties and parades. Really, humans had a hard time getting along with each other, much less with a totally alien species.

The pain and hurt of it all continued to consume me. Later, I understood that this was a sort of hysteria fueled by magic. But at the time, I simply sank into a dark, gooey despair.

"Rory..."

I heard a distant voice that gradually pulled me out of the abyss I was wallowing in. I raised my head and with detachment noticed that I was now rocking back and forth on the floor. And next to me squatted Aerona, shaking my shoulder and looking into my eyes.

"Rory, pull yourself together! Hey, look at me, darling. The magic is doing this, it's okay. It's pop psychology. Throw some stuff around and then you'll be fine. Plus, you have streams."

"What kind of streams?" I asked sluggishly, looking at Aerona. She looked almost modest: She wore a long, dark green dress with silver stitching and a single slit, although yes, it went from her throat to her navel. The fabric was sturdier than usual, and didn't hug her curves.

"You see, when the Tree unites a couple, it's like their energy flows are interconnected. And we feel each other at a distance. With you, all this began with the awakening of your magic. And it simply came together just now. It was a truly difficult process, but it's done now. With me and my husband, it was days before we got out of bed. As for Doran, I think he'd be willing to stay in bed with you to facilitate the process."

Unwittingly, Aerona had hit a sore spot.

"He destroyed my pills."

"What?"

"I had pills to prevent pregnancy. I... we said too much to each other. I couldn't stop myself."

"Join the club," the King's sister murmured. "Get up, crawl into bed."

"No!"

"Rory, either go to bed or I'll stun you. And then you'll end up being put to bed just the same."

"You don't understand!" I wailed, jumping up. I moved so swiftly that Aerona recoiled in surprise.

"Your brother lied to everyone! Including to me! There was no plan to help the faeries out of their situation. All he'd wanted really was to see if faeries really needed to be among people. You stopped giving birth when you came here, you know? I pondered it, and pondered it some more and suddenly got it. It's outside the realm of science. But just the same, it's so ... so logical."

"You're scaring me."

"The King suspected that there was some kind of symbiosis between humans and fairies, but he wanted proof. And he also wanted a treatment of some sort. And now that he knows our child is destined to be the strongest of the faeries, he will most likely stop me from participating in the search for a cure. And he won't take this bracelet off me and ..."

"What's symbiosis?" Aerona asked.

I gasped and fell silent, trying to catch my breath. My heart was thundering in my ears, and my hands trembled. Yes, out and out hysteria. Unfortunately, I didn't have a sedative. Nor did I have any antidepressants. *Take this for six months and you'll be good as new.*

"Well, let's presuppose that we can, in fact, take that bracelet off of you," a purring voice said from the door. Zephyr, still a panther, entered the room and sat next to Aerona. She bowed her head respectfully and threw me a quick glance.

"Symbiosis is the mutually beneficial coexistence of two organisms," Zephyr explained. "In this case, for centuries Faeries and Humans lived side by side, but neither one understood that they depended on the other."

"What do humans get from being around faeries?" I asked, unable to say "us," thereby counting myself among the faeries. I just couldn't do it.

"I don't know," Zephyr said, "I am indifferent to people. As I am to faeries, as well. But the faeries have given me the opportunity to feel. This is new, and fun. And so far, I'm still enjoying it. But Aurora, you cannot go back to Earth, no. There, they'd pick you up and start conducting experiments on you. Would you want to investigate *you* if you were really a human scientist?"

"How do you know?"

"Hello. I'm Chaos," Zephyr said, and I could see him mentally shrug his shoulders. "The Wild Hunt brings back a lot of interesting news from the human world. Yes, indeed, on Earth, Doran would easily find you. To him, you'd be radioactive, like a nuclear reactor."

He was right. Yes. Only that staying here made me physically ill. I might be the latest greatest thing around, but it didn't mean jack if I wasn't respected and if what I thought wasn't taken seriously.

It was so hard to be so offended by someone you'd somehow, without even knowing it, fallen in love with.

"And how's the captive doing? I mean Jioladh," I asked Aerona.

She shrugged and looked at Zephyr. "He's getting better," she said. "Do you want to see him?"

Yes, I did. I knew he was in on Haedyn's plan to abduct me, but just the same, he seemed okay to me. Perhaps rather befuddled or something. Whatever, I wanted to see him again. I felt it — he wouldn't survive it if he were to remain in the torture chamber.

"Doran won't let anyone in to see him — just the healers," Aerona said. "He's stationed Shadows, and also guards there."

"There is no one near the prisoner now," Zephyrs said. "And there won't be for another half hour. Have a talk."

His green, almond-shaped eyes blinked, and Aerona and I both gasped: Jioladh suddenly lying right there, on the floor.

I gulped: If this was what they called on the mend, then what did he look like before? The red-headed charmer's throat was ripped apart, and his entire body was seriously mauled, while the bones of his legs seemed to stick out at odd angles, but on the good side, his arms and hands seemed to be okay.

"The healers focused on his internal status."

"I don't need the details on how they did this to him," I muttered, struggling to not turn away. And I'm not the type to shy away from the sight of blood.

"What's he to you," asked Aerona, disgusted. She leaned over Jioladh and almost poked him with the toe of her shoe. Just think, not so long ago she'd been lovey-dovey with him in the dark of the dudgeon.

"I myself don't know," I admitted. I felt sorry for Jioladh, and I didn't know why. I couldn't help but remember how he'd looked at me when I'd pushed him aside to save him from the assassination attempt. Or how upset he was in Komina's house. Really, I'm not the best at reading people, and even worse at understanding faeries, but right now my heart ached as I looked at the battered Jioladh.

What a fool I can be. This was what I was thinking when I leaned over the red-haired charmer and touched him with the palm of my hand. I felt something warm and a little prickly emerging from within me. For some reason, a golden-orange light flowed from my hand.

"I ..." Aerona began and paused, looking at me in astonishment. Zephyr was now like a translucent statue, staring at what was happening.

And I, too, froze, as a pale orange light now flowed from my fingers. It spread over Jioladh, enveloping him.

And began working wonders on him. Rather, it was as if the wounds and injuries were peeling off of him. And ten minutes later, he was whole again. Meanwhile, I was trembling inside, and my head was spinning. I dropped to my knees and realized that I was now soaked in sweat. In contrast, Jioladh, still very pale, opened his eyes and looked around him with cloudy eyes. He clearly was still unable to understand what was happening.

"Rory ..." Aerona whispered. "I'm....you....I'm almost afraid of you."

"What?"

"You turned back time for the prisoner," Zephyr said drily. "This magic is from Chaos. Doran refuses to employ it."

"B-b-but why?" Right, now it was me who was stuttering.

"He said that playing with time was serious business. And dangerous."

And in this regard, I agreed with the King. I believed in the butterfly effect. Because now I was sitting there bathed in sweat, wondering if I was in for it now.

"Fear not," Chaos again read my thoughts. "You'll be okay, but you'd be wise to not misuse this."

"I don't..."

Jioladh groaned, and we all switched our attention to him.

"Can you talk?"

"I...I think so," Jioladh still had a smooth, rather enchanting voice. But now I was immune to it. Meanwhile, Aerona's eyes sparkled dangerously, but for the time being she contained herself.

"They'll keep on torturing you," I said, looking him in the eyes. "It will go on and on. Until you tell him about Haedyn's plan. And about me, who I am. Do you hear me?"

"Loud and clear." Jioladh felt his throat and grimaced. "What happened?" he asked.

"The hounds of the Wild Hunt had a go at you, and then I healed you.".

"You've awakened," Jioladh exhaled, somehow hopelessly. "So now what? Do you want to jeer at me before your King has his turn?"

My throat felt suddenly tight, and I swallowed. "He is not my King. What am I?"

"You can of course torture me," Jioladh said with a sigh, "but it won't get you anywhere. I don't know what you are, Rory."

I sighed in disappointment, but then Jioladh went on. "But I know who might be able to help you. It was Haedyn who knew what was what. And Komina. I was just a bystander. I'm not afraid of torture, though I have yet to experience it. But if you let you me go, I can take you there."

"Are you laying down the terms here?" Aerona snarled. "You?!"

"I really don't want to be tortured," Jioladh admitted.

"Give me a minute," I said. And I walked away. I was flooded with thoughts, and I had to take several deep breaths before I could more or less calm down. What I was thinking seemed stark raving mad. But it was at least a way out of my dilemma.

I couldn't return to Earth, but I sure didn't want to stay here. No. I felt ill when I thought about how Doran had crushed my pills. It was like being stabbed in the heart. He was taking his stand and showing me my place.

"This shall come to be — I will not have it otherwise!"

I hugged myself, and almost groaned out loud. Well, I'd be an idiot to think for a moment that Doran could behave like a human being. Or see me as his equal. Even now, he was showing me my place in no uncertain terms.

I went back over to the others, still shaking over the decision I'd made. But I was crystal-clear in my head.

"You," I indicated the red-haired charmer. "Zephyr...Chaos, is there some kind of spell that will make him value me more?"

"There is. Mine."

I kept my eyes on Jioladh. "Swear to me that you will be true to me, you will not betray me, you will not sell me out to anyone, and that you will lay down your life to defend me."

"No, no," Chaos reassured me. "I've got this covered." And turning to Jioladh, he said. "Do you swear?"

"Yes," Jioladh said quietly.

The cat stretched out his paw and touched the naked Jioladh's shoulder. He arched in pain, but relaxed almost immediately. And on his shoulder, a brand in the shape of a paw emerged.

"Now, if he hurts you or betrays you, he will be roasted alive in my flames. This is a very slow, painful fate."

Jioladh turned even paler, which was

really remarkable.

Then Aerona asked, "Wait a minute, Rory, where are you going?"

"I cannot go back to Earth, but your brother sees me as his beautiful toy who can suddenly bear his child."

"So you want to run off with *him*?!" she asked, indicating Jioladh.

Exchanging glances with Jioladh, I nodded. "Yes. I want to find out what I am, and also give Doran a chance to think about our future. You won't tell him, will you?"

"You're out of your mind," Aerona said hopelessly. "Ji, where will you take her?"

"To the Wasteland."

"Oh my," Zephyr joined in. "What a dangerous place – yet fascinating. And you can fend for yourself. If you want to."

"Rory, this fairy is going with you, too," Aerona said.

I stared at Aerona, amazed. She raised her chin defiantly and narrowed her eyes: "What?"

"I'm selfish, Sweetie. You promised me I'd be a mother someday, so I'm not letting you out of my sight, got it? And you have greater chances of surviving with me along. And anyway, my husband and I need a break to renew our relationship. It'd be good for him to worry about me. All the more so since I've longed to see the Wasteland. There are so many stories about it. When we came here, the magic came with us. All of it. But then some of it settled in the Wasteland. So there's a lot to see out there..."

"Good god, what am I doing? What am I getting myself into? And where am I going?"

"You, Rory, are crazy," Aerona continued, "but it's all good. I should call Doran now. So that he puts a stop to this. But guess what? I don't want to. You shouldn't just fuck the one you're destined to be with, you must also respect her. So I'm with you, yes. And I can also ensure that Ji doesn't betray you."

"I won't betray this one," the redhead said quietly. "I have no intention of doing so. I didn't like Haedyn's plan, but I was already too deeply involved. And Rory saved my life. So I am indebted."

I looked at Zephyr. "Do you understand that I'm going to flee this place?"

Instead of answering, he tapped my wrist with his paw and the bracelet simply evaporated. There were no special effects, nor did I feel any different. But my wrist was now cleansed, freed from the bracelet. I could hardly believe it, and pinched myself to make sure I wasn't dreaming. *It was that easy?!*

"You must cross the borders of Ruadh to open the portal to the Wasteland," Zephyr said. "I can hide the prisoner from inquisitive eyes, but you have to get yourself there. Once you're outside the palace, the Shadows will quickly take you to the border. Once there, I will help you with the portal."

"Why are you helping me?" I asked. Zephyr looked at me as if I was a child.

"It's elementary, Aurora. I promised you I would help. And that's what I'm doing. The King needs to learn how to manage a wealth of new feelings. It really is best that you leave him for awhile. And because a sliver of me resides within you, you can summon the Shadows even when you're beyond the borders of Ruadh, if only for a short while. They will protect you and tell me about the new lands.

"Yes, I foresee learning many new things," he continued. "But first, you need to flee, get out of here."

It was hard for me to believe that all this was really happening. My arms and legs were icy, while inside I felt like I was on fire.

I felt like I was in a dream as I changed into the jacket and pants that Aerona brought me. All the while I saw Doran's face before me. Then, it was like an invisible dam suddenly burst and the tears gushed out. Inside I was grieving, outwardly I brushed the tears from my cheeks, all the while readying myself for the journey. No one tried to comfort me, but I saw a glint of sympathy in Aerona's gaze.

Forgive me, Doran, but you have to give love a chance to breathe.

And I'm tired of being your toy.

I need to find out for myself what I am. I need to learn how to use my magic. I may not be entirely human, but I am a scientist, and this will help me evolve into a better magician than all of the faeries put together.

Never again will anyone dare to put a collar around me!

END OF BOOK ONE

Want to be the first to know about our latest LitRPG, sci fi and fantasy titles from your favorite authors?

Subscribe to our *New Releases* newsletter:
http://eepurl.com/b7niIL

Thank you for reading *Captive of the Shadow!*
If you like what you've read, check out other LitRPG,
fantasy and science fiction novels published by Magic
Dome Books:

Level Up LitRPG series by Dan Sugralinov:
Re-Start
Hero
The Final Trial
Level Up: The Knockout (with Max Lagno)

The Way of the Shaman LitRPG series
by Vasily Mahanenko:
Survival Quest
The Kartoss Gambit
The Secret of the Dark Forest
The Phantom Castle
The Karmadont Chess Set
Shaman's Revenge
Clans War

Dark Paladin LitRPG series by Vasily Mahanenko:
The Beginning
The Quest
Restart

Galactogon LitRPG series by Vasily Mahanenko:
Start the Game!
In Search of the Uldans

The Bard from Barliona LitRPG series
by Eugenia Dmitrieva and Vasily Mahanenko:
The Renegades
A Song of Shadow

The Neuro LitRPG series by Andrei Livadny:
The Crystal Sphere
The Curse of Rion Castle
The Reapers

In order to have new books of the series translated faster, we need your help and support! Please consider leaving a review or spread the word by recommending *Captive of the Shadow* to your friends and posting the link on social media. The more people buy the book, the sooner we'll be able to make new translations available.

Thank you!

Till next time!